PENGUIN BOOKS

THE INK TRUCK

William Kennedy is the author of the universally acclaimed cycle of Albany novels, *Legs, Billy Phelan's Greatest Game*, and *Ironweed*, which received both the Pulitzer Prize and the National Book Critics Circle Award for Fiction. He is also the author of a nonfiction work on his hometown, *O Albany!*. In 1984 he received a New York State Governor's Arts Award.

WILLIAM KENNEDY

THE INK TRUCK

PENGUIN BOOKS

PENGUIN BOOKS

Viking Penguin Inc., 40 West 23rd Street, New York, New York 10010, U.S.A.
Penguin Books Ltd, Harmondsworth, Middlesex, England
Penguin Books Australia Ltd, Ringwood, Victoria, Australia
Penguin Books Canada Limited, 2801 John Street, Markham, Ontario, Canada L3R 1B4
Penguin Books (N.Z.) Ltd, 182–190 Wairau Road, Auckland 10, New Zealand

First published in the United States of America by The Dial Press, Inc., 1969
First published in Great Britain by Macdonald & Co. Ltd. 1970
Published with a new Author's Note by Viking Penguin Inc. 1984
Published in Penguin Books 1985

LIBRARY OF CONGRESS CATALOGING IN PUBLICATION DATA
Kennedy, William, 1928–
The ink truck.
I. Title.
PS3561.E428I5   1985   813'.54   85-6508
ISBN 0 14 00.7674 3

Grateful acknowledgment is made to the following for permission to reprint copyrighted material:

Avon Books: "For My Part I'll Smoke a Good Ten Cent Cigar," by William Saroyan. From 48 Saroyan Stories, copyright 1938, 1939, 1942 by William Saroyan.

The Bollingen Foundation: For The Hero With a Thousand Faces, by Joseph Campbell, Bollingen Series XVII (Princeton University Press, revised edition, 1968). Copyright 1949 by the Bollingen Foundation.

Doubleday & Company, Inc.: An excerpt from archy and mehitabel, by don marquis. Copyright 1927 by don marquis.

Harper & Row, Publishers: Epigram from "Maxims from the Chinese" in My Ten Years in a Quandary and How They Grew, by Robert Benchley. Copyright 1936 by Robert Benchley; renewed 1964 by Gertrude Benchley. Reprinted by permission of Harper & Row, Publishers, Inc.

D.C. Heath and Company: For material from Hundreds of Turkeys, by E. Osswald and M.M. Reed. Copyright © 1941 by D.C. Heath and Company, A Division of Raytheon Education Company, Boston, Massachusetts.

Macmillan Publishing Company and A.P. Watt Ltd: "To a Friend Whose Work Has Come to Nothing," from The Poems of W.B. Yeats, edited by Richard J. Finneran. Copyright 1916 by Macmillan Publishing Co., Inc., renewed 1944 by Bertha Georgie Yeats.

Stratemeyer Syndicate: Selections from Tom Swift and His Undersea Search, copyright 1920 by Grosset & Dunlap. Copyright renewed 1948 by Victor Appleton; copyright assigned to Stratemeyer Syndicate in 1978.

The Welk Music Group: Lyrics from "They Always Pick on Me," written by Stanley Murphy and Harry Von Tilzer. Copyright 1911 by Harry Von Tilzer Music Publishing Company. Copyright renewed (c/o The Welk Music Group, Santa Monica, California 90401). International copyright secured. All rights reserved.

Printed in the United States of America by
R. R. Donnelley & Sons Company, Harrisonburg, Virginia
Set in Times Roman

This book is for
the three elegant ladies I live with:

Ana Daisy
Dana Elizabeth
and
Katherine Anne

Author's Note

All that needs saying is that this is not a book about an anonymous city, but about Albany, N.Y., and a few of its dynamics during two centuries. Nothing has been changed from the 1969 edition except the design of newspaper headlines on the part title pages, their original galumphishness now banished.

What pleases me most is that the political wisdom that most allowed me to survive a hostile decade has not rotted away. Bailey confronts it most vividly when the Lord Mayor of Cork, Terence MacSwiney, tells him: "Try very hard to..."

Bailey listens, hears.

1984

EXTRA!

A
BIZARRE BOLLY
FOLLOWS
INK CARRIER

WHAT'S
A BOLLY?
PEOPLE ASK

The wise man moves fast, yet a great many times it is hard to catch him. This is because he has no soul. This is because he lives up there with all those radicals.

—ROBERT BENCHLEY
Maxims from the Chinese

Again Bailey dreamed, just before opening his eyes, of an essential oil that when massaged on eyelids became the quicksilver of the brain. The eyes did not then window the soul: They reflected truths of here and there, now and then. But when he opened the eyes and looked at the acoustical-tile ceiling of his bedroom he wondered what kept driving him to such a dream. He had all the truth he could stand. Any more truth about himself or others would tip the balance, turn him into an ape, a goat, a pig.

Bailey rose jerkily from a bed of anguish and plot. Sitting up, he looked through the window of his pajama crotch, saw his pubes growing wild, plucked a few, held one. The Puerto Ricans had a word for it: *pendejo*. A pube. A jerk.

Who's calling?

Mr. Pendejo.

Make a noise like a glug and float away with the bath water.

Bailey looked at the sunless day, remembered this was the twelve-month anniversary of the Guild strike. As usual he prepared to go forth to new reversals, a mental habit of Guildsmen. But the anniversary set the day apart. He felt the need to be creative. No sitting in the Guild room waiting for something to happen. No trivial brooding. Something radical was called for.

But before that there was the chore. Mr. Otto.

Bailey looked at Grace, sleeping beside him. Let sleeping animals lie. He stood and dressed himself, shaved and washed quietly. He swallowed half a quart of milk, thinking how the news magazines had convinced him the thip-thip-th-th-thip-thip of his heart was cholesterolated irregularity. Must ingest polyunsaturates. Keep the balance. Chew some corn-oil margarine for lunch.

From the hall closet Bailey took down his checkered sport jacket, his green muffler which dangled to hip length after a once-around twirl, his black cossack hat and his black corduroy car coat with the black fur collar. He tiptoed across the room, opened the door quietly, closed it just as quietly and went down one flight of stairs. He knocked at another apartment door. Knock-knock, knock-knock. Feet shuffled toward the door and from the other side came a hoarse whisper. "Bailey?"

He repeated the double knock-knock. The door opened and a woman in a ragged, coffee-stained nightgown and loose black hair, snarled all the way to her shoulders, smiled at him through sleepy eyes.

"Is your husband home, Mavis?"

Mavis shook her head.

"In that case may I use your telephone?"

Mavis smiled and opened the door wider. When she'd closed it Bailey took her by the shoulders and kissed her lightly on the left eye, then went to the phone on the table beside the bed. He sat on the bed and Mavis lay down beside him, scratching the back of his neck. Bailey dialed the newspaper office and asked for Mr. Otto, the sportswriter.

"Otto here."

"Sir, my name is Batchford. I believe we have common interests in a matter concerning a person with the initials G.B."

"Who is this?"

"Batchford, sir. Sterling Batchford. I'm a graduate student of osteopathy and I do believe that the news about G.B. is crucial. I burn to tell you of it, sir."

"What news? Who's G.B.?"

"One doesn't discuss such matters on the telephone, sir. I suggest a meeting at a place convenient to you, say the tavern near your newspaper. Fobie's, isn't it? Shall we say ten minutes?"

"I don't know what this is all about."

"It behooves you, sir, to find out. It is, in its own way, a survival matter. I shall await you in Fobie's."

"You're a tease," Mavis told him. "I thought you came to see me."

"But I did. Two birds at once. I could have called from Fobie's."

"You can't see much in ten minutes."

"The briefest of looks is a feast," Bailey said, raising her nightgown to neck level, patting her here, pat-pat, pat-pat, and there, pat-patty-pat-pat, then pulling the gown back into place.

"Soon," the woman said. "It's been such a long time."

"Soon," Bailey said, going out the door, escaping, having saved a dime.

He sat on a barstool at Fobie's, one of five customers, one of two drinking beer, the other three swallowing Fobie's pale coffee and greasy doughnuts. He sat where he couldn't be seen from either the window or the doorway and watched for Otto through the back-bar mirror.

Otto entered and stood by the door, looking over the five customers. Bailey swerved on the barstool and confronted Otto suddenly. Otto's face widened in recognition. He opened the door, started to run, Bailey following.

"The coffee hour is on you, you Jew stick."

Rosenthal nodded, grunted once and hung up the phone. He stroked his pencil-line moustache, looked at the work on his desk: one sheet of paper with a list of names and phone numbers. Poverty of duty. From the closet he took his black cape off its hook, put on his Tyrolean hat with a fat red feather in its band and grabbed his swaggerstick from the shelf. Bailey said he dressed like a sartorially confused British jewel thief. But he had pursued a specialized image ever since Shirley, his wife, said he had none. He zigzagged from cap to beret, from cane to umbrella, and settled on the cape, an anachronism. What's out is in. But why did he have to be in? Why did he need an image? Without it you cast no shadow, Shirley said. Look at Bailey's image, and look at the shadow he casts.

Rosenthal left the Guild room and walked over old snow toward Fobie's. It was a cold morning, overcast, new snow in the air. Would the winter ever end? At Fobie's he found Bailey with a captive audience, a stranger who watched Bailey's face as if it were a television screen. Rosenthal stayed back, listened.

"As a boy," Bailey was telling the stranger, not loudly for the benefit of all present but with a resonance Rosenthal could tune in, even from a distance, "I wanted to be Jesus. But I got that out of my system and decided to be Ben Franklin. If I couldn't save people, redeem their spirit, I could at least invent bifocals for them, or the harmonica. I later played the harmonica, trying to make music for them, trying to be a minstrel of my time. But the harmonica didn't make it, and when I added the ukulele I found that too missed the mark."

The stranger stared vacuously at Bailey. Compulsive Bailey, Rosenthal thought. You'll talk to anybody. But talk that deceives, that never gets to the Bailey center. Never gets to the unspoken Bailey. The unspeakable Bailey.

"I found my mother lode in the news columns," Bailey went on. "I invented new phases of bifocalism, figuratively, of course, and shot everything through with a little bit of Jesus stuff, set to music. And they loved it. They paid me big money, shoveled the old honors at me. I was all set for my skyrocket time—there he goes, the Bailey comet. I was on edge, I tell you. Ready to ride. And then we went on strike."

The stranger blinked only when Bailey stopped talking. Bailey drank his beer, licked his lips. Rosenthal moved in.

"What a coincidence finding you here," Rosenthal said. "I didn't know you drank."

"I came in to dry my underwear," Bailey said.

"I'll have a drink."

"No coffee?"

"It's been a bad morning."

"Drinks, Fobie," Bailey said to the owner-bartender, "for all the true men in the house. My trucking friend here," and the stranger nodded, "plus one for yourself of course, you old piddlebox. And one for this elegant strand of spaghetti here, this paragon of style and suavity, this Tyrolean feather duster. But none for the scabs, Fobie. You don't serve scabs, anyway, do you, old boy?"

Fobie snarled at the thrust. A sickly little man, he was renowned for his lectures on the evils of fresh bread and World War One cooties, and for having described a Negro customer as being black as the ace of coal. As the Guildsmen's number diminished from the long strike and they faded away from Fobie's, he made new customers of the scabs. Now he resented their being made uncomfortable, resented Guildsmen bickering with them, fighting them.

"Scabs are the pus people," Bailey said. "Cans of rich vomit. Bottles of pee."

Rosenthal looked down the bar at the customers he knew to be scabs. They ignored Bailey. None of them wanted another fight. Bailey was built like a black bear, an ox, a rhinoceros. The scabs called him a maniac, a communist. His image at Fobie's changed regularly, depending on his last outrage. With the lady customers it was something else. Look out, girls. Here comes the wicked-eyed Baileywhaley down the street in his sperm suit.

Fobie set up three beers.

"You make enough noise for two dozen things," Fobie told Bailey.

Bailey smiled, turned to Rosenthal. "You have something on your secret Jewish mind," he said. "You stride up here like a regular Yiddisha barleycorn when I know you hate the stuff, long for absinthian cups from the exotic tongue spots of Europe. You crave the Jewish continental culture. You favor pumpernickel. You loathe the American proletariat."

"Mushmouth," Rosenthal began, "I have a message to you from our leader."

"From our leader," Bailey said, removing his Russian hat and placing it over his heart.

"There is to be a motorcade."

"Oh, my sweet bottom."

"Tonight."

"Oh, no. No. How could he still believe in motorcades?"

"Don't ask absurd questions."

"But we don't have any motors."

"Do you think Jarvis really cares about such details?"

Bailey considered the development. The last motorcade drew only twelve members and five cars, plus two volunteers from other unions. That was a month and a half ago to celebrate Jarvis' birthday and to harass drivers getting a fat pre-Christmas edition on the street. The motorcade delayed one truck eight minutes. Jarvis scored it a victory and turned forty in a haze of glee.

"We're getting lax in our militancy," Rosenthal said.

"Is that what he thinks?"

"So we'll harass the ink truck that we hear is due in tonight from New Jersey. We'll ride round and round and make them nervous over there."

"Ink truck," said Bailey.

"But no violence. Just militancy. His precise word was fuss."

"Fuss him," Bailey said. "I'll bomb the son of a bitch when it gets here."

Rosenthal smiled, battened down his hat, put on his gloves.

"Got to get back and call the membership."

"Nobody will come," Bailey said. "Don't waste your time."

"It's an order."

"You're a fool."

"I know it," Rosenthal said.

"You sit up there making phone calls, making notes, following Jarvis' orders. Sometimes I think you believe the man who does his duty will end up all right. But if you accept the framework, you're done for. Drink is oil for unauthorized movement. A wrench in the gears of doom. Have another beer. There's not enough time for us to win this strike."

"You may be right."

"You really are a fool."

"Right again," Rosenthal said, holding his beer in his gloved hand, finishing it. He adjusted his cape and picked his swaggerstick off the bar.

"Listen," Bailey said. "Come to lunch today at the house."

"What house?"

"My house."

"Your house?"

"Exactly."

"What time?"

"Lunchtime."

"I used to drive an ink truck," the truck driver said.

"Ink truck?" said Bailey.

"I heard you say ink truck. I used to drive one."

"You drove an ink truck," Bailey said.

"I heard you talkin' about one."

"You heard us talking."

"This is too deep for me," Rosenthal said. "See you at lunch," and he went out.

"Now," Bailey said to the driver.

"No. Not now. I used to."

"I'm afraid I don't understand."

"I say I used to drive an ink truck."

"An ink truck," Bailey said.

Rosenthal approached an alley half a block down the street from Fobie's at the approximate moment that an ambulance pulled to a stop in front of it. The attendants lifted a stretcher onto the sidewalk, wheeled it toward the alley, then lifted a bloody-headed figure out of the snowcapped rubble and onto the stretcher's white sheet. As they covered the man with a blanket Rosenthal saw a bone sticking through bleeding elbow flesh, heard the man groan, seemed to recognize him as a scab from the editorial department. But with such a bloodied face Rosenthal couldn't be sure.

The phone was ringing when he entered the empty Guild room.

"Guild," he said.

"Listen," Bailey said. "I could throw one grenade into the motor of the truck and another through the press-room window."

"Did you forget that the press-room windows are reinforced with steel mesh? A grenade would just bounce off."

"You gutless scab," Bailey said, and hung up.

Rosenthal put his clothes in the closet and waited for Bailey to call back. When the phone rang he picked it up and said, "Uh huh."

"Hang one grenade on the wire mesh," Bailey said, "and when that explodes toss a second one through the breach."

"What about the guards? What about the floodlights? You think you can sneak across that yard?"

"You yellow-bellied pimp," Bailey said, and hung up again.

Rosenthal debated whether Bailey would call a third time. He decided he wouldn't and so began his own calls, musing on what the company man who tapped the phone would make of Bailey's conversation. Maybe he was used to such talk by this time. The phone had been tapped since the first week of the strike.

Rosenthal said nothing specific when he called the membership beyond telling them that a doughnut party was planned for eight o'clock. Nobody bothered to refuse. When he dialed Irma's number he thought of her profile below the neck. Hillocky hummocky.

"Irma, please."

"She's not here. This is Francie. Who's calling?"

"Rosenthal from the Guild."

"Irma is no longer in the Guild."

"She's what?"

"You got good ears."

"When is she coming back?"

"Never. She's engaged."

"To whom?"

"A tall fellow with nice straight teeth. He works for a living."

"You know his name then? We'd like to send congratulations."

"Eppis. Mr. Eppis."

"From the Eppis Mortuary?"

"The same," Francie said. "Now will you birds down there please leave my sister alone? Quit sucking her blood?"

Rosenthal noted Irma's resignation in his ledger. She was the 247th defection, leaving only eighteen members. But only Jarvis, Bailey and Rosenthal, with Irma now gone, worked daily in the Guild room. The fifteen others made only sporadic, conscience-stricken appearances; and so for two months hired pickets had marched on the line.

Rosenthal thought of Irma's case: Her assignment for two weeks had been to urge funeral directors not to place paid death notices in the newspaper, the eleventh such campaign since the strike started. No doubt she met her undertaker on the phone. It won't be the same without Irma around, Rosenthal thought, deeply saddened not only by this but by the ever-present thoughts of galloping Guild decay. If this was the sorriest Guild local in all the Judeo-Christian world, and it surely must be, why was he afflicted with duty toward it? When would duty burn itself out? He knew it was the same with Bailey: mired in hope, wedded to a black death. Yet Bailey did not plan to die. He behaved as if revolution were possible and he talked like a madman. Bailey believed in possibility. Not dead yet, Bailey said. And he could smell death, an Irish trick. It came from eating so many rotten potatoes for hundreds of years. The stink of decay was in their nostrils at birth, and nothing fooled a sniffer like that. Mystic Irish. Rosenthal saw Bailey as an innocent warrior. And in self-punishing moments he saw himself as a trained mouse from Hamelin (self-trained was he?) who followed the death piper over the hill to nowhere (piped the tune himself, did he?). Will the secrets of power ever be revealed to the likes of us? Rosenthal wondered.

Jarvis came down from the roof bundled in his oversize overcoat and knitted cap, the cap smothering his eyebrows and ears, the sleeves of the coat hiding all but the first two joints of his fingers. The buckles on his overshoes jingled as he came.

"What's the reconnaissance?" Rosenthal asked him.

"No news," Jarvis said.

"How's the weather?"

"It keeps up."

"Any birds in the air?"

"Negative."

"It looks like snow."

"What does?"

"The general scene."

"You think I give a rap?"

"Everybody should give a rap about snow."

"Not me," Jarvis said. "I don't give a rap."

Jarvis went to the roof each afternoon and studied the situation in the company yard down the street. The Guild-room window also overlooked the yard but Jarvis preferred the roof. From there he could count the pickets, see whether they were marching all the way to the corner as he always instructed them. Sometimes they turned around three or four feet before the corner, which enraged him. We picket the whole block, he told them.

From his pocket Jarvis took a sheet of paper and dropped it in front of Rosenthal, his report on the latest negotiations with Stanley, the company's lawyer-negotiator. Jarvis went back to the roof as Rosenthal read:

> Called Stanley five times before he accepted call. He agrees company should split tuxedo-trouser-and-cummerbund rental costs for reporters who attend formal functions on news assignments. But insists reporters are notorious gravy spillers and must pay for their own dress shirt and jacket. Stanley says our 57th proposal unacceptable without changes. He refuses to specify which changes. Hinted even with changes he wouldn't like it.

As he went out for lunch at Bailey's house Rosenthal hung the report on the bulletin board atop all the others. Sometimes he hung Jarvis' reports sideways.

Grace Bailey, forty turning fifty, opened the door when Rosenthal knocked. She looked at him but said nothing.

"I'm Rosenthal."

"Come in, sit down, he's out, how do you do?"

It was Rosenthal's first visit to the Bailey apartment in all the years he had known Bailey. Among Guildsmen only Matsu, the photographer, had ever been inside: on a night he carried Bailey home drunk. Matsu brought back a tale of furniture piled everywhere and nothing at all in one room but an ashtray of burning incense on the floor. Grace talked to Matsu from behind the half-closed kitchen door, told him she couldn't come out because she was getting rid of a pooka. Everybody thought Grace sounded like a card.

Rosenthal looked around the living room, captured immediately by an enormous poster of Mrs. Bailey in a roller-derby costume, coming at the viewer with skates skyward, buttocks forward, about to land with a fracturing thump. Scowling, helmeted skaters in the background moved menacingly forward. Beneath the photo a large printed message suggested:

DROP IN
& see
GROOVY GRACE
The Toughest Broad on Wheels
—Queen Of The Camden Bloomer Busters—
Madison Square Garden
Tuesday, Dec. 4, 1943
8 P.M.

On another wall Rosenthal recognized bits of Bailey's taste: a magazine cartoon sketch by Ronald Searle of a decapitated James Joyce climbing down the rocks beside the

Martello Tower with his eyepatched head under his left arm, clutching his ashplant with his right hand; and above him a screaming hawk flying off with a copy of *Ulysses* in its claws. Beside the sketch was a framed Playbill from the Abbey Theatre, and below these, three composite photos, each with a head superimposed on Bailey's torso, the torso recognizable anywhere for it was wrapped in the same checkered sport coat Bailey had worn day and night at the Guild room and the office for the past two years, time out only for semiannual cleanings. (Bailey believed a man ought to have a trademark.) The heads on his torso belonged to a blue pig, a hound with his tongue out and a cross-eyed tiger.

"So he's a professional Irisher at home, is he?" Rosenthal said to Grace. "He probably kissed the Blarney Stone."

"You can't knock him to me," she said. "Tell him what you think. What he does with stuff is his business. That's his wall."

She left Rosenthal abruptly, went to the bedroom and came back with an envelope on which Bailey had written: "My latest column. Please react."

"He said to give this to you," Grace said. "Don't ask me what it is. I don't read his things."

Bailey's column had been syndicated in twenty-eight newspapers before the strike began. But focusing on the strike, obsessed with settling it, obsessed with harassing the company, obsessed with every tortured nuance which might lead the Guild back into daylight, he neglected deadlines, missed weeks at a time. Rosenthal could have told him how narrow his vision had grown: How can you expect to sustain reader interest permanently in strike commentary? How can you expect management capitalists to subsidize propaganda against themselves? Ah, Bailey. Poor bear. To Rosenthal the fear was not that Bailey would crack but that he would shrivel. Rosenthal plopped in the sofa against Bailey's wall, sensing that sitting under the airborne Grace would bring her wrath down upon him. He opened the envelope and read:

THIS WRITER HAS A PROBLEM

I recently received a letter from a reader who claims he has forgotten how to live. "I try to recapture the bright days of past pooka," my reader writes, "when I felt I was really living. But am so overwhelmed by frustration, uncertainty and the emptiness of all pooka except efforts at exchanging love with those who seem to pooka you and whom you seem to pooka in return, that at length I find myself wallowing in a pool of pity, snuffling up a snoutful like a pig in muck and hosing myself with it, like an elephant pooka bathing pooka pooka. Then from this flows the understanding that the ego is so knotted up with itself that it becomes incapable of extending sympathy, friendship or pooka toward another. Then follows the pooka to apologize for this failing and the wish to explain it away by admitting self-pooka. And all this, oddly, is accompanied by a glorious sense of pooka, for this is life intensified, new pooka. But then it turns black pooka, and you see it as opportunistic, cheap, battening on your own suffering pooka. One then resolves not to pooka oneself, or at least, that being impossible, to keep pooka quiet in the mind and stop using it as a substitute for genuine pooka. Can you help me?"

I responded to my reader with two aphorisms: "In wartime, an antitank gun will also blow up a corporal." And: "Trouble is like a lady's garter. It will get to you whether you snap it or not."

"One must self-suffice," I added. "Please send word if you discover how."

My reader then replied: "Thank you for your pooka. I have discarded pooka pooka pooka and am getting down to some serious pooka pooka. If you ever get out this way stop in for a pooka. Yours truly, Joe the dog."

Bailey is mad, Rosenthal thought. Over the line at last. Bailey the believer. Believes in the intensity of others. They will study me with clear eyes, Bailey thinks. They will read me with full attention, no matter how I say it. Bailey the jerk. Rosenthal put the column back in the envelope.

Grace came out of the kitchen and Rosenthal half-spoke the first word of an empty but congenial thought. But she ignored him and sat in a rocker, staring at the door with eyes abulge, breasts pushing out of her soiled and low-cut baby-blue sheath. He sensed that her face was moving toward the door, that she was willing herself forward. Yet she did not move. Rosenthal sneezed and when he looked back at Grace she had pushed her chair two feet nearer the door. She fluffed her rag-doll hair, crossed and uncrossed her legs, stringy with old muscles. A noise in the hall drove her straight up, fingers rubbing one another. But the noise passed and she sat, only to stand again and lift her skirt, pull up her stocking, readjust her garters, tweak her panty elastic and throw the skirt down again.

"He'll see," she said, and pushed up her breasts with both hands.

When a key penetrated the lock of the Bailey door, Grace fled to the kitchen. Bailey stood in the doorway, looking at the empty rocker facing the door.

"You're late for lunch," Rosenthal said, "but early for tea."

"Is that you, doll?" Grace called. "You caught me in the middle of a casserole. The phone just rang and I thought it was you."

Rosenthal didn't remember the phone ringing since he'd arrived.

"Who was it?" Bailey asked. "Bernardo?"

Grace leaned against the kitchen doorframe with shoulder forward, skirt tight against her thighs, outlining what was beneath, a familiar pinup pose. She smiled, androgynous head atop a body reduced from roller-derby plump to emaciated sensual.

"Bernardo who?" She licked her lips.

"Bernardo the scrivener. The fellow who wrote you the letter I just got out of the mailbox. Shall I read it?"

"Not in front of me," Rosenthal said. "Skip the personal problems."

"But this goes well beyond the personal," Bailey said. "It's why I wanted you here. The letter is an added dividend, but it's all part of the scheme." He read the letter:

Dearest Bug,

I yearn for Fridays when you come to the supermarket. I dream of you all day behind the meat counter. I see your loins in every lamb chop. I carve your whatsie and your whosies out of sausage meat, sometimes top round ground. If your dumb husband doesn't appreciate you, never forget that I do. I will count the days until you round the corner by the ginger ale.

Your fool and tool,
Bernardo

"I don't know who that bird is," Grace said. "I don't know why he writes to me."

"This is a wife for you," Bailey said.

"Why don't we have lunch," Rosenthal said, "and save private problems for some other time?"

"But this is Mata Hari you see before you," Bailey said. "My very own Mata Hari. Don't feel uncomfortable. If you saw it in the movies you'd probably sit through a second show."

"He writes me all the time," Grace said. "What the hell does he mean, comparing me to a lamb chop?"

"She thinks I can take it seriously," Bailey said.

"How's all your sluts?" Grace asked.

"This too is part of it," Bailey said. "One begets the other, you see. Imaginary betrayal into imaginary distrust. The only one who sees it all clearly is my pooka, and Gracie can't stand him in the house. She thinks he tracks up the walls and ceiling."

Bailey opened the bedroom door, looked at the ceiling.

"No tracks," he said.

"You didn't bring that damn thing back, did you?" Grace ran to the bedroom and inspected it, then the bathroom, the kitchen, behind the sofa and all the chairs, under the table, behind the sketch of James Joyce. "You bastard. If you brought him in . . ."

"She doesn't even know what size he is," Bailey said, "and yet she hates him."

"Are pookas any particular size?"

"Pookas," said Bailey, "are how you find them."

"I always thought they were invisible."

"Only if you can't see them."

"Of course. And is your pooka any particular shape? Like a horse? Or a goat?"

"More goat than horse," said Bailey, "but more pig than goat."

"We got enough pigs in this house," Grace said, backing out of the hall closet.

"Right you are if you think you are," Bailey said.

When she leaped at his throat Bailey caught her wrists and held them behind her. She rubbed herself on him, then kissed him with great ferocity. When he let her go they fondled each other and Rosenthal stood up and looked over Bailey's wall. The Abbey Theatre Playbill was from Saturday, April 12, 1952, for the play "The Money Doesn't Matter," When Bailey saw him looking at it he dumped Grace on the sofa.

"I can't remember the play," he said, taking off his overcoat, wadding it and throwing it at her, "but when I found it in the trunk last year the title reached me." He looked at

Grace, who was watching him with moon eyes. "Didn't it, love?" And Grace nodded.

"The title spoke for all of us down in that squalid little room. Our jolly commitments to some abstraction or other. They'll lower us into the grave with it painted on our tombstones: 'Questing for glory, they died as they lived: dirty and broke. Unemployed agitators attacking the system, all out for number one. They might have had great wealth, but they opted for emotional bunko and the spiritual con. Hot-shit abstractionists. Good riddance.' "

Bailey was a speechmaker when the spirit moved him; sometimes just a buncombe artist, but always with a smile. Rosenthal now could see only grimness as Bailey leaned against the wall, his green muffler hanging loose, his cossack hat in place.

"You talk like a man making some kind of marvelous discovery that the stars don't really twinkle," Rosenthal said.

"Of course. But when you see this thing in others it has a sinister quality. It's a disease. No question about it. Progressive, often fatal and quite contagious. Even my little pussy cat here"—he stroked Grace's stringy hair—"had slipped on the goo of an abstraction. It used to be simple with Grace. Throw her a quick one and she survived happily till the next one came along, as it always did. But now she fears she's losing touch, that feeling is draining out of her like blood dripping from a high-hanging goose. Pretty soon a dry carcass. And a woman like Grace who's been oiled with the juices of love all her life finds this hard to accept. Topped, tossed, tiddled, it's not enough for old Grace anymore. The very idea of pleasure has grabbed her, the need to arouse her own desire, and she sinks deeper and deeper into the morass of intellectualized fuckery."

"He's makin' that stuff up," Grace said. "Oiled by the juices of love."

She tried to sound angry but it was obvious to Rosenthal

that talking about it revved up her engine. She rubbed Bailey's neck, pushed a finger in and out of his ear.

"The next step for Grace would seem to be sexual fits, but that would be a misreading of the abstraction. That would drag it into the real world, and that isn't where it leads anybody. It's led Grace to intrigue. Do you remember that Stanley knew of our last proposal before we called him about it? We suspected a burglar. Recall how the guards anticipated me when I entered the building with the stink bombs? Why go on? I discovered last night at Fobie's from a scab with mixed loyalties that a gay dog from the company, with an oily telephone manner and a pretense toward roller-derby fanatacism, has been calling Grace and talking to her in romantic obscenities and sports jargon, all the while pumping her for news of the Guild. He's off that job now, just today. I wanted you to know all this. Verify it."

"I never told anything," Grace said. "It's a lousy thing to say I did. It's Bernardo who calls."

"I'm on to Bernardo," Bailey said. "That intrigue is also over."

"Intrigue?"

"He overstayed his welcome."

"You take me for granted," Grace said, pouting. "You think nobody wants my body anymore. I'll bring Bernardo right into that bedroom and give you double moose horns."

"Watch out for the pooka in there."

"You did bring that hairy thing back. I'll get rid of it."

She rifled the drawer of an end table for incense and lit it in an Oriental ashtray. She put the tray on the bedroom floor, opened the room's window and closed its door, then rechecked all the other rooms.

"Grace and I are at an ending," Bailey said to Rosenthal. "Our abstractions have become mutually exclusive. There was a time when I sensed that I was divinely favored in discovering Grace because life took on a primitive tone with her, and I've always been drawn back to primitive times. With her I felt I'd reached some essential level of behavior, had plunged beneath the crust of sophistication. But it was just another deception, another trap set by the cult of simplicity. I'm no more pure animal than I am pure spirit. What I am, Rosy old man, is a fuck-up. A man people see as a noble boob, a worthy sucker. Quite an image, eh? But I'm out to change all that. I'm heading for new depths. No more fresh starts for Bailey. I'm after mutation now, lopping off parts till the species is as slick and streamlined as a buttered bullet. Eventually I may be able to sell myself to a freak museum as the Transmogrified Man. He cut out his vital parts and fed the birds and the sewers. He opened his veins and dribbled out his blood to thirsty pigs. And he sold his brain to raise funds for a fashionable supermarket. What you see before you, ladies and gentlemen, is the vile corpse. Note that it has petrified ears, vulcanized genitals and a calcified liver. Proceeds from this exhibition will go to the former owner, who has since become an anopheles mosquito."

Grace came out of the bedroom in time to hear the last of Bailey's comments.

"You were always a mosquito," she said.

"You know, don't you," Bailey said to her, "that the ginger ale is nowhere near the meat counter."

Grace's eyes pulsed. Her eyebrows arched.

"He sees me through the mirror," she said.

"Furthermore, I recognize your handwriting. The way you cross your *t*'s gives you away."

She stared out of a face slowly giving way to defeat.

"Treason drains women of their sexuality," Bailey told her. "It's not the same as infidelity. It's only a matter of weeks before your tits turn to marble."

Grace wheeled around, snatched the casserole off the kitchen stove and poured it over Bailey's overcoat on the sofa. Then she threw the pan, hitting his forehead and opening a vertical cut. Bailey twisted her arm behind her, lifted her skirt with his free hand and sat her down on the steaming food.

"This, of course," he told Rosenthal, "spoils our lunch."

Rosenthal cleared his throat politely and picked up his coat. Bailey took another coat from a closet, twirled his muffler once around, and they moved gingerly out of the room and down the stairs into the sunlight.

"**D**id you read my column?" Bailey asked as they walked along the snowy street.

"Unusual, I'd call it. Will your editor approve?"

"I've modeled my pooka after him. A soulful drunk named Fagin."

"Well, your readers, then. It's a jazzy column, but you've got to admit it's also pretty nutsy."

"My readers are loyal," Bailey said. "If I'm nutsy it's not a problem for them."

"A nice arrangement," Rosenthal said.

When they entered the Guild room Rosenthal went to his desk and Bailey, with a solemn look, sat in his chair. As always when he came into the room, he felt a pinch of joy, a twinge of doom. Now doom stuck a rod in his belly, shooting agony-to-come through him. Once again we must go tilting, each in his own way. The Bailey way was not the Jarvis way. A fuss for Jarvis. But the truck driver in Fobie's had painted a dark vision in Bailey's imagination: spilled ink. The driver knew how to pull the pin on an ink truck, let the black blood of the company flow over the street. The joy of such a vision. Bailey trembled from it. But would it fruit out? What difference would it make?

Bailey stared at the bulletin board. He saw the new report from Jarvis spiked atop all the others. Oh, no, he wouldn't read it. He was too full of good things, vicious things, to let Jarvis spoil the mood. He sat quietly, calmed by the potential of his thoughts, comforted by the familiar contours of chair and wall. His eyes turned once again, O inescapable ritual, to the photo of Rosenthal, Jarvis, Irma, himself and others long gone, taken the first night of the strike when they all so enthusiastically walked off the job. What joy on those faces of last year! What radiance! What anticipation! No enraptured face of childhood could ooze innocence more than those happy strikers. But now innocence was gone. In the days that followed that singular night, scores of Guildsmen trooped through the Guild room in snowboots, ski clothes, thermal jackets, fur caps. They dropped paper cups and the ashes of thousands of cigars and cigarettes on the unvarnished floor. They consumed untabulated gallons of donated coffee from Fobie's (Fobie revoked his donation after two months, claiming hardship). New camaraderies were established among the members, many of whom had never before communicated. They settled into particular corners of the room, favorite chairs; and the whole Guild room took on a fixed appearance that never changed. Lists of scabs and strikebreakers hung on the wall, long out of date, for there had been a heavy turnover of scab labor. Memos on committees caught dust, as did cartoons spoofing company aides and early Guild optimism. The letter from Adam Popkin, the third alternate delegate of the International Guild, sent after the first two weeks of futile picketing and negotiations, still mocked its readers with its capital letters and fading red underlines. Popkin wrote: "I salute you all with the words of Alexandre Dumas the elder, who said: 'All human wisdom is summed up in two words— wait and hope.' I believe that no greater message exists." Popkin's letter grew yellow beside letters of encouragement from other unions. No one moved anything anymore. Nothing changed. There was no disorderly crowd anymore, no chaotic anger, no happy banter. Bailey, never bored with this condition, always mystified by it, took comfort from the emptiness, the fixed quality, preferred it to that formless clot of old.

"I forgot to tell you," Rosenthal said. "Irma quit."

Bailey looked up, stared at Rosenthal, took off his hat. Rosenthal told him the story of his conversation with Francie. Gongs clanged, sirens wailed in Bailey's head. Irma is on fire.

"Eppis, you say?"

"The same," said Rosenthal.

"Have to set her straight, poor girl; probably gone mad. I'll call her and give aid and comfort. Is that or is that not an idea? You straw. You Jew hero. You sliver. Am I right, or would you leave the poor girl alone?"

"I hate to see her go. She's our last contact with sex."

"You circumcised pig. Just because Irma has mountains like the Alps, a valley like the Rhine and the lips of a queen bee, you forget she has a mind. Curb your Semitic dangle, Rosenthal. Remember there's more to life than humpybumps."

Bailey telephoned and identified himself as a representative of the Sundown Burial Squadron, but Irma recognized his voice immediately.

"I'm through," she said. "Don't try to wheedle me back."

"I just want your reasons. What did it?"

"Easy. I stopped kidding myself we'd ever go back to work. I hate that Guild room and that phony picket line. I was even getting to hate you and Rosenthal. You and your damn old endurance, your rotten nobility."

"But the straw, lovey, what was the straw?"

"The hairy wart on Jarvis' chin."

"It's his best feature."

"I kept getting the urge to cut it off with a scissors. I kept thinking: If I cut it off we'll go back to work. Yesterday I picked up the scissors."

"We'll miss you, dovetail."

"Mutualwise, me too." She paused, then through a whimper added: "See ya around the campus. And don't take any wooden pickets, you dumb jerks. Dumb, dumb, dumb. Oh!"

She was in tears.

"She thinks she won," Bailey said to Rosenthal as he hung up. "She thinks she's dead at last. At ease. First she called the undertaker and now she's crying over her own corpse, worrying about us from the next world."

He buttoned his coat, twirled his muffler, covered his great crop of wiry black hair with his cossack hat.

"Doughnuts at eight," Rosenthal said as Bailey strode out.

When he stepped across her threshold, Irma licked his cheek, as a cat kisses after it bites.

"You bastard," she said. "What are you after?"

They were lovers after the strike exploded. He rubbed up against her at Guild meetings, walked with her on the picket line. She talked to him of meditations at sunset, of Robert Frost and Bette Davis. He found out she wore medium Kotex and thought of herself as a squirrel: bushy-tailed nut collector. Bailey took that two ways. Irma said he was right to do that.

"Kiddo, I don't believe what you said on the phone. You didn't tell all."

"I knew you'd say that," Irma said. "As soon as you came in I knew why you were here."

"Irma full of eyes."

"Sometimes I can't stand to look at you."

"Does it eat you I'm not as heroic as I look?"

"Who said you looked heroic?"

"You did. Months ago in the time when we worried over moon phases."

"I watch you," she said, "and you don't shatter. You never shatter. Bailey's not fragile. He'll never break. But I see you erode. I see your eyes wander when they used to be steady. I hear your talk fuzz over like a lawn gone to weeds. Poor Bailey, I say. Poor Bailey. You think I can hang around pitying you?"

"Cross your legs like you used to."

"No."

"Do you know that I love you now?" he said.

Irma laughed with luxurious pleasure, without mockery. Bailey saw beautiful, rounded flesh: a soft, white inner tube: no bones: only a great, pliant whiteness.

"I love you too, bubbykins," she said.

She mixed the drinks and raised her bourbon in a toast to their love. Both had professed it when it was only gilded affection, but after the settling in, Irma backed away from Bailey, the ogre-souled outlaw. Scab lifter. Garter snapper. Titty pincher. Oh, Bailey, you dirty bird. He burned her ears with his language, he scorched her heart with his hot love. Oh you Bailey. Irma backed off. She's no animal. She's a thirty-four-year-old career girl with a clean heart. It was lovely, Bailey, but after all, you've got Grace. Irma quested for reality too. And you're taken, Bailey. You're a career striker, and you're taken.

"How's Grace?" Irma asked him.

"She's conventionally ill," Bailey said.

"Oh, I'm sorry."

"It's chronic now. Don't feel bad. Grace is a brick about it."

"What is it?"

"The madness. It's on her."

"Oh, I'm sorry."

"We all have our crosses," Bailey said.

Lust crept up Bailey's pantleg and tickled him. He wondered about its cause, conjectured on Irma's stockings and her probable garter belt as catalysts, for he knew her chiefly as a ski-pants type in the filthy winter of the early strike. And later, in the springtime, when she was no longer his and had reverted to skirts (was she fending off the winter cold or the Bailey heat with those pants, now that he thinks of it?), he didn't pay much attention. But now the time of Irma's pantslessness had arrived. Bailey looked at her beautiful curve of soft black hair across her forehead, her sweet and simple smile that deceptively covered her toughness. He studied her, thinking: Go quietly, don't push the girl. After all, she's engaged. Let magic ignite the dust. But he didn't wait. The bourbon had loosened his tongue.

"Do you understand it? I'm not sure I do."

"What, bubie? Your love?"

"It's so quiet. It goes on even without you."

"Oh, what glop, Bailey. I never knew you to be sentimental."

He smiled, knowing her to be quite sentimental, and slid his hand up her nylon until he touched flesh. He stroked it gently.

"What are you after, a little massage to perk up the afternoon, or the whole works?"

"Whatever you're prepared to give," he said.

"What kind of a son of a bitch are you, coming in here like this and testing me? You want to tie it all in, don't you? Love, the Guild, sex, resistance, and rescuing the damsel."

"I didn't organize my motives."

"The hell you didn't. Rub Irma's leg. Aladdin and his magic friction machine. She'll come back. She'll get the meaning."

"I see you drifting off, and I want to stop that. But if you're dead, I want to know it. When I lose what I love, I want full reality."

"How delightfully absurd of you to say that," Irma said. She paced and smoked and smirked. Bette Davis–style, Bailey noted. "It really does betray you, you know. On the march to sweet reality. You wouldn't know the real thing if it walked up and grabbed you by the fanny." She shook her head, tossed her hair. "Incredible how you believe we're all committed to that stupid strike. You sound like my aunt telling me it'll end soon because she had a novena said. Well, I don't have that kind of faith. I refuse to go on believing impossible things are possible. I want to be alive during my life."

"Is that why you took up with the undertaker?"

"He pets me, he feeds me, he gives me things. So what if he smells of formaldehyde? I feel normal with him. What did you ever give me?"

"Nothing at all. I took from you steadily."

Irma sat on the sofa across the room and stared at Bailey. What should a girl do with a bastard like Bailey? See him smile. See him leer. Him and his heavyweight crotch. I got over him. I don't need him. The hell with him. She said. Then nostalgia crept into her silence and she crossed her legs in the old way. But certain types of behavior are not necessarily what they seem. What Irma decided to do in the moments immediately following was to carry a relationship to its conclusion. She viewed it as punctuation: nostalgic and funereal. Bang, Bailey. You're dead.

The ink truck bled of its ink grew larger as Bailey thought of it. A gesture at last that would be more than a gesture. It would be the transfiguration of a protest. He would be done with the mortifying slouch of the timid piss ant. Something moved in his center, urging itself upward from the grave. Seeds. Transfigured. Up, up! The crust of the grave began to crack. Isn't it grand what a little call to adventure can do for you, Bailey. Does Bailey love a challenge? Do eggsuckers suck eggs?

He entered the Guild room, sat once again, stared at the photo once again, felt at ease in old contours once again, was swept over with joy, doom, nostalgia and rancor once again, but with a difference: Black ink covered all doom, ebony beautiful. The viscous gook swamped all piss ants. The stink of hot life drove away the poops, suffocated the finks. Bailey giant-stepped through the mire in the hip boots of a rubbery spirit, inhaling the fumes that polluted the lungs of all but the fittest. Up, up, seeds. Up through the black crust. Up!

"We have a volunteer," Rosenthal told him, and Bailey looked at the stranger, a curlytop youth, cultivated torso, cocksure young bear swaggering with collegiate improvidence, shorn of innocence, cloaked in early wisdom. I know the score, said the collegian's face.

"His name is Deek, and he wants to join the Guild."

Bailey smiled at that. Now that he's wise he wants to be a hero.

"He's been reading protest literature and he says our strike is the only thing around that grabs him."

Sad for you, young bear. There are no more heroic protests. No more heroes. Chivalry is even dead as a memory. Now the cycle is so complete that the damsels are out with their lances, protecting the men. Mother Irma, Dame Irma, protectress, gone from us. Our last touch with unified concubinage, sis, mom and Miss Prim, total female, gone.

"This is Bailey, Deek. Our prize bull. He'll tell you about the strike, won't you, Bailey?" Rosenthal continued with the phone calls.

"I like you guys," Deek said, pushing out a sophisticated lip. "The way you buck the odds. My father sells ads for the company and talks about you all the time. He says you're all crazy. He won't even come near this block. He says one of you's got a sniper-scope BB pistol and that you take pot shots at company people. That's cool."

"You're not a spy, are you?" Bailey inquired. "The company hardly needs another spy. They infiltrated us months ago, and now they have the gypsies."

"I'm no spy. My father'd flip if he knew I was here."

"Tell him about our demands," Rosenthal said. "That's what he wants to know."

"Tell the young man our demands," Bailey said. "Of course. Tell the young man the secret of the pomegranate. All right. We began asking for $292 a week, not a lordly sum in a time when expense-account thieves live their lives without ever touching their salaries. Yet $292 was far more than the company would give. What's more, they knew we weren't out for money, which armed them. We talked about it over the table. We readjusted, compromised. I was our negotiator in those days, having regular conferences with Stanley, the company man. Stanley often confounded me by knowing our proposals in advance: those spies in our ranks, of course, selling us to the devil. But it mattered little. When I tried for a wage raise with a surprise offer to cut back on paid holidays, Stanley would counter with abolition of paid vacations. The low point of my time came when I offered a return to the prestrike status quo in return for the right to charge lunches at the company coffee shop. When Stanley refused this I knew we were in for a bad time. Seven months of strike were already gone. Currently the company stipulates that no strikers be permitted to eat in the lunchroom when the strike ends.

"Jarvis took over when I gave up the mastermind role. But ever since he agreed to a forty-percent salary cut below pre-strike levels, his grip on reality has weakened. We understood the depth of his distraction last month when he set up a seafood luncheon meeting with Stanley and tried to send Rosenthal to the pet shop to buy clams. At the moment, Jarvis is still our only contact with the company. Labor lawyers have abandoned us as hopeless, arbitrators have advised us to seek new professions, politicians have found no reason to even recognize our existence now that our position is so weak and our number so small. Jarvis perseveres and Stanley sometimes deigns to meet with him, and we will survive, I presume, as long as the International Guild continues to recognize through its weekly dole that we got into this thing through their original organizational efforts. But when the dole goes, so go we. And until that bleak tomorrow we live on the edge of possibility, believing some white bird of circumstance will one morning light on our shoulders and whisper the secrets of transcendence into our ears. Jarvis negotiates with all the strength in him, then sends in his reports. We avoid reading them since they only spur us to new depressions. Our manner, in a word, is aloof, perhaps even a bit royal.

"So do you see where we stand? You don't. I can tell by the question mark on your forehead. But don't feel bad. Don't count the pomegranate seeds as a means of discovering the riddle of the royal fruit. If you've got the time and the stomach, I suggest you stick around, stay at the edge of our world for a few more hours. We've got an adventure in mind for tonight, and maybe that will illuminate something for you. Transcendence is a sticky business, not given to mathematical purity. Join the onlookers. Watch the Guildsmen. See how they run. At the very least you'll be entertained."

Once in the Guild room, Bailey had the compulsion to leave; once out, to return. Six o'clock. Two hours until the ink truck's scheduled arrival, hour and a half until the pin-pulling technologist met him again at Fobie's. As he walked, the snow began. Grand. Black on white. Black pool spoiling sweet whiteness. Bailey walked toward the company and stood across the street from where he estimated the ink truck would park, where the ink would gush out of the truck spigot, splash into a widening black puddle, rise to sidewalk level and move sluggishly down the gutter toward the sewer. Pool of blackness, blood flowing. More than a gesture. Orgasm of doom. Climax of a dream.

Why did Bailey's dreams turn to garbage? Garbage that stank only in his own nose. Not a great stink, not an unbearable stink, not a stink Bailey would die from. Was it because all dreams were timid dreams? Dreams that shook no foundations, diverted no rivers? Not grand enough to survive the garbage fate? Timid Bailey, you once talked of dynamite on Stanley's doorstep, but you talked of it uncapped. You fought the scabs, whipped them and sent them off with tucked tails. Establish the meaning of that. You picketed until your knees gave out. Establish the validity of such loyalty. You outlasted almost everyone and if you survive you will outlast the rest. Chart the route of your perseverance to indicate where you began, how long you traveled, where you are now. What does this traveling mean?

Only the black vision comforted Bailey.

When he heard a door open behind him he turned, saw Smith the gypsy standing in the doorway of the storefront across from the newspaper. For a month the gypsies had occupied the store, owned by the company and for years used only for stockpiling of newsprint in times of emergency. Seven gypsies lived in a trailer behind the store, led by Putzina, the presumed queen. The gypsies had descended on the storefront suddenly, without reason, bringing back the unknown past to Bailey. Six of the gypsies he did not know, but Putzina was a romantic figure out of his Uncle Melvin's life. Though his uncle never spoke of the woman, relatives recounted the legend: that Melvin and Putzina were the family's conjugal low point: a tug captain and his gypsy scum.

Smith, Putzina's son, watched Bailey now, hand in trouser pocket, mole eyes questioning Bailey's presence in front of the store. Few approached the store since the gypsies arrived; only company people who went in bunches to have their fortunes told by Putzina at lunch hour. And since a half-frozen Negro youth had been found unconscious in the snow beneath a gypsy window, ankles and wrists bound with wire, unwilling to explain why he was there or what had happened to him, terrified to be asked about it, the cautious walked on the opposite side of the street.

When the gypsies first arrived, Smith worked four days as a news photographer; but the company fired him for pawning an enlarger. After that no gypsies were allowed in the main building. They worked out of the storefront as company menials: janitors' helpers, snow shovelers, garbage carriers. Also they watched Guildsmen, reported their movements to the company.

Bailey stared at Smith with an easy eye, without fear of his mystery. Then he walked toward the door and faced the gypsy, their noses inches apart, Smith's bald head agleam, a pendant earring motionless in his left ear. Bailey's eyes leaped from baldness to earring to mole eyes to pucker mouth. Smith took his hand from his pocket, a knife in it. He opened the large blade with his thumbnail and held it like a torch, the blade pointing at the ceiling. Bailey raised his right hand slowly to the same position and doubled his fist. His left hand rose to the defense of his stomach. Bailey saw figures moving behind Smith, but his eye fixed on the blade. A trickle of black fluid ran slowly down from the tip, as if it had been dipped in the ink Bailey had just envisioned in the gutter across the street. Bailey wanted to believe it was oil, but it had a deep, shining blackness unlike even the filthiest of oils. As Bailey watched the trickle, Smith slammed the door and pulled down the shade. Bailey drew back his fist to smash the glass, but held the blow, wondering whether his fantasy had gone wild.

For half an hour after Bailey left the Guild room Deek sat in silence across the table from Rosenthal, listening to the repetitive announcement of a doughnut party, coming to understand, from Rosenthal's tone and the workings of his eyes, the consistently negative response from the other end of the line. Knowing nothing of what eight o'clock would bring only stoked his imagination. These two men seemed capable of mad deeds. He thought of the Molly Maguires and the Wobblies that he knew from history books, and all the labor strife that belonged to times long gone. Neither the dapper seediness of Rosenthal nor the hulking, erudite wildness of Bailey fit any image of workingmen that Deek ever had. His father, with an expanding belly and a thumping heart, had eased himself out of such concerns, if concerns they had ever been, at a young age and had opted for the quiet life of a deskbound salesman.

Anarchy was not in Deek as it was in others of his generation. He craved the rising of his own blood in willful deed: the overwakefulness of heroic action. He did not know Bailey yet, but he sensed that Bailey knew of such things. To be that was to be a horned and toothy beast in a wild field of gazelles.

Rosenthal feared new violence. He understood Bailey's mood and Jarvis' plan only too well, an absurd intersection. He never doubted that the motorcade would descend into hand-to-hand combat, for which Guildsmen were unarmed, unequal. He watched the snow, wishful that it would mount to such heights that the motorcade would be impossible. But there was not enough time for such a wish to be realized. It would only be deep enough to enrich the hazard of wild driving. Rosenthal feared the inequity of the violence. The guards had behaved like wild dogs ever since Bailey broke the nose of one with an elbow jab, and Matsu, the Japanese photographer, almost killed another with a karate chop to the windpipe. Matsu lost an eye in the beating two brutes gave him the week after that incident. They bulled into his flat and dragged him to the yard, where neighbors heard his screams and pulled him off a garbage pile. No one blamed Matsu for leaving the city. The police took a neutral position on the incident, as they'd done throughout the strike, considering it a double dose of pox. They favored the Guild only once, after a guard broke Bailey's left shoulder with a clubbing. They clubbed the guard in retaliation, for Bailey was a man they cared about. He wrote often in his column about shorter hours, better pay for cops.

Bailey bent his head to listen.

"If it's a Mack, the overflow is regulated by a petcock that sits up behind the temperature gauge. On the Internationals there's no petcock. You got a small tube that angles out from the top spigot. But that's only for overflow. The pin is under the belly of the tank. It looks like a doorknob on the Macks, and on some of the Internationals it's got a mushroom top. This you turn clockwise, except on the GM jobs, when it's counterclockwise. And on them it's more like a screwdriver handle with ridges in it, and you got to turn it, then pull. It's got a ratchet inside, so you got to get it just right or it won't come out. Except on the Macks, where there's no ratchet, but there is a sliding panel like a bolt, and you got to shift that back, or up on some models. If it's a White truck, then you got to open the overflow spigot before the pin can come out. The petcock serves as a secondary control that locks the pin in. The ratchet on this one is beveled, so you got to swing it up to the left a little before you get the teeth just right; then you pull and the thing pops out halfway and you slide it up. That's on late models. On the early ones it's got no pin at all and you need a seven-eighths-inch Phillips-head wrench to give it at least three turns. Then it opens out like a door, and you reach under and turn the rotator . . ."

Bailey nodded.

At ten minutes to the ink-truck hour Rosenthal considered calling Fobie's to remind Bailey of the duty. But Bailey would know the time. He would be contemptuous of being nudged. Rosenthal worried over Bailey and all his talk of bombs. He saw him as an aristocrat of the spirit living in an era when aristocrats were lined up at the guillotine. Better to be a little more compliant. What good is a headless spirit? But who could reason with Bailey?

Rosenthal was used to failure. He knew how to deal with it, roll over and up again. But Bailey fanned the breeze, flailing at it. Bailey the magic balloon. Knock him down, see him pop up again twice his old size. Bailey, thought Rosenthal, stop behaving like a balloon. You know what happens to balloons.

Jarvis' voice crackled through the walkie-talkie: "Eight minutes to Yuma."

Rosenthal acknowledged: "Eight minutes. Yuma."

Jarvis spoke from the roof. He stayed out of the Guild room, sensitive to the insolence of his subordinates. He would direct the start of the motorcade from the roof via the walkie-talkie, which Rosenthal would carry. Then when it began he would leave the roof, direct operations from the window of the empty Guild room.

Deek wanted to ask the significance of Yuma. He wanted to know why there was a sign on the wall above the mimeograph machine that read: DON'T SIT HERE. He wanted to know why Rosenthal spent two hours calling people on the phone and why nobody came. He wanted to know what a doughnut party was, where Bailey was, why Jarvis stayed on the roof in such cold weather, and what happened to bring things to such confusion. Deek was full of questions he did not feel he should ask.

Bailey arrived precisely at eight o'clock, sat in the chair and stared at the bulletin board. Then he got up and took a ukulele from a shelf in the closet behind Rosenthal's desk, and stripped it of its cloth case. He ragged a few chords, then softly sang three old songs of the Irish rebellion: "Nell Flaherty's Drake," "Kevin Barry," "By the Rising of the Moon."

Wretched, sentimental bosh, Rosenthal thought. Beautiful, thought Deek. On the roof Jarvis heard the music and spat. Bailey finished the song and laid the ukulele on a chair. He took off his cossack hat and put it beside the uke, knelt and raised his hands prayerfully.

"Salvation must come from the pooka," he said, and solemnly chanted:

Now we go to motorcade
Pride of pookas on parade,
If we wake before we die,
Pooka, pooka, pooka pie.

Rosenthal brewed a cup of instant coffee for Bailey, who took it and stared at the wall.

"Is he all right?" Deek whispered to Rosenthal.

Since he had no answer, Rosenthal ignored the question.

A long, motionless silence was broken by Jarvis, again on the walkie-talkie, his voice wrapped in static, but booming through in ominous monotone.

"Prepare the motorcade."

"I remind you there are only two of us," Rosenthal said. "None of the members have shown up. That leaves us with only two cars."

"The orders," Jarvis said with uninflected purpose, "are prepare the motorcade."

"A two-car motorcade?"

"A one-car motorcade if necessary."

"And if there are no cars?"

"Who are you—Mr. Question Mark? Get moving."

Rosenthal walked to the window and looked toward the company yard, where the ink truck's black hood was visible. Bailey put on his hat. Deek stood, to find his leg asleep, lurched and collapsed on Bailey's ukulele. His knee shattered its box and its strings went limp.

"Garbage," said Bailey. He held the dead uke aloft by its broken neck, then carried it outside and shoved it into an old snowbank until it disappeared. Rosenthal steered the aerial of his radio through the doorway, and Deek followed, pushing into his corduroy coat, pocketing his glasses.

"What should I do?" Deek asked as they walked down the hill toward the company yard.

"Stand clear," said Rosenthal.

Bailey stood on the corner watching the four hired pickets

approach. Rosenthal came up behind him, and Deek crossed the street, leaned against a phone pole.

"Join the line," Jarvis advised. "Study the lay of things."

Rosenthal and Bailey stayed in the shadowy corner. Just before the line about-faced at the corner, Rosenthal signaled with his eye to the picket captain, a hireling, that the plan was under way. The rear of the ink truck was blocked from view by two guards who stood by it with folded arms. Bailey, his collar up to hide his face, searched the empty street for his specialist, finding only a newsboy, no more than ten, who stood beside a pile of first editions of the newspaper, protecting them from the heavy, wet snow with a piece of canvas. He offered a paper to the pickets each time they passed him. Bailey admired his insolence.

"Commence motorcade," came Jarvis' voice from beneath Rosenthal's overcoat. Rosenthal touched Bailey's arm, and together they walked across the street, past the gypsy store and toward the dark parking lot.

"They won't even notice our two cars," Rosenthal said.

"They'll notice us," Bailey said. "But I've got to find somebody first." He told Rosenthal his plan to pull the ink-truck pin. Rosenthal listened, excited by Bailey's picture of a river of ink.

"I'll block the back end of the truck," Rosenthal said.

Deek, who had followed them to the parking lot, stood by politely, waiting to be noticed.

"I want to help, whatever you're going to do," he said.

"Do you have a car?" Rosenthal asked.

"My father's."

"You can block the front end of the truck then. Park down by the corner, facing the truck. When Bailey signals with his lights, nose in front of the truck, but don't get out of your car. The guards might get violent. If they ask you to move, stall, and if they threaten you, move, then come back and park a different way. But don't fight guards or cops. This isn't your trouble."

"It's all right. I like you guys."

He shook hands with Bailey and Rosenthal.

"Up the Guild," he said, and ran off.

Bailey drove down the block toward Fobie's to find his man and Rosenthal waited in his car with motor running, lights off, watching the ink truck and waiting for the driver to come out of the building. He expected more elaborate preparations, for the company certainly knew something was up. But the guard remained at four, a smug number.

Bailey left his motor running and peered through Fobie's window. The specialist was alone at the end of the bar. Bailey went in, grabbed his arm.

"Ready."

The truck driver gave him a glazed look.

"What's this worth to you, pal?"

Bailey drank the trucker's beer and pulled him by the arm out the door.

"You're a volunteer," Bailey told him on the sidewalk. But the trucker wagged a finger in Bailey's face.

"Fifty now or no action."

Bailey grabbed him by the collar and coattail and dunked him head first into a snowbank, grabbed his ankles, shoved him deeper in.

When Rosenthal saw the ink-truck driver come out, he flicked on his lights. No time for Bailey. He dimmed the lights twice as a signal to Deek, who might or might not be watching, and with wheels spinning in the deepening snow he sped toward the truck. He braked to a skid and guided the car into the truck's rear bumper, then slumped over the wheel. Two guards were quickly at his window, whispering. Rosenthal's head pained from a whiplash and his knee hurt where it had hit the dashboard. But he did not move. He heard another car stop, a door slam, and then Bailey's voice.

"Is he hurt? Did you bother to find out?"

But Rosenthal knew the guards never replied directly to the public. Bailey opened the door.

"He looks like a victim of pooka," Bailey told the guards. "Do you know what that means?"

No answer.

"I didn't think you knew."

Bailey raised Rosenthal's head, eased him into a restful position.

"This man has pooka dust all over him. Call an ambulance."

"He's a fake," one guard said. "It's a trick. They're strikers."

"The pooka one looks familiar," another guard said.

Rosenthal heard Jarvis signaling on the intercom, humming the Guild theme song: "Whistle While You Work." Jarvis hummed because he couldn't whistle. Rosenthal pulled his coat tighter to muffle the sound. No time for Jarvis. An ambulance, if it arrived, would clutter the street further, give Bailey's specialist time to get at the pin. A guard grabbed Rosenthal's wrist and tugged. Rosenthal smiled, screamed painfully.

When Deek saw Bailey angle in at the side of the truck he gunned his own motor and with tires all but tractionless on the wet snow, he spun slowly across the intersection and nosed into the front of the truck. He saw Rosenthal sitting as if dead in his car, Bailey bent over the rear of the ink truck, inspecting the damage to Rosenthal's front end. Deek leaped out of the car as the ink-truck driver left the cab of the truck and came toward him.

"What's the big cockamamie idea," Deek said, "parking trucks in the middle of the cockamamie street?"

The stillness of an instant: all sound gone from around Bailey, his shoulders epauleted with new snow, his neck wet from it, a halo caught in the crown of his black hat. He gripped the twisted car bumper and knelt with one knee on the street. Rosenthal was an upright shadow, the guards silhouettes of belligerence behind him, and Deek was screaming at the ink-truck driver like a voiceless figure in a dream. He did not feel the ground wet beneath him, nor the bumper cold in his gloveless hand. He stared at the bull's-eye of black, the outer circle of gray on the white floor of the street beneath the truck.

Drippings.

There were no petcocks, no gauges, no spigots, no knobs, no ratchets, no panels, no bolts, no bevelings, no teeth, no doors, no caps, no rotators, no pin: only a smooth sheet of steel which covered the entire rear of the truck, hinged at one side, padlocked stoutly at the other.

From an unseen source inside the steel sheet, ink dripped, only one drip since this instant began, but it caught his eye. It had soaked outward into the snow in concentric circles, black into gray into white. At the center, where it fell, where it had fallen for all the time that the ink truck was parked, the ebony blackness shone up like the eye of a devil. Transfixed by the spot, he stared into timelessness and the futility of his deeds. Why did he rely on others? Why did he yield to the seduction of impossible dreams? He knew he was better than his failures, but in the center of himself a seed burst and a black flower bloomed. Did only the seeds of new abominations lurk beneath the crust?

Another drop.

It might have fallen onto the tip of Smith's upraised knife. Challenge unanswered. Dare undared. When the company (was it Stanley?) hired the gypsies, Guildsmen shrank inside their fear, fell away. The gypsies stood their sullen watch in front of private homes. Who can live under the hostile eye? Who can live under the upraised knife? There were a few, and Bailey was one. The driven Bailey. But what did it mean to live eye to eye with the sallow, the sullen, the silent face? What did it mean to dream, only dream, of black rivers? Another timid dream out of an innocent, bygone Bailey age.

Now the devil's eye looked at Bailey and drew him out of
innocence. Behold my blackness. Let it seep in and nourish
the black flower. Change your ways, Bailey. Make your mark,
Bailey. You thought you were done with piss-ant behavior,
but you fooled yourself again. You covered yourself. Look at
your hat Bailey. See the halo. See how much whiteness still
hovers over you. Burn it, Bailey. Burn the whiteness. You see
now the abominations that only wait to be born in you. Seek
the abominable, Bailey. Burn the abominable, Bailey. O most
abominable Bailey, burn, burn, burn.

In marijuana clarity Deek once leaped over his father's
head from a standing position. Barely touching the ground, he
leaped back again, then forward, until he was leaping twice
as high as his father. He leaped over his house, then back.
He leaped over his block, his neighborhood. With exultation
he was readying a leap over the city, but he hesitated too long,
and everything changed. No temporizing now. In front of the
company garage at the edge of the yard he heard himself
yelling at the truck driver and at the guard, who said nothing
but watched with his hand on his smooth, brown club. Deek
wore no hat, as did Bailey, but what did that matter? He took
the measure of the guard, felt equal. The guard had no gun.
Deek was not playing to the gathering crowd, but so many
faces buoyed him, protected him. In his suede jacket and with
Levi's tucked into ski boots, he knew his uniform was correct
for the task at hand. Nothing cumbersome, the foot a weapon.
Also he looked as he should: tight, formed, knowing.
"You guys think you own the road."
"Okay, sonny," the guard said. "Move that car."
Behind Deek the garage door went up. He looked into the
black interior, saw a form receding, oil cans along the wall.
A siren. The police at last. Time running away.
"Let him move the truck."
The club touched his suede chest, and he pushed it away,
stepping back. It rose again on the hinge of the guard's fingers,

and he stepped back again, cocked his arm in the shadows.
When the police car whined to a halt he did not look. Keep
your eye on the ball. But the guard looked toward the police,
and the tension went out of Deek's half-raised arm, his fingers
began to uncurl. He then felt an arm tighten around his neck,
pulling him into the darkness.

When the window would not yield to his push, Bailey
smashed it with his fist, then hid behind the snowcapped
hedges, determined to do what he would do even if someone
answered the crash. But no one came, and he unlocked the
window, crawled inside. The shades were all down; yet he
lighted only a moving circle of floor as he stepped carefully
across the room. Willful. Abomination. He wanted first to
see what they did in this room.

He moved along the walls, finding wooden chairs, an
empty table; in a corner a waist-high pile of newspapers. He
found Putzina's crystal ball, not even a ball; just a half-round
magnifying glass set into a hollowed-out piece of wood and
draped with a purple rag. The white eye of his flashlight stared
doubly out of the glass, and his own hand rose up from its
depths as he moved the light closer. He edged around the
entire room, seeing only filthy walls, unpainted floorboards,
and he whispered to himself: "They work with nothing at all."

He felt the wet rag in his pocket, soaking through his
coat, his pants, dampening his flesh even though he had
wrapped it in a newspaper. He took it out now, smelling its
power. It had taken him almost five freezing minutes to wet
it through, dipping its loose twists into the open carburetor of
a car in the shadows of the parking lot, then pulling the link-
age until the ejaculated spray had saturated it.

Now, he thought, you are giving it back to them in a
way they'll understand. Now you have changed. You are done
with empty works. Master of the Order of the Black Flower.
Company of one.

The pile was neat. He lit the match.

The policeman had told Rosenthal twice to get out of the car. Twice he did not move. The third time the policeman said only: "Out or I drag you out."

Rosenthal, with a great show of pain, slid across the seat away from the policeman's face, toward the sidewalk. Jarvis hummed frantically under his coat. And where was Bailey? And his pin man? Rosenthal had seen Deek in the garage doorway, then when he looked again he was gone. Now a police tow truck had backed up, a policeman hooking a chain to Deek's bumper. How would Mr. Dad explain this to the company in the morning? A guard hovered as Rosenthal slid off the edge of the seat and dropped his feet into the snow. Rosenthal stood, leaned, slid along the outside of the rear door as the guard slammed the front door. Leaning with one arm on the car roof, Rosenthal edged back toward the front end and looked at the damage. He bent over, saw the smashed area and realized only then that his knee was seriously hurt. It gave way then and he fell on his side in the snow. The walkie-talkie slipped out and lay in front of his face. Jarvis. Old Jarvis. He pressed the button.

"I wonder if you have any instructions," he said softly into the radio.

"You see that kid by the corner?" came Jarvis' voice.

Rosenthal looked at the newsboy, who was selling the first edition to the crowd with great success.

"I see him."

"Put a picket on him," Jarvis said.

Rosenthal put Jarvis back in his pocket and sat up. There were no pickets anywhere. Even the picket captain had fled. The tow truck backed up to Rosenthal's car and lifted its rear end, pulled it to the parking lot and left it. Deek's car was already off the street. So was Bailey's. Rosenthal was in control of his knee but content to sit in the snow. Then Bailey broke through the crowd and came over with his hand out. They walked slowly to the corner.

"Is Jarvis coming down? Is he sending any help?"

"I'll ask," Rosenthal said. He pressed the button again. "We could use reinforcements, Jarvis. Did anybody show up?"

But no answer came, and when they looked up at the Guild room window where Jarvis had been standing, he was not in sight.

"He's gone," Rosenthal said.

"You suppose he went to dinner?"

"It's possible, but he usually eats earlier than this."

"He may have had a late lunch."

"Not Jarvis. What happened to your friend who knew about ink-truck pins?"

"Weaseled out. Did you notice the fire?"

Rosenthal turned to see the gypsy storefront in flames, guards running toward it. A policeman called for fire apparatus on the tow truck's radio.

"I wonder how that happened," Rosenthal said.

The mob increased as the fire engines arrived. Firemen hosed the flames as Bailey and Rosenthal watched silently from across the street. Rosenthal knew; knew from Bailey's curious smile, and silence. A vision of the penitentiary loomed.

"I lost track of Deek," Rosenthal said.

"A game kid," Bailey said. "I like his style."

The womb must be like this, Deek thought, doubled into the fetal position, swinging helplessly in the air inside the bag of darkness. When they pulled him into the garage and closed the door, the guard drove the wind out of him with two blows of the club and tied his hands and feet with wire.

"Who is he?" the guard asked.

The man with the earring who grabbed him from behind spoke as he wound the wire around.

"I don't know him, but he was with them all day. New blood from outside is my guess."

They bound his hands over his groin and held them fast with wire around his thighs. Then they shoved him into the burlap sack and hoisted him high. Only the taillights of a company truck illuminated the area while they worked, but inside the bag Deek could see no light at all. He made no sound when the first blow landed. The bag spun. The second blow curved around his back. A hose. Another slammed across his face. He felt the welts rising as he spun, tasted blood. He thought they would kill him, but for what? He would get them if he didn't die. He had seen both their faces. He buried his bloody face away from the new blows. No, I won't die from this, he thought.

"Now," he heard, and the bag plummeted to the floor, but from what height, Deek did not have a chance to guess.

Rosenthal saw the garage door open and stared at it, only a fraction of the interior blackness visible from where he stood. But he did not see Deek rolled into the snow of the company yard, for at that instant he heard the woman's shriek and looked back to the fire to see Putzina in her long skirt, her bandanna around her head, running across the crisscross of fire hoses, through the axed door with its broken glass and into the building. A fireman screamed at her, ran to grab her skirt, but she was inside. He turned a twisted mouth to the others on the sidewalk who had been as helpless as he in stopping her. Less than a minute, Rosenthal guessed, and she came running as she had gone, but with her coat, her bandanna, her skirt flaming. The fireman clutched her to his black rubber coat, threw her into the pile of snow in front of the building and smothered her body with his own. In her hands she held a newspaper, folded like a fish wrapper. She beat out its flaming edges on the snow in which she lay. Even from across the street Rosenthal could recognize the money as it flew out with each new thwack of the paper on the snow.

"That old woman," Bailey said.

Rosenthal heard the garage door close and only then saw Deek's crumpled body. He nudged Bailey and they ran to Deek, hovered over him.

"I think one of my legs is broken," Deek said. Blood oozed from his forehead, his cheeks, his swollen lips.

Bailey shook his head. "I don't know what to do about this," he said.

"There's nothing to be done," said Rosenthal. "Just get him to a hospital."

"We blocked the bugger for a little bit," Deek said.

"They won't forget us for a while," Rosenthal told Deek.

Bailey stared at Deek's bloody face. "Garbage," he said.

Rosenthal looked up to see that the truck had been moved to the inner wall of the company yard. Its driver stood beside the truck's spigot, monitoring the flow of ink into the press room. Bailey threw off his hat and like a goaded bull, head down, charged across the yard and butted the back of a guard who stood beside the driver. As the guard went down, two others converged on Bailey with clubs, and when he went limp they dragged him to the sidewalk and dropped him face down in the snow. Rosenthal pillowed Deek's head with Bailey's hat and limped toward Bailey. As he dragged him toward his car, Irma ran out of the crowd, and together they lifted Bailey into the back seat. The front wall of the burning building collapsed into a river of slush. Deek grunted with pain as they carried him to the car and laid him on the floor. Irma sat with her feet straddling Deek's chest, Bailey's head in her lap, blotting his blood with her bright orange scarf.

Bailey opened his eyes and looked up at her.

"The trouble with richly endowed women like yourself," he said, "is that they lack a sense of humor about life."

"Shut up and quit bleeding," Irma said.

As Rosenthal drove, the bent fender rubbed against the tire, humming like a giant fly suffering an insecticidal death. Yet it was not without its musical quality and as Bailey regained full consciousness near the hospital, it was a fit orchestration for the banal thoughts that passed through his head.

EXTRA!

MISSING STRIKER MAY BE VICTIM OF FOUL PLAGUE

BLACK SPOTS MIGHT BE SORE POINTS

Characteristic it was of Tom Swift to act calmly in times of stress and danger, and he ran true to form now. Only for an instant did he show any sign of perturbation. Then with calmness and deliberation the young inventor quickly did a number of things to the controls within his reach.

—VICTOR APPLETON
Tom Swift and His Undersea Search

Rosenthal's knee had grown to half again its size, and so he too lay on a stretcher beside Bailey and Deek, all of them behind a white curtain in a partition of the emergency room. An intern had treated all their visible wounds and now Irma ministered to the three with words and a cold towel, waiting for the nurse to wheel them individually to the X-ray room.

"Oh, you stupid, stupid people."

She pitied the three men on the stretchers: sweet Rosenthal, the new and gorgeous young Deek, and Bailey. She could love them all. Cuddle and coddle them. Pet them. Bring them inside. Smother their trouble with her breasts. Talk to them, listen to them. Such marvelous men who would never grow old because they would never grow up. Bailey was almost thirty-five but he was as young as Deek, really. And Rosenthal, gentle man with an indestructible vanity. No, they wouldn't age; they would die running, die on top of a woman or with a fist in the face of an enemy. Give up the Guild? Why, she might as well give up God. Give up Bailey? How? Bailey was born under a star. He was born with a caul; he told her that. He was an outlaw now. She knew he set the fire; he was the only one capable of it. But that was because he was always an outlaw. Now others would see what Irma had long known: that most of his character was buried. Bailey the iceberg. Bailey the tree with roots as deep as his leaves were tall.

"Irma, wipe my forehead," Bailey said.

She heard the gypsies arrive before she saw them: humming, wailing softly as they shuffled in behind the stretcher that bore their queen. The ambulance attendants put Putzina in a private room just off the emergency-ward corridor, and in front of the closed door six gypsies took up their vigil. Smith sat nearest the door, a movie camera on his lap.

The wailing, broken by sudden silences and then begun

anew, drew Irma away from her stretcher cases to the doorway, where she watched the tableau. She feared the gypsies as everyone feared their secret ways. Did they really want to be left alone as they said? Smith seemed to contradict that notion. She heard him talking for the benefit of a crowd of scabs one night in Fobie's. The scabs were admiring his earring, a gold, scimitar-shaped baseball bat that dangled from his right earlobe. Irma saw his eyes shine when he explained that the bat bore the facsimile signature of Ted Williams. "Remember the day," Smith added in glory tones, "when Ted hit the home run and then gave all his fans the finger?"

Bailey said Smith wasn't his real name. Bailey knew from his uncle that his true name was Séptimo Ascensor, which meant seventh elevator, but that he changed it to Séptimo Smith because he wanted to be an American.

The more Irma studied the gypsy grief, the more her fear gave way, the more love burgeoned in her heart for an outcast people. Smith was a repulsive little bald man; she did not want to love him. But she could console him, mother him a little in a moment when his own mother was so gravely hurt. He was all rumples in his ill-fitting suit coat and pants, his shirt long unwashed and his ten-cent-store pretied necktie undone from the collar and hanging down his shirtfront like a broken flower.

"I hope your mother isn't too badly hurt," Irma said.

Smith did not speak, did not look at her. The gypsies around him stopped their wails.

"Is that your camera? Do you take movies?"

He gave her a blank look.

"I thought you quit the Guild," he said.

"I did," she said, "but only today. How could you know?"

He wound his camera and photographed Irma from her shoes to her head.

"You didn't answer me. And why are you taking pictures?"

"Channel Eight will do a special if Putzina dies. And there's a Paris director who's been after me for years for films of a queen's funeral. Five thousand if he likes it. Not bad, eh?"

"You're pretty cool about it, I'd say. Your own mother and all."

"If I get worked up, I get eczema. No sense in making a thing out of it if she doesn't die. And if she does, well, after all, she's a queen. She belongs to the world. What a selfish son I'd be if I kept her death all to myself."

Smith stood up and photographed the gypsies lined against the wall, closed in on the number nailed to Putzina's door, opened it and photographed through the crack.

"May I go in?" Irma asked. "I'd like to pay my respects to the queen."

Smith shrugged and let her walk ahead of him into the sickroom.

What Irma could see of Putzina's ancient, fleshless body was smeared with orange ointment. Her greasy and matted hair, much of it singed, had soiled the pillowcase, and her arms trembled outside the soiled sheet. Her pushed-up face, oily and brown, was without teeth, giving her mouth the shape of half an eggshell. Irma leaned over, and Putzina looked up.

"I hope you're not in too much pain," Irma said. "I know you don't know me, but I know someone who knows you. Mr. Bailey's Uncle Melvin. I work with Mr. Bailey, and he says his uncle speaks about you fondly."

The old woman gave Irma a long stare.

"Melvin is a perverted old bastard."

"He remembers you lovingly, from what I hear."

"He left his Putz. He left me for a cat."

"Oh," said Irma. "I didn't know."

"Busne," Putzina snarled. She spat at Irma. "Meripen pa busne."

Irma turned to Smith, who stood behind her in the doorway, filming the scene.

"What did she say?" Irma whispered.

"Meripen pa busne," Smith said, and he spat in Irma's eye.

Irma backed away from the bed just as Putzina sat up and
grabbed for her, sensing the old woman wanted to claw away
a fistful of her flesh. A plump nurse who had been standing in
a corner took Putzina by the shoulders and forced her to lie
back. Then the nurse ran from the room. Outside the door
Irma gave Smith a dirty look.

"You should get your pants pressed," she said.

"There's no room in America for vanity," Smith said, and
humming a snatch of tune that seemed to Irma vaguely patri-
otic, he photographed her as she walked back to the emergency
room.

When Irma told her trio about the gypsies, they insisted
on a look, and so one by one she rolled their stretchers into
the hallway and elevated their heads with the crank. Smith
was on the floor again when the nurse returned on the run with
a doctor. The gypsies sat quietly and wailed softly until one
old gypsy man with a grassy moustache stood before the
sickroom door and rocked in rhythm with the wailing. All the
gypsies stood then and rocked. Smith filmed it. The sight of the
camera seemed to send one young gypsy girl into a leaping
fit. She jumped onto the only bench in the corridor and wailed
with both index fingers up her nose. Smith followed her
with his camera as she buried her face in her hands, leaped
off the bench and prostrated herself. The mustachioed gypsy
sat on her buttocks, wailing in his own style, slapping her on
the thighs, holding an imaginary set of reins and riding her
as if she were a horse.

The plump nurse came out and spoke to Smith: "You're
her son?"

"You got it right," Smith said, photographing the nurse.

"You'd better come in."

"Right," he said, keeping his camera on her as she re-
entered the sickroom. He followed her and closed the door.

The six gypsies took off their hats and coats and piled
them a few feet from the door. Then they circled the pile,

mumbling and wailing, the women in a falsetto, the men's
mumbles turning into Spanish-sounding words that echoed
what Putzina said to Irma:

"Get it down," Bailey called to Irma. And she scribbled
what she could get:

Meripen pa busne,
Majaro Undebel.
Ful pa busne,
Majaro Undebel.
Chinela janreles busne,
Majaro Undebel.

In the pile of clothing Irma discovered a pattern: a catafalque with a built-in corpse. One fur hat was the head, and a
buttoned coat, with arms crossed, lay supine atop the other
clothes. The gypsies circled it faster, the men clapping, then
pausing and clapping again, then leaping little hop-leaps with
feet together. As the pace quickened the leaps increased in
number, the claps took on a frantic ryhthm and the women's
wails soared into new falsettoed heights. The sickroom door
slammed open, ending the dance abruptly. Smith stood in
the doorway with the limp body of his mother in his arms. He
placed her gently on the catafalque, retrieved his camera from
the sickroom and photographed the scene. Slowly, as if they
had not previously reached a crescendo, the other six gypsies
resumed their dance.

Smith shot pictures from above, standing on a chair; he
lay on the floor beside his mother and shot upward into the
circle of dancing faces. He stood and photographed Putzina,
beginning with her feet and traversing her length, past her
criscrossed legs up to her stomach, where her hands lay flat,
index fingers pointing at each other, past her invisible breasts
and then to her face and stringy hair that was wet from the
ultimate sweat. The men clapped faster, leaped higher, the
wailing now at scream pitch. Nurses made feeble, failing
efforts to halt the dance. The women pulled at their hair
between claps and leaps, and the men beat their chests with

both hands. They clawed their faces, and blood flowed from the scratches. Doctors, patients, nurses jammed the hallway; old people in wheelchairs, in casts, supported by canes and crutches, nightrobed, barefoot: They all gawked.

The self-scratching became competitive among the women. They tore open their blouses and dresses at the neck and raked the skin of their breasts. As they shook themselves the blood flew, speckling the floor and walls and even the ceiling. One woman marked Putzina's face with her drippings, and Smith howled, dropped his camera, pushed the woman out of the circle and blotted the dead face with his coat sleeve, then his handkerchief. The gypsies watched mutely as he knelt and smoothed his mother's hair, ran his thumbs over her eyebrows, then faced Irma and the three stretchers.

Two men in overcoats and fedoras with brims turned down all around pushed through the gawkers. Smith rose slowly, staring at Bailey. He threw his arms in the air, arched his back like a cheerleader and yelled: "Slow, busne, it will be slow," simultaneously taking a knife from his coat pocket and flicking open its blade. He started for Bailey, knife held like a lance. The men in hats grabbed his arms, and one rapped him with a blackjack. The knife clattered across the corridor and he fell. The men lifted him, two male gypsies lifted Putzina, and the rest snatched up the clothes and camera. In swift procession they strode down the corridor, ignoring protesting doctors and nurses who threatened, then pleaded for them to return the body. But they pushed through the swinging doors and were gone.

"The knife," Bailey said to Irma.

She found it in the shadows. As Bailey studied it, finding no black fluid, Irma saw that like Smith's gold earring it bore Ted Williams' signature on one side, the fleur-de-lis on the other. Built into it were a removable toothpick, a corkscrew and a nail file; and the smaller blade, near where it hinged, was usable as a bottle opener.

The pain in Rosenthal's knee receded under the power of a pill; also under the anesthetic of gypsy distraction and under the concentration of absurdities that danced holes in his brain with their jackass hooves. Seeing Jarvis come down the hallway sent his dancers into a wild jig, but also brought Rosenthal a sensation of comfort. He always knew Jarvis was inept as a leader, rather above average in ineptitude. Yet Jarvis still held a power over him. Are you a sheep, Rosenthal? No. I have wielded power over others and understand the process. The first time was when he helped run a machine-shop tool room in late adolescence and controlled the tools of master mechanics. He was much like Jarvis then. You want inside micrometers, do you? Well, they're not here. Wait awhile. And you. Where's your check? No tools without a check. Two-inch reamer? Broken. Wait. Just wait. He did not withhold tools any more than Jarvis withheld meaningful direction from the Guild. Neither he nor Jarvis could be held responsible for the complex needs of others. But of course they were. The mechanics had cursed him, just as Guildsmen cursed Jarvis, for being inadequate; for the role was contemptible. And of course, he was a duty figure still. His wife demanded it of him. The Guild demanded it. He demanded it of himself. Yet the duty had nothing to do with his deepest needs. It was merely therapeutic; about as relevant as hair collecting. But as long as he kept busy, then the failure of all Guild effort would seem only temporary.

The comfort from Jarvis' oncoming presence was like that: an illusion that nothing had changed and that there was a chance still. What, after all, is more unsettling than the break-up of the club? Yet he dreamed of change, dreamed of running the Guild himself, with Jarvis out of the way. It would be a slow process to rebuild, for the Guild was as burned out as the gypsy storefront. But there was a foundation, and block by block it could rise. Slowly, yes. Excruciatingly, perhaps. But it could rise.

A nurse wheeled Deek toward the X-ray room. Jarvis stopped and watched him go. Then he clomped up to Bailey's and Rosenthal's stretchers. His face was drawn and sunken, product of collapse: All my teeth fell out early. His eyes, Rosenthal thought, were clear pools of ink eradicator. Life would make no mark they wouldn't remove. Or was that being unjust to old Jar? Hopeless sap. He deserves better too.

"We missed you," Rosenthal told him. "I tried to get you on the radio."

"I must have been in the bathroom."

"I looked for you after the fray too. We could have used a hand, as you can see."

"My wife called. She wanted to borrow the dog."

"How's your wife?"

"The hell with her."

"How's everything else then?"

"We're in trouble. Stanley called. He's marked us for removal."

"Like urban blight?"

Bailey lay with his eyes closed, hands on his belly like a corpse.

"Tell him about Putzina," Bailey said.

"She just died," Rosenthal said. He told Jarvis of the gypsy ritual and Smith's attack, showed him Smith's knife. Jarvis opened the blade, picked his teeth with the toothpick, cleaned his left thumbnail with the nail file.

"Let me check this out," he said. "This doesn't look like a gypsy weapon to me. I'll have it researched. I'm suspicious of it."

The nurse who had wheeled Deek away returned with an empty stretcher. Deek's leg was broken, she said, and he'd be admitted. Now they would check Bailey.

"Here I go to the picture show," Bailey said.

"If Stanley presses for arson charges," Jarvis told Rosenthal and Irma, "he says the police will want to talk to all of us."

"Who said it was arson?" Irma asked.

"Nobody yet."

"There's the birds who slugged Smith," Rosenthal said.

Jarvis walked down the hall toward the hatted men for a better look, but when he neared them they went out the door.

"You call them gypsies?" Jarvis asked Rosenthal. "They're company guards. One is Fats Morelli. We used to bowl together. He used a fingertip grip. His father came to America from Naples with two barrels of olive oil. The other one's Clubber Reilly. He was our milkman years ago. Lived with his mother up on Goat Hill. He kept leaving skim milk when what we wanted was buttermilk. Or sometimes we'd ask for the regular milk and he'd leave heavy cream."

"Never mind the irrelevancies," Rosenthal said.

"These are specifics. Did you know that the old woman had two thousand smackeroonies wrapped in that newspaper?"

"I didn't know the amount."

"We'll have this out," Jarvis said. "You guys put on a lousy motorcade."

"I could use a sandwich," Irma said.

"I've got to go get the dog and feed him," Jarvis said. "We'll meet tomorrow at two o'clock. You all better be there."

Irma went for sandwiches at the hospital coffee shop. She brought one for Deek, but he was asleep under a sedative. When she went back to the emergency room Rosenthal was gone. She found him at the X-ray room with no broken bones. She went back up for his clothes and found Bailey's clothes too, but no Bailey.

Rosenthal stood up from his stretcher and fastened his black cape, then tipped his Tyrolean hat at a jaunty angle.

"Bailey is playing hide and seek," he said.

"Nobody in emergency's seen him," Irma said.

"I got his chart here," the X-ray attendant said, "and there's the stretcher he came down on. But when I got ready to take him he was gone."

"Did you see any strange-looking people around?" Irma asked.

"Everybody looks strange in this joint," he said. "Take him, for instance." He gestured at the dashing Rosenthal.

They checked the admitting office, emergency again, but Bailey was not in the hospital. As they stepped out into the snowy night Rosenthal looked at Irma.

"Welcome," he said, "to dry gulch."

As Irma took his arm and they picked their way over the slippery slush, Rosenthal tried to form an action plan, but could not. How to rescue Bailey when you could not say with certainty that he required rescuing, that he had not done something outlandish on his own? Sudden departures were hardly new to the Bailey style. Yet there was a portentous quality about this one. There was absence of his allegiance to the continuity of a Guild moment. It was un-Baileyesque not to see things through to the conclusion.

Irma's arm distracted Rosenthal.

Irma saw two winter birds fly to the shelter of a ledge beneath the eaves of the hospital. Swiftly she recapitulated her recurring dream: the flock of blackbirds landing on the fence that protected the plowed field, the beginning of a sudden snowfall as harbinger of a wave of frigid air; the temperature swiftly dropping seventy-five degrees and blast-freezing the blackbirds to their perch, inside their coverlets of snow; television news cameramen coming to photograph the phenomenon of hundreds of birds frozen to the fence; commentators marveling at the scene; thousands of curiosity seekers passing by. Only Irma noticed the few winter birds that flew over the scene and perched on the limb of an apple tree, studying the curious as well as the corpses.

"I wonder," Rosenthal said, "what would happen if we won the strike. Or even if we won just a round."

"The sun would stand still in the heavens," Irma said. "And the whole schmeer would melt."

"Bailey is a fixed idea."

"So I noticed."

"I keep wanting to change his ways, correct him."

"You should seek more rewarding work."

Rosenthal opened the door of his Mercedes for Irma. As she got in, her skirt went up to mid-thigh. Rosenthal saw, stared perhaps two seconds too long.

Confronting the possibility of Bailey's death, Rosenthal also confronted his own. The piper's tune beckoned. But where did it lead? The odd thing was that it always led back to where it began: concentric life. Here we go round the sameberry bush. Yet what else was there to do? Why hadn't he or Bailey ever gone on to higher tasks, or even another Guild local, where they could function at least in the old way, the way they functioned before the strike? Ah, that was the question, was it not? It was easy to answer that the old way was the old way, which was true, but a riddle. Rosenthal could conceive of nothing that would improve his present condition. It seemed he had felt that way since the beginning of the strike. Now even winning the strike might not improve anything for him. He might continue to sit in the Guild room each day, working for Jarvis, answering the phone, posting new notices. Habit might dictate what dream once motivated.

Without lipsticks Irma's lips were provocative.

Irma wondered if she really understood what was happening in Rosenthal's mind. She saw his eyes reflecting apparent boldness of thought, which might or might not become action, and it annoyed her. She did not really blame Rosenthal for his aggression. He had always kept himself in gentlemanly balance. But the nasty animal that growled within all men, that did what it damn well pleased: that, at the moment, was what she despised.

"What's your best guess on where he is?" she asked.

"With the gypsies," Rosenthal said. "Where else?"

He started the car and pulled slowly out of the hospital parking lot, the gypsy trailer his first destination. Irma crossed her knees, revealing nothing. Rosenthal turned his head at the movement nevertheless. Another habit pattern. Since he had no self-doubt that tried to shake him from his patterns, he assumed they were correct for him, even if they were also ritualistic, seemingly mindless, often absurd and sometimes deadly. His wife wanted him different. Grace wanted Bailey different. Bailey wanted everybody different. People corrected their neighbor in their own image. Yet there was a smugness in himself and in Bailey that seemed to assume that self-correction on certain matters was no longer profitable. The way was fixed for them and they understood its terms. Rosenthal concluded that such understanding might be the beginning of self-sufficiency. But weren't hermits also self-sufficient? Ah, to be a hermit, now that death is near. How does a hermit fail?

Irma's nakedness was now in his mind.

As they neared the company yard, Irma saw that her preconception of the scene was askew. There was no army of guards as she had anticipated, no cordon of police around the building, no firemen raking over the ashes of the burned storefront. One company car with two uniformed guards in the front seat idled near the spot where the inert Bailey had been dropped into the snow after the beating.

"We'll ask them," she said.

"Ask them what?"

"Selected questions."

"I don't think you should."

"Their reaction might mean something even if they don't tell me anything."

"That's freshman talk."

She shrugged and smiled, and as Rosenthal's hand moved toward her in a gesture whose meaning she could not assess with certainty, she slid quickly out of the door and walked toward the guards at quick-pace. The sidewalk now seemed strange, though she had picketed along it for a year, knew all its blemishes. Now it seemed like a path on the moon. Beyond the snow-covered embers of the storefront Irma saw an empty lot, the gypsy trailer gone. Two more subtractions. Where would the gypsies go next? How could Bailey be traced? They might take him anywhere. Across the ocean. To Mexico. There are even gypsies in China, so they say. Life suddenly seemed very odd around her. What if Bailey were gone for good? Nothing was like it had been. Even Rosenthal's reaching hand had no basis in Rosenthal history. Was Rosy mutating? Odd. Not unpleasant. After so many months of predictable boredom, ridiculous failure, useless violence and futile hope, a bit of mystery amid the verities seemed a gift from oblique gods. She strode up to the side of the guards' car, whose motor was running, and spoke through a half-open window to the one on the passenger side.

"I'm looking for Mr. Smith," she said. "He's one of the gypsies." The guard looked at her and dragged on his cigar, then blew a smoke ring at her.

"She says she's looking for Smith," he said to the driver, who smiled. Then both men looked ahead through the windshield.

"Well, have you seen him? Do you know where I can find him? Or any of the gypsies?"

The driver raced the motor, drowning out some of her words.

"If you can't tell me about Smith and the gypsies, maybe you'll be able to give me Stanley's home phone number."

Both guards killed their smiles. The driver shoved the shift lever into reverse and backed across the yard with a screech of tires. He nosed the car around, flicked on the headlights and began moving toward Irma, who was already in motion, running toward Rosenthal. The guard stopped only a few feet away as Rosenthal pulled in at the curb, his car door swinging open, and yanked Irma inside.

His arm was on her shoulder as he sped off, and the thought came to him: There is trial and error in all relationships. Have courage. Sometimes we draw strength from one another. We don't always bleed one another dry, and the trick is caution. But no matter how cautious he might be, he knew there were stumbling blocks in any new relationship with Irma. They were blocks he had stepped over all his life, never picking them up. He seemed in puberty again, groping to understand his animality. He held Irma's arm as if it were a fragile vase. He was oddly awed that after such violence he was able to concentrate only on her. He could see a great deal of her left thigh the way she was sitting, and he eyed it without turning his head.

"You saved my life," Irma told him.

"That's a fringe benefit from Guild membership. I'd let nonmembers and scabs make it on their own."

"Everything suddenly seems different," she said, "like we all died and went nowhere."

"Don't dwell on death. You're all right. Bailey'll be all right too."

"Says who?"

"I'm going to call Stanley."

"You don't know his number. You'll never get through."

"I'll call the company."

He parked by a drugstore and Irma followed him to the phone booth. He left the booth door open so she could hear.

"This is Mr. Rosenthal from the Guild," he told the company operator. "I want to speak to Stanley."

"He's gone for the day."

"Connect me with his home then. This is life or death."

"I am unable to do that. Sorry."

"Will you see he gets a message then?"

"That's what I'm here for, bozo."

"All right. Tell Stanley that I know the gypsies have abducted my friend Bailey, and that I will consider it a holy crusade to avenge through Stanley any harm done to Bailey. Tell Stanley I would therefore massacre all of his relatives and desecrate their graves at the earliest opportunity. Tell him that I would blow up his house and car, poison his pets and destroy all that he owns in the world. And when done with that I would seek him out and strangle him slowly over a twenty-four- or perhaps forty-eight-hour period. Do you have that?"

Silence.

"I say, do you have that?"

"To be sure," came the operator's abstracted whisper.

"Excellent," Rosenthal. "And so good night. And thirty."

Irma took his arm when he came out of the booth, kissed his cheek.

The difference between Bailey and Rosenthal, Irma thought, is that Bailey confronts the flow of life by running into the middle of it. Rosenthal waits for it to wet his foot. But they both swim in it. Lovely, she thought, feeling great warmth toward Rosenthal. But when he leaned toward her, moved his hands past the gearshift, stopped briefly on the tan leather seat and then bounced onto the inside of her thigh, she frowned and lifted the hand away.

"What the hell," she said, "don't you even inquire?"

"Does Bailey?"

"Ah ha, you fiend."

"Fair's fair."

"I'm not attracted to you, Rosy. Not bedwise."

"I'm exceptionally well hung."

"Medical science may be interested."

"I've always thought you were desirable."

"That's lovely, and nice for my ego, but what's the point? Twenty minutes in the back seat to bleed your bioemotional need? Then what?"

"I hadn't carried it beyond a beginning."

"Well, goddamn it," she said, suddenly angered, "carry it beyond. Don't just sit there sending out feelers that make sense only inside your head. Find out what's in *my* head, why don't you? Establish *my* reality. You think I hang around just to relieve your glands?"

But when he dipped his eyes, she thought: Poor Rosy, sulking now. Inside his cape. Under his feather. He never hated himself in all the Guild times. Failure couldn't do that to him. Will he despise himself now for insulting a lady? And guessing wrong?

"I'm not insulted," Irma said. "I really am flattered. I didn't mean to yell."

"I'm not very good at seduction," Rosenthal said. "I got bashful as I grew older. You wouldn't have known me in college. I used to take off my pants in public for a gag." He paused. "You're the only one I've told that to in twenty years."

"I'm flattered again."

"I could tell you things."

"I hope so."

"Last year when we needed money I got a part-time job as the Easter Bunny. My wife doesn't know that either."

"Don't confess everything. You don't have to win me over. You and Bailey are the best men in the world. It just happens that it's Bailey who turns me on."

"Bailey said I was a fool, but he's the fool. He makes himself ridiculous. He doesn't care how people see him. He probably wouldn't mind if they saw him dressed like the Easter Bunny."

"You've got Bailey pegged," Irma said, pulling her skirt over her knees.

Demons danced. They cackled out of a hellish haze that reeked of rotten eggs and animal dung. Up from dead regions they flew and burrowed, over the haze, through it. Faces turned into bats, bodies into flying corpses. Arms became penises with pitchfork heads. Bats turned into flying vaginas. The laughter of the demons belched out of cavernous throats while a choir of maggots chanted the *Dies Irae* in squeaky celebration of happy evil. Locusts swarmed over the maggots and devoured them, then turned into flecks of salt. A dragon with a cow face licked the flecks away with a smoking tongue. The booming voice of god zagged through walls of smoke, falling on the ears of demons like thunderbolts. The god-words made no sense. God spoke in static. The demons laughed louder. The locusts and maggots returned, crawling, flying, dancing with joy.

Bailey knew he was dead.

He opened his eyes to see the demons more clearly. Always he sought to give shape to the shapeless, dust his spooks with the ashes of his fear. Given shape, they assumed substance. Bailey feared few things of substance.

Faces watched him: blubber lips under the old man's moustache; gold teeth flashing in the flicker of light; and nippled beads the size of cherries hanging to the waist of the long-nosed, sensual young woman: that dancer. The child (Bailey took him for a deaf mute) seemed to hear nothing through his large ears. His mouth shaped sounds but made none. Beside the child Smith sat, and beside Smith the gold-smiling woman who might have been fifty. She was the only one who smiled.

Bailey knew he was not dead. Not yet. He saw the gypsies by the light of the kerosene lantern which sat on a half-box. Smith stood when he saw Bailey's eyes open, paced, kicked the hay on the floor. They were all in the barn, which was as empty of useful objects as the store had been. Snow fell inside

the barn, through the broken roof and onto the warped floorboards. But they all sat beneath the empty hayloft, and no
snow touched them. Bailey's head throbbed from the beating
and from the final blow that had darkened his mind. The
pain in his body seemed general, so many places had he
been struck. And now he shivered on the floor without coat,
hat or muffler. The two men who had attacked Smith in the
corridor had taken Bailey by surprise near the X-ray room.
They had gagged him, trussed him swiftly at knifepoint, and
then dragged and carried him out a fire exit to the car where
Smith, conscious by then, was waiting. Immobile in the car between Smith and the old gypsy man, Bailey wondered: Is
this the last ride? Will my life end like a cheap movie? The
smiling gypsy woman drove, the child and the dancer in the
front seat beside her. They drove out of the city and onto a
dirt road that led to the desolate farmhouse and barn, both so
empty, so tipped by time and weather that the sides of both
had sagged with rot. The buildings were a century and a half
old: small, primitive, the beginnings of fertility gone to a
natural, weed-choked death. He knew approximately where
he was: in the city still, but on the edge of wild, hilly land
that in the time of the early immigration had been called
Cabbageville.

The old man and Smith had pulled Bailey out of the car, his
head and torso aching even then from the beating by the
guards. Smith slammed the car door and in almost the same
motion punched Bailey in the stomach, then about the head.
The old man delivered the blow to the temple that sent Bailey
to his knees, onto his face, and into blackness.

In the phantasmagoria that stank and danced, fading now
as the light of kerosene chased the fog, Bailey sensed a beginning, an ending. Never before had he been so helpless: bound
with wire hand and foot and alone amid vengeful, violent
gypsies. The time of the early strike, when he was one with
hundreds, when those hundreds knew there were hundreds

more of like mind waiting, even eager to lend aid, comfort, money, food, even blood to brother or sister in trouble, seemed like a paleozoic age away with only fossilized memories to remind him of a reality that once was, or purported to be. He could count on nothing now to help him. Help might come, but as from a comet: out of nowhere, unsought, unexpected. Also, it might not come. He could die as meaninglessly as a bug dies, having lived only to procreate. And he had not even done that. Outdone by a bug. And done in by his own hand. For he knew he had brought himself to this situation. It was he who brought on the gypsies. They descended like a mysterious plague after he twice outraged the company on successive days, first loosening the brake, kicking away the wheel blocks and watching a newsprint-loaded trailer truck roll back and smash away a section of company wall; and again, in the disguise of a delivery man, parking a rented truck in front of the building, carrying a parcel past the door and elevator guards, pressing forward for personal delivery of the package to Mr. Klopp, the advertising manager, leaving it by the elevator door in the advertising office, one end of the parcel loose enough to permit the eventual, curious emergence of its contents: a male skunk; and thereafter storing up the legends of that day's chaos and evacuation to warm his heart in arctic times to come.

He smiled now, remembering, and saw Smith scowling. Gypsy. Counterforce from Stanley. His own counterforce in his mind, the fire, flaming in his cortex. Smith paced while the others sat on the shelf that might once have been a farmer's workbench before the farm had failed of its promise.

"I want to know did anyone actually see him," Smith said. "Did anyone see anything at all, is what I want to know."

The boy formed a soundless word. The others did not speak and paid the boy no attention.

"Does anyone doubt that he did it before we go on? Tonya, do you?"

Smiling through her metallic mouth, Tonya revealed nothing.

"Mr. Joe?"

The old man shook his head. "Busne," he said.

"Stephanie?"

The dancer looked at Bailey, staring into his eyes for a clue to the liar's mask. Bailey had admitted nothing, even as Smith was hitting him beside the car and screaming with every blow: "Killer of mothers. What part of your hell is reserved for killers of mothers?" How would they interpret his silence? Would it mitigate?

"Well, Stephanie?"

"I've watched him," she said. "He's not a coward. And Putzina killed herself."

"Shit," said Smith.

"Putzina died in his fire," Mr. Joe said. "I heard her curse the Guild people. She named him, cursed him."

"Putzina cursed everyone," Stephanie said.

"Killer of mothers," Smith said.

"Busne," said Mr. Joe.

Tonya leaped down from her perch, laughing, and came toward Bailey with heavy, wrinkled breasts swinging loose in her dress beneath her open coat. She pushed her face close to his, stroked his cheek with her fingertips, stroked lightly with her nails. Then she dug the nails into his cheek and raked it, drawing blood. She laughed hysterically and pulled her coat tight, sat down. Mr. Joe tapped the boy on the shoulder and spoke: "Mutra, Pito."

The child opened his pants and pointed his spray at Bailey's chest, but as the fountain spouted, Bailey pushed the boy with his feet; Pito, a rotating geyser, wet the legs of the others. Mr. Joe slapped the child, who collapsed in his own puddle, eyes collapsing too but without a tear or sound. Mr. Joe walked behind Bailey and stepped on his fingers, twisting the toe of his shoe to grind them into the hay.

"Animal," Stephanie screamed; too loudly, Bailey thought. Where did all her human quality suddenly bubble from? Hadn't she danced wildly at Putzina's door? A schizo, perhaps. He wouldn't fight it. She knelt by Bailey and with her flowered skirt dried the blood from his scratches, the tears of pain from his cheeks. He felt the only reason he did not pass out from the pain was the injection they'd given him at the hospital to quiet his other tremors. He sensed his fingers must be bleeding but he could not only not see them, he could not even feel them individually. He felt only pain as behind his back Stephanie leaned over to his hands and sucked the injured fingers, cleaned Mr. Joe's dirt out of the bleeding scratches, patted them with her red flowers. Bailey thought she smelled like faintly rancid meat.

"Thank you," he said to her. "I take you for an angel."

The door creaked, opened. Bailey saw the lantern first, then the man. As he stepped into the barn, the snow dancing in cyclonic patterns, Bailey recognized Skin, the traitor. It wasn't correct to call him a traitor, for that implied a switching of allegiances, and Skin had no allegiances to which he could be traitorous. Still, he had switched sides physically, active turncoat, the only Guildsman to have done that. Many had gone back to work for the company out of economic desperation, or having been otherwise subverted. But only Skin had left the Guild to work against it. Bailey, watching Skin close the door, did not see Smith's foot coming. The kick caught the calf of his right leg, then the left. The kicks spun him on his hip.

"Killer of mothers," Smith said.

"Kill him, and you're on your own," Skin said in a flat, boyish voice. "I bring that advice from Stanley. Kill him, and you'll have Stanley to deal with. Stanley says don't hurt him. Stanley has other plans for him. Stanley wants him back in one piece."

The news strengthened Bailey. But was he yet safe from im-

minent death? Watching Smith pace like a beast, he knew the
potentiality for irrational violence. How deep did Smith's sense
of self-preservation go? Did he fear Stanley? Was he a mother-
lover extraordinary? Would he die for her corpse?

"Where did you come from?" Smith asked Skin.

"Stanley told me to find you. He heard you'd taken him, so
I came here. Where else do you ever take anybody?"

Stephanie, still sitting behind Bailey on the floor, leaned
toward him and whispered in his ear: "I'm a third-generation
gypsy. I don't think like the others."

"You. Get away from him," Skin said to Stephanie, his tone
suddenly harsh. Stephanie stood and patted Bailey's hair,
stroked its waves, tousled it with her fingers as she would the
hair on a dog's neck. He did not mind her smell at all now.
He wanted it. But he lost the comfort of that, the smell of a
friendly body, when she sat on the workbench. He raised his
nose, tried to smell her across the distance of those few feet,
but the smell of the hay, wet from the snow that came through
the roof, overpowered her odor.

"I wanted him to die slowly," Smith said. "Take his life
away piece by piece. Make him suffer the way my mother
suffered. And now you say we can do nothing with him?"

"Stanley says that," Skin said.

"There are things we can do," Mr. Joe said. "Nasula."

"Eeeeee," squealed Tonya. "Nasula." She leaped down
and hugged Mr. Joe. Smith sneered, and Tonya stuck out her
tongue in retaliation, then waggled her half-naked old breasts
at Smith, who turned away in disgust. Tonya turned her back
on him, threw up her skirt and thrust her naked buttocks at
him.

"Gypsy women are great cockteasers," Bailey said. "But
they don't follow through."

Everyone stared at him, struck silent. He knew it was an
absurd thing to say. With his life in the balance, gratuitously

insulting the matron of the group, however batty she might be, was the act of a deranged man. But even as these thoughts sped through his mind, Bailey spoke again. "Gypsy women steal anything. They even take out the bottoms of copper pots and put in papier mâché. Most gypsies are filthy swine who eat carrion. Half of them are cannibals."

Smith's foot came out of the silence and caught Bailey under the chin, sent him reeling backward. Sitting still, he had almost forgotten the pain of the wires on his legs and wrists, but now they dug into his flesh as he rolled. He looked at the raw and bleeding ankles and imagined his wrists to be far worse. While he lay still, the mute gypsy boy urinated his last drops on Bailey's shoes. Tonya patted the child on the head.

"We'll vote on what to do," Smith said, and pulled the others into a huddle. Skin stood apart, staring at Bailey, who caught none of the gypsy whispering. When they broke from the huddle they circled him. Mr. Joe waved his arms over Bailey's head, mumbling inaudibly as the others stood with heads bowed. Then Mr. Joe spoke slowly and clearly, and with a sense of high delight:

"Majaro undebel, may he die with pain. May he die regretting he ever lived. May he die reaching for water. May he die slowly, as a snail moves, suffering many sicknesses. May his children be imbeciles. May his stick fail ever to rise. May chancres grow on it. May his sack of stones become boulders. May his teeth turn to cinders. May great itching hives drive him to madness. May food be sour on his tongue and wine bitter in his mouth. May all women deceive him and all men betray him. May the spirit of his mother forget him. May the wrath of the just god give him raging fevers. May the hollow of his bowels burn with an endless itch. May his bladder leak. May his kidneys explode. May his bones break in many places. May his blood grow watery. May his eyes weaken. May the pox cover his body with running sores. May his brain be

stricken to simple whiteness. May fungus grow in his throat.
May his urine burn like flaming acid. May cancers grow in
his belly and lungs. May lice infest his hair. May his body
stink. May his toenails grow inward. May his loves turn to
dust. May his works be spoiled by time as well as men. May
he never finish another task. May he fail in all things. May
he wander forever in his mind, finding nothing. May every foul
evil of the earth crawl on his life like vicious worms and
smother this killer of mothers in putrid garbage."

The gypsies all spat on Bailey and threw hay dust on the
spittle. Then they circled him again.

"May the good god grant us these wishes. Querela Nasula.
Majaro Undebel."

As they backed away from Bailey Skin asked them: "Are
you through?"

"For the moment," Smith said.

"Then I'll take him," Skin said.

"Don't take him too far," Smith said.

"Help me with him, Stephanie," said Skin.

The girl and Skin carried him to Skin's car and put him
in the back seat. He moved to let his head rest against the
window, the wires again cutting into his wrists, his ankles.
He knew the absurdity of his position, of everything that had
happened to him, and of his own behavior most of all. But
it was not untypical. In the midst of great endeavors of the past
he would suddenly find himself picking lint from the rug. He
was like the flowers that grew in the yard of his childhood. The
Stupids. They grew with roots partly exposed, vulnerable. They
grew tall and blossomed, healthy and beautiful. And in the
midst of bloom they fell over, their blossoms top-heavy, and
they died groveling. Yes, Bailey thought, I am as absurd as
the Stupids. But I am not groveling yet. Down, but not dead.
Not yet.

The thought buoyed him and he felt a swelling in his chest
that he diagnosed as growing pains of the spirit. Trouble, if it

doesn't kill you, strengthens you. No noble boob now. Beaten almost to death, covered with blood, hay dust, gypsy spit and kiddie pee, Bailey smiled. As the car began to move, he claimed victory.

He awoke in a dark room, remembering nothing of how he arrived, assuming his body had succumbed at last to hospital drugs and exhaustion. Through a window he saw tall city buildings with scattered lights in upper stories and long-dead flowers standing upright in a whiskey bottle, silhouetted against the moonlight. It was still snowing. He was still bound with the wire and lying on a sofa. His arms and shoulders ached with a pain more pervasive than he had ever known, his head throbbed as if nails had been driven into his skull and the swellings in his legs where Smith had kicked him had fused with the pain of his ankles. He felt his legs had been stripped of skin and that his flesh, macerated in its own blood, lay open to receive the infections of a polluted sky.

He searched the darkness, saw a chair, a bed, and on it a human form. Skin. He tried to reach the wire on his wrists with the fingers that Mr. Joe had stepped on, tested the wire for looseness because the flesh it had broken and the bones it had rubbed could not convey such a message. He bent his knees and fingered the wire on his ankles but found nothing but smooth coilings, no twist he might untwist, only wire, and wet flesh. He quit trying and swung his legs off the sofa, thrust his torso to a sitting position. He saw another human form then, on the floor along the wall. Stephanie. Balancing himself with fingers on the sofa arm, Bailey thrust his body upward, feeling the wire gouge his wrists again, but he fell back. He slid slowly to the floor and began to move forward on his buttocks, slowly and quietly, discovering new pain in his hips. He reached the door and with back against the wall, hands as suction cups, he raised himself. Noiselessly he turned the knob, and when the door opened he saw he was at the end of a long hallway in which the dimmest of light came up from a lower landing. He saw the stairway at the far end and hopped toward it. But he lost his balance and fell into a cardboard box half full of orange peels, meat scraps, coffee grounds, eggshells.

"Where you goin'?"

When he did not move he was moved, rolled onto his back, caught under the ribs and tugged. Skin wore a blue work-shirt and jeans. Bailey stared at his cowlicks of dirty blond hair, at the pimples on his face, his neck, his arms, his ears. Skin dumped him back on the sofa and lit a candle on the table beside the dead flowers. From under the bed he pulled a tape recorder and turned it on. Sounds Bailey could not always recognize came from the machine: a prolonged buzzing, a fizzing, a rush of water, familiar street noises, the whee of auto wheels, footsteps and horns.

"I take it you're not going to unwire me," Bailey said.

"If I did that you'd leave."

"Do you see what the wire is doing to my ankles and wrists?"

"You won't die. You're tough. I've studied you."

An airplane landed, another took off. Maybe. A coffeepot perked.

"You like my sounds? They're the sounds of life."

"Is that what they are? I don't recognize some."

"You've got to listen a long time, like anything else. Do you think they're real?"

"They're real sounds. What time is it?"

Skin looked out the window. Something exploded. A rocket? A dynamite charge? A glass broke. Metal struck metal.

"I can't tell by the moon from here. Since I moved I don't know which way is west."

"Do you have any whiskey?"

"I don't drink whiskey anymore. What about my sounds?"

Someone typed. Someone hammered. Bailey listened. A door opened, creaked, closed.

"What I mean is, that was a real door."

"Was it?"

"Just because the door's not here doesn't mean it's not real."

"So you're onto reality."

"I'm a student of humanity."

"My heart takes wings. Have you got any aspirin? I tell you, I'm in pain. What does your humanity say to my bloody wrists and ankles?"

Skin pushed a chair close to the sofa and talked into Bailey's face. Someone chewed corn flakes or potato chips. Birds' wings flapped, or a hundred bats flew. Skin stank like sour sneakers.

"I know blood," Skin said. "I've been inside my own body. Plenty of times I got to the threshold of perceiving my blood before I crossed over. First I saw the blood in my throat and I started to dissolve. I got scared and wouldn't go over. Then I saw a girl floating in a bathtub full of blood and I chickened out again. But when I saw my blood cells I liked them, so I walked through my veins and found a Tibetan monster that started to eat me. I kind of liked that too, but I knew it was only an illusion. Finally I turned red and was in the middle of my heart. It threw me around with every beat, like a tympani gone crazy. After a while I got the knack, like learning how to go with a trampoline."

"So my blood doesn't mean much after that."

"Pictures of ripe tomatoes get to me. And I got some twinges studying your ankles and wrists. That's really raw meat."

"Why don't you help me? Or have you got something else in mind?"

"Don't rush it, dad. I want to talk to you about your body. How is it now?"

"It hurts."

"Think you can get outside it? Step out of it like a space suit?"

"It'd be a pleasure."

"Try it, dad. Contemplate. Close your eyes and watch the
pineal gland between them. It turns purple. Keep watching,
see how you turn into a single thought. When you do that,
you can get outside yourself."

Bailey closed his eyes to get away from Skin. An alarm
clock rang. Or was it a burglar alarm? A fire engine clanged
and its siren screamed. Then ploop, the sound of a finger
snapped out of a tight mouth, or was it a popped cork? The
siren brought back the gypsy store collapsing in slush: chain
of causation to the moment. The chain was clear, except for
the impetus to set the fire. That devil's eye? Why succumb to
that? Was it the pussy-foot life? And what made him think he
lived such a life? Because no one feared him? Because no
one worried when Bailey entered a room? A gentleman,
Bailey was. Mothers didn't tuck away their daughters when
Bailey arrived. Animals didn't run from his foot. Always kind.
Then why are your hands so scarred from fighting, Bailey?
And why so many notches on the dorque, Bailey? Few men
have done so much, and so many, unless they made it their
career. Bailey, you don't know what you are. A pussyfoot
milquetoast who breaks rocks and noses, bleeds the lady's
heart as he ups and unders. You're more than you think, less
than you wish, Bailey, and you're something you don't even
understand, for why would you be here otherwise? What is
this madman up to? Hatchet job for Stanley?

Skin had been with the newspaper only a few months when
the strike began. Unwashed Phi Beta Kappa, precocious
husband whose wife left him for an even filthier figure, he had
worked as a police reporter, packaging an existential flower
message with every accident story, an approach to the news
which quickly earned him pasture in suburbia. There, report-
ing on sewer district meetings, he drew provocative analogies
to Roman aqueducts and subtle Rabelaisian and Chaucerian
cloacalisms, none of which reached print. When the strike
began he was put on the publicity committee and in the early

chaos wrote releases for radio stations which, he found, would broadcast anything. "Jesus Christ is the favorite person of striking Guildsmen, an informal poll revealed today . . ." Catholic Guildsmen thought it profane to refer to Jesus as a person. Jewish members took exception to the poll's conclusion. Skin was put back on the picket line.

In those days Bailey enjoyed the anarchy of Skin's vision, but anarchy without end palled, and Bailey lost interest. When Skin defected, few sorrowed. His thesis that the Guild was top-heavy with jerks was no longer a revolutionary notion, and his sweatshirt had become unbearably gamy. Caught short on the picket line one afternoon, Skin used the company toilet, where he met Stanley, who was taken with his compulsively spoken anti-Guild views and encouraged his defection. Skin reported the subversion attempt to Jarvis, who made a note of it. Three days later Skin was screaming anti-Guild slogans from the gypsy store: "Radicals are manic-depressives," he shouted. "Guildsmen are phony lumpen proletariat." Putzina pulled him inside, and after that he worked behind the scenes.

"Are you making it, dad? Are you outside yet?"

Bailey opened his eyes, stared, proving he was making it, then closed them, wondering whether this would tick off the bomb in Skin's head.

"Keep focused on the old pineal," Skin said. "You won't need a shrink to get out like I did. I know the route and I want to show you, get you arhat status because I like your style, Bailey. You deserve better than that shitty Guild, and you know it. Be an arhat, that's the answer, and screw the Guild. That's how you reach for the sun when you live at the bottom of the tarpit. All that violence, Bailey, all that stupid hanging around, that's not you. You don't have the talent for it. As a rebel you're a flop, just like I was. You know there used to be an ogre outside my room but I got past him, bounced over his mind. Then this soft little plastic jackal came at me and I picked him up, watched him squirm in my fist and threw him under the bed. But I couldn't let him wiggle there on his terms and come at me when I wasn't ready. So I put him in a shoe box and wrote OM on it and turned up the music and listened to its colors to take away the smelly sound of that jackal. I looked into the corner of my eye and saw the white light, just an edge, but the rest of it was around the corner and I knew that. So with quite a bit of confidence for a man who didn't used to be able to decide whether to eat his potato or his vegetable first, I moved toward it. And, dad, I knew I was safe, because God loves me. And right away I understood Aztec geometry and what it means when you say paradise is a milk bottle. But what the hell has knowledge got to do with anything? Think about it, dad. Twenty years from now, what will all your Guild wisdom amount to? Will you have figured out how to die in God's arms? That's the anthill everybody's looking for."

"Wrong," Bailey said. "It's a duplex pad with a built-in altar under a picture window that looks out on Glory City. Two Porsches in every pot, everybody in love with us, name in the papers and a girl friend who wears no panties. You believe in God, I'll buy old Nietzsch the Peach, that we want to create a world we can kneel to."

"Crass, Bailey, crass. That's beneath you."

"Take off the wires."

"You'd hurt me if I took them off."

"No, I wouldn't hurt you."

"I don't trust anybody not to hurt me," Skin said. "And, hey, you're not concentrating. Think about killing that old woman. That'll help. You've got terrifically interesting problems. Just focus on that old lady and don't let her become anything else. I used to think about an X ray of a snake digesting an X ray of a hamster. Wild. But it got me into the tunnel, dad, all white light, white as the hole in a diamond and going about sixty, and then purple lights on both sides giving me the royal welcome. Two zillion miles up anyway, and no signposts, and I look around and say to myself, okay, this is an interesting place, but where did I come from? I got restless. No action, no God. How do I get back? I drifted and saw little lights away off but couldn't get there, and then I wondered what I used to be. And, dad, that shook me. Thank God I had a thought. I remembered my body, but I couldn't find it. Saw it in a closet and took it out but then lost it again. Finally I dove into it and wondered, is this my body? But it didn't matter. That's my message, dad. That's what God taught me up in the void, that bodies don't matter. And even if this old house is destroyed, that diamond crystal that was floating around up there will still go on and on and on. All the talents, memories, desires that make up the old Skin don't have anything to do with that diamond crystal. You dig, dad? That made me an arhat. Are you making it?"

Bailey suffered the irony badly, being lectured on the soul. He'd had a soul and gotten rid of it when Skin was just a sausage. Now he was being tortured into a reacquisition of it under another name. What a laugh. What's more, Bailey was positive that the underside of Skin's proselytizing was another of Stanley's subversion efforts. From the beginning, the Guild leaders had viewed Stanley's every act as a move by a chess master. But that was romanticizing by boobs. It was only in later months that Stanley truly became devious. He began blatantly, wooing desperate strikers with promises of pay raises to return to work; and though he paid off in pay cuts, they stayed with the company, flip-floppers unwelcome at the Guild, of course. Then he moved with a goon squad and the beatings and shadowings scared a handful of Guildsmen out of town, another few back to the company. Reciprocal terror, the shadowing of scabs holding down key company jobs, neutralized Stanley's goons and forced him to more subtle measures. He flooded the Guild neighborhood and Fobie's bar with circulars offering a month-long all-expenses-paid vacation at the Beauty Spot, the company-owned resort in Florida. Two-dozen winter-weary strikers hypocritically grabbed at the free holiday, chuckling at Stanley's gullibility, and vowing to return to the strike with renewed fervor after a rest. But none returned. To a man they rejoined the company ranks, creating the great subversion coup of the strike. But all the Guildsmen agreed that the peak of Stanley's inventiveness was aimed at a much smaller group, the half-dozen Guild members over sixty-five. Stanley rented an empty office on the floor above the Guild and for two days staged a series of Granny strip shows. Stanley knew his audience. The old men never came back.

Now he was dueling individually; Bailey the single enemy. But did Stanley really think a raunchy Zen missionary could riddle his commitment? Cut off my head, Bailey thought; that might work. He opened his eyes and saw Skin studying his bloody ankles.

"You know I might be dying," Bailey said.

"Only your body," Skin said. "Don't worry about it. I'll get you to God before that happens. But you've got to break the old patterns. I picked up a copy of Freud while I was walking through my blood vessels, and I really had to laugh. 'Siggie,' I said, 'if you only knew.' I threw the book to my monster and he ate it up. He'd eat anything."

Bailey closed his eyes and imagined reading a story in the morning newspaper about the strike being settled, all Guildsmen back on the job with raises and equal chances for advancement, no grievances aroused during the strike to have any validity. Bosses and Guildsmen must be nice, fair, honest with each other. Above the strike story was a photo of Jarvis shaking hands with Stanley, and behind Jarvis stood Rosenthal, Irma and Bailey himself, with smiles that established the invalidity of past trouble. As he dwelled on the photo, Bailey realized he hadn't changed. Around him the world had changed, but he had not. He had committed certain acts he'd never committed before, but along the walls of his brain the same pictures hung, the same file cabinets stored the same old answers to the same old questions that no one expected to be asked anymore.

"I'm hungry."

Bailey opened his eyes at that, Stephanie's voice.

"God," Skin said.

"Where's the food?"

"There isn't any."

"What does that mean, there isn't any?"

"It means we have no food. God."

"Well, we better have food, skinny boy."

"We don't, though."

"I bought food."

"I know."

"Where is it?"

"Gone."

"I don't remember seeing it go."

"That's true enough. You were probably asleep."

"I bought and paid for it."

"The eggs were rotten. The coffee was full of bugs. The oranges were dry. The meat was foul and green."

"What did you do with it?"

"I ate it."

"That was my food," Stephanie said. "I only go this way once, and all I got is what I eat, and my friends."

"We share on this planet."

"I didn't get my share. Not quite."

"I can get you plenty of food," Bailey said.

Stephanie yawned and stretched felinely, smiled at Bailey as she spoke to him. "I thought I'd choke when you said Tonya wouldn't follow through. If there was ever anybody who loved to follow through, it's her."

"I said that on impulse," Bailey said. Looking at Stephanie,

Bailey remembered her rancid odor but could not smell it.
Possibly it came from eating green meat.

"How's my boy making out?" Stephanie said to Bailey,
gesturing at Skin. "Did he convert you yet?"

"He's telling me things," Bailey said. "Why don't you take
my wires off?"

She stood up and walked close to Bailey.

"You like to fickydick?" she asked.

"I'm game," he said.

"I only go this way once, and I take all opportunities. It's
rotten. The whole rotten thing is rotten. Everything is rotten.
There are worms in the apple, my friend."

"There's truth in what you say," Bailey said.

"I'm sick of gypsy stuff," Stephanie said. "I want elegance.
I only go this way once, and what I need is a palace, a castle
maybe. Rent some of them big candleholders and live on
truffles for two weeks. And drink only wine from grapes
squashed by monks' feet. And two or three surprises in the
closet, like you."

"Take off my wires," Bailey said. He tried to make it sound
sexy.

"You can't do this," Skin said to her. "I'm not finished with
him."

"Little boy jealous."

"What do you think of an ego like that?" Skin said to
Bailey. "She barges into the middle of a spiritual quest with
her empty belly and itchy twat and pushes it right into the
middle of everything. God. Wouldn't you think some people'd
have the decent manners goats were born with?"

"Do you have any water?" Bailey asked.

Stephanie and Skin looked at one another.

"Don't look at me," she said. "I didn't bring him in."

"All he wants is water."

"You brought him in, you take care of him. You clean up
after him."

She lay back on the bed and rolled into a sleeping posture. An oogah sounded, a drummer drummed, a bird chirped. Bailey could conceive of no way out. He could think only of his pain and the futility of expecting humane treatment from Skin and his gypsy crackpot. Death was a clock on the wall that he could not see. But he could hear it tick, knew its hands moved. Death had never been so clear in his mind. He had never been so helpless. Any act might tip the madness the wrong way. He saw Christ in a red canoe about to go over Niagara Falls to his death. Christ stepped out of the canoe to walk on the waters and raised his hands. But signals got mixed and the Falls parted like the Red Sea and Christ hurtled into the black chasm while God's voice chased him in descent, trailing apologetic static. Bailey looked at Skin, thinking: Screw it; thinking: Thank God I had a thought.

"God you're a bore," Bailey said. "A monumental goddamn bore."

"That's a crummy thing to say."

"You and your arhat and your crystalware."

"I don't want to impose myself where I'm not wanted," Skin said.

"A toad, that's what you are. A goddamn boring hoptoad."

Stephanie laughed. She rolled off the bed and walked over to Skin. She nuzzled him, kissed his pimples.

"My bumpy little toad," she said.

Skin held her by the buttocks and pressed his cheek into her belly.

"I failed Stanley again," he said.

"Don't you worry," Stephanie said. "There'll be other times."

"The wires," Bailey screamed. "Take off the goddamn wires!" He kicked the arm of the sofa with both feet, knocking it loose from the frame.

"Now look what you've done," Skin said.

He picked up the broken sofa arm and studied its raw

wood and torn mohair. He raised it over his head and brought it down on Bailey's stomach. A dog barked. A car started. As Bailey passed into unconsciousness, a telephone rang. Was it a real telephone? Skin would say yes.

"**G**ood mor-ning!"

The greeting was a song but Bailey again awoke in darkness, smelling after-shave lotion. Then suddenly the room was in full light, a female's bedroom, a young woman in a negligee carrying a breakfast tray toward him. His body ached and his stomach region was aflame with pain. His hands were in front of him for the first time since he'd left the hospital and his wrists bandaged with gauze and adhesive. But he was handcuffed. He raised the bedclothes and discovered himself in royal-blue silken pajamas. His ankles were also manacled, and like his wrists, had been treated. He touched his cheek, discovering new pain in his arms, found himself smooth-shaven and knew the shaving-lotion odor was on his face.

"My, do you look different," the young woman said. "Deliciously bully."

She put the tray on a bedside table, readjusted the bedclothes and fluffed and propped the pillow behind him. She helped him sit up and put the tray across his lap.

"Am I supposed to eat in handcuffs?"

"Can't you manage? They seem to give you some leeway. It's better than having them behind your back, isn't it?"

"That's true enough."

"You don't seem to know me."

"Miss Blue, isn't it?"

"Oh, you do. How nice."

He knew her as a company secretary, one of a long line of Stanley's concubines. She wore her hair blond, cut like a poodle. She dressed in miniskirts and cornucopian sweaters and she waddled.

"Why am I here?" Bailey asked her.

"Mr. Smith dropped you by and asked me to fix your cuts. I must say you were a mess. The things men get themselves into."

"Smith, you say? Did he tell you to put me in cuffs?"

"That was my idea," Miss Blue said, and she winked. "He said you were a maniac and I didn't want to get attacked. At least not right away."

"What else did Smith say?"

"Not much. He was with that young boy with the pimples who cried all the while he was here. He wasn't at all the sort of person Mr. Smith usually brings me, but then neither are you."

"Is this your bed I'm in?"

She nodded and winked again. Bailey drank the orange juice from the tray, holding the glass with both hands and studying the transparent section of Miss Blue's negligee. Then, with wrists crossed and using only one hand, he ate boiled eggs, toast, marmalade, coffee. Miss Blue followed his movements with a relish equivalent to his own appreciation of the food.

"Does Stanley know I'm here?"

"I couldn't care less," she said, an answer Bailey thought evasive.

"Did you shave me? Bandage me? Dress me up?"

"You are some yummy thing," Miss Blue said, nodding and winking.

"I don't know why I didn't wake up."

"I kept chloroforming you. I knew you needed the sleep."

"And the handcuffs? You always keep two pair around the house?"

"A guard from the company gave them to me. I've done him a few favors." She winked. "A girl needs all the tools she can get."

"Of course you wouldn't think of taking them off me."

"If you'd do me a favor."

"Anything."

"I want you to help me with my pacifier."

"Let's get at it. What's a pacifier?"

"Something Mr. Smith helped me build."

"You seem to be close to Smith."

"Not really clo-ose," she said, winking. "He's not much of anything, really. A kind of neuter, if you know what I mean. But he can get anything done, and I do mean anything." She winked again. "After all, Stanley isn't as young as he used to be, though he has his moments." She ran her hand under the bedclothes, inside Bailey's pajamas and massaged his thickness between thumb and forefinger.

"Is that what you call the pacifier?" Bailey said.

"Don't be so conceited."

"A bit aggressive of you, I'd say."

"Don't you like aggressive women?"

"Only if they're really women."

"Oh, I'm a woman, all right, can't you tell?"

"It's easy to be deceived."

Miss Blue stood and dropped her nightgown, revealing pearly breasts the size of cantaloupes. Body paint had made bull's-eyes of her nipples, and above them was a message:

which radiated in blue tattoo toward Bailey. Across her stomach another tattoo stared,

luring Bailey like a button-nosed, spade-bearded lady, one tattooed eye wide, the other bellyfolded to a wink as Miss Blue bent a knee in relaxation.

"I suppose you wonder where I got the tattoos."

"Don't feel you have to explain."

"Everybody has their little quirks. That's what makes life interesting, I think."

"I couldn't agree more. Take off my handcuffs."

"All in good time, Rodney."

"Bailey's the name."

"I call all my intimate friends Rodney. It's such a picturesque name."

"You do have little quirks."

"It's just I'm being the real me. Ever since high school I've understood that if I wasn't *me*, why then I was nothing at all. My mother was a bearded lady in the circus and she had a thing going with the tattooed man. But I'd never have dreamed of getting tattooed if I hadn't run across the little old tattoo artist near the high school. He was about seventy and he paid fifty cents a look and a dollar a slurp and used to sit us young girls on this old shoeshine stand in the back of his tattoo parlor. He had hair on his fingers up near the nails, which he chewed. His tongue was about a yard long. But we didn't mind because we were just young kids out for fun and profit. He was fun too, for a while, but I never really got excited. You know, oo-oo-oo kind of excited. So after graduation I went with a clown who had eyes for me, but nothing happened until he wore his clown suit, and that got me. Then there was a divinity student, a police sergeant, an Eagle Scout, a pastry chef, two ushers and six sailors and even though my excitement never happened, I knew I had a thing for uniforms. I began to read a lot, all porn of course, because I knew reading would help me get at my essence. I remember reading a beautiful thing about Theodora of Rome. What a woman! They said she wished she had a fourth altar on which to pour the libations of love. I never forgot that, though for myself, none of the altars ever make much difference. Most things in this world just don't have enough passion in them. But then one night I was having a go with a Canadian Mountie and I was so bored I started to read a kid's book I found on the bus and suddenly visions of Rodney the tattoo man and Rodney the Eagle Scout and Rodney the two ushers and Rodney the six sailors all loomed up in front of me. I figured it was the combination of uniform, book and memory, and I knew I was onto something. If I could just get the right combination, just once, I might really find out who I was. So I kept on with street cleaners and elevator operators and mailmen and bellhops and Pinkertons for just months. Would you believe I never came near that feeling again? Oh, it was fun, don't get me wrong. Even when it's bad it's still pretty good. But you know, don't you, that without that extra something, that sand, that twinkle, that life is just terribly, terribly ordinary? Anyway, I bumped into Mr. Smith one day at the company lunch counter, and before I knew it he was up here filling me up with new ideas. I tried, you know, to coax him into something, but he said he couldn't because of his up-bringing, which I thought was nice. Which of us, really, lives by his principles that way? He said he only liked to watch. That's why he built the machine and got me the pizzle. He had an awful time finding one. Just nobody stocks them. Would you like to see it?"

She let go of Bailey and from a closet shelf took down a small mahogany chest with a green velvet lining. She displayed its contents across outstretched palms for Bailey's scrutiny.

"It's been cured or pickled or something," she said. "It can't go bad or get meaty."

"Is this the pacifier?"

"Just a small part. Would you like to see the rest?"

"I wouldn't miss it."

"You'll have to get into costume. That's my rule."

"What about the handcuffs?"

"You keep your bargain, I'll keep mine. I'm a person that keeps their word."

"I'm no welcher either," Bailey said.

"Ooo," said Miss Blue.

She put her treasure box on the bed and pulled Bailey to a standing position, then cut his pajamas away with a scissors.

"Don't move now," she said, and rummaged again in the closet. She came toward him with a white cloak that hung from his shoulders to the floor.

"Now the headpiece," she said, and from the closest shelf took a bull mask with large, curved horns. Bailey felt it, found it rubbery.

"Let me see you," Miss Blue said, and slipped it over his head. Looking through the eye holes, Bailey saw Miss Blue in what seemed to be the beginning of a swoon.

"Oo-oo," she said. "Ooo-ooo."

She took his hand and shuffled slowly beside him to the living room. He thought of what he must look like in the bull getup and felt absurd beyond words, but helpless to change anything; more helpless than he'd been with Skin, for at least he could argue with Skin. There was no argument possible with Miss Blue. He felt debased through ridiculousness and failed to understand how early wisdom, early promise, early glory, could have gone so cockeyed. But then possibility went in both directions, did it not? For every realm of glory, wasn't there a parallel universe of the grotesque? This is my beloved son, in whom I am well pleased. But what if Jesus had gone the other way with Mary Magdalene? What would he have come to? But that was unreal. Forget that. The bull costume was real, oh yes. Another silly event in a silly cosmos, and Bailey, one of the silliest of molecular structures. Bailey thought: An absurd self is a hated self; and he considered the possibility of a conspiracy to reduce him to an absurd condition.

Miss Blue pulled a drawstring which parted a set of wall drapes, then tugged a knob, pulling an elaborate wooden construction out from the wall.

"Isn't it something?" she asked.

"I'll say."

"It's got two parts. The toro machine and the cow frame. You play toro, and guess who I play."

Bailey raised his headdress for a better look at the machine, but Miss Blue pulled it down again.

"Mustn't break the mood," she said. She dashed to the bedroom and returned wearing a cow headdress and clutching the pizzle.

"Now I put this on toro first," she said, and by means of a leather strap she fastened the pizzle to a small rod on the front of the toro machine. "I call this gadget my connecting rodney," she explained with a wink. She draped Bailey's cloak behind him over the toro's barrel-shaped torso, then strapped him onto the front of the apparatus, the toro seat, so that he remained in a restful but standing position. He felt like the decorative prow of a ship. The pizzle protruded with formidable girth and length at his knee level.

"Comfy?" Miss Blue asked.

"No, but don't fret. Just get on with it."

Every muscle in his body ached, his head still pained. He took comfort that his wounds were closed, their rawness a physical torture but no longer a mental one. Pollution would have to find other entrances. But had it already found one? How deadly a pollution was the vision of oneself as absurd? Now he was convinced that Stanley's order had dropped him into this mechanized insanity. Yielding to the marathon galumph of Miss Blue, a man could lose his balance, begin to grow wild hair on his gums, break wind erratically. Once stability began to wane, the whole system of equilibrium could blow out. Stanley, thought Bailey, you are a diabolical fiend, but I'm on to you.

"Get ready," Miss Blue said. "Move your feet up and down

on the pedals when I say go." Bailey pressed and felt them give and rise like player-piano pedals, activating gears which moved the pizzle back and forth. Miss Blue swept the rug off the floor, a brown and white cowhide, and flung it over the cow frame, then climbed backward into the back end of the frame and past the dangling tow-rope tail. She reclined at about a thirty-degree angle, pushed her legs into delivery-room-style knee rests and switched on a small light over her head. She took a book from a wall compartment and asked Bailey: "Are you ready?"

"I suppose you'd call it that."

"Bully," she said. "You are a good sport."

She pressed a button, and a foam-rubber mitt rose suddenly from beneath Bailey and cradled his extension. Simultaneously the toro machine began to move forward. Miss Blue loosed one long cry in basso tones: "Moooooo." Then she pulled a lever and the cow's tail flew up like a pump handle.

"Pedal now," she said. "Moooooo."

Bailey pedaled and the toro machine coupled like a freight car with the cow frame, the pizzle finding its mark and exciting a tremor in Miss Blue. Bailey felt unused. After a few minutes of pedaling, however, Miss Blue sat up halfway and gave him some attention. But his concern even then was less with himself than with what she did all by herself. When she fell back again she put her book on a reading stand that accordioned out from the cow's interior wall and read out loud:

"Hundreds of turkeys. Eggs! More eggs! Hundreds of eggs. We have hundreds of eggs. We want hundreds of turkeys. Hundreds of eggs. Hundreds of eggs in the incubator. We must wait and wait. We must wait four weeks. We must work and work. We must clean the sheds. We must work and work. We must fix the fences. We must get feed. We must get grit. One, two, three, four weeks! We worked four weeks. We cleaned the sheds. We fixed the fences . . ."

Baffled, Bailey pedaled on, and slowly Miss Blue's face changed. Her eyes widened, her eyes rolled back, her tongue hung out. The book fell away, but she recited from memory: "We must get grit . . ." The rhythm of the combination had begun to lull Bailey, but then Miss Blue shivered, a monstrous tremor that looked to Bailey not at all like a conventional climax but as if the effort would explode her brain. He stopped pedaling. She sat up as he unstrapped himself.

"Don't you want to finish?"

"I've played my fill," he said, climbing down.

"A little longer. I almost made it that time. We can try the bed, and you hold the pizzle."

"Handcuffs," Bailey said.

"You're like all the rest. You can't trust a man."

She clambered down, pouting. But she unlocked the cuffs and brought Bailey his clothes. He looked at himself in the mirror, a mass of welts, cuts, bruises, and in his stomach a great pain where Skin had hit him. Yet he was whole. Nothing absurd, nothing ridiculous about that altogetherness. Altogether basic, it was. Ah, Stanley, the best-laid plans. And poor Blue. Another Stanley tool. Nice try, though.

"Kiss me one time," she said.

Bailey slid into shoes, pants, shirt, coat, ran his fingers tenderly over her hair. She smiled, bovine eyes blinking, magnificent milk pods trembling like new Jell-o. She pushed herself toward him, naked and puckered, and with soft thumbs he closed her eyes.

"Don't move," he told her. While she held the pose he fled into the morning.

EXTRA!

GUILD MEMBERS BESET BY WEIRDNESS

A BIG MYSTERY IT SEEMS

i once heard the survivors of a colony of ants that had been par-
tially obliterated by a cow's foot seriously debating the intention
of the gods towards their civilization

—DON MARQUIS
as Archy, the cockroach

The Guild room was crowded when Bailey entered, an ex-copy boy sitting in his chair, Jarvis at Rosenthal's desk, and all the familiar faces of absentee members filling the room with the buzz of small talk. Bailey saw Irma across the room, talking with a man he recognized as Adam Popkin. He pushed toward them through the crowd which parted silently. Irma threw her arms around him, kissed him.

"Bubie, you're all bumps and cuts. And your wrists. Those bandages."

"I got it worse than I thought from those guards," he said.

"But where did you go? We thought they'd taken you off and boiled you down to make candles. And who bandaged you up?"

"It's a long story, love. You'll have to read my memoirs. Do you know where my car is?"

"In the lot where the tow truck left it."

She handed him his coat, hat and muffler that she'd taken from the hospital.

"That's Popkin, isn't it?" he said.

"Oh, right." She grabbed Popkin's arm. "Doesn't he have a lovely moustache?"

Popkin's moustache, a huge bush with flat ends and tapering in the middle like a bow tie, overpowered the rest of him. Bailey knew him only from stories and photos in the Guild newspaper and from his early letter of support. But like other exalted leaders of the International Guild, he found it unnecessary to give much attention to this particular local: the all-time champion loser among locals. Yet here he was now, in person.

"Things must be worse than I thought if you're here," Bailey said.

"Unbelievably bad," said Popkin.

"What's going to happen?"

"We'll get the rascals."

"Great," Bailey said. "Glad to hear that kind of talk from on high."

"Who are you?"

"This is Bailey," Irma said.

"Oh," said Popkin, and slithered into the crowd.

"Well, is that a creep or is that a creep?" said Irma.

"Where's Rosenthal? And why all these people?"

"I don't know where Rosenthal is, but Jarvis called these people, or so he says."

"Jarvis?"

Bailey weaved through the crowd to the desk where Jarvis was busy making notes. Bailey looked over his shoulder and read:

dogfood
Bailey
Rosenthal

"Some crowd," Bailey said. "This your work?"

"I called the meeting, if that's what you mean. Is that what you mean?"

"You convinced everybody to come here? You?"

"I've got things to do."

Bailey watched as Jarvis added lice powder to his list. He looked back and saw Bailey watching and scratched out the lice powder, protecting, Bailey presumed, the dog's reputation.

"What ails you Jarvis?"

"I didn't ask for this job."

Bailey rejoined Irma, and Jarvis tapped to get the crowd's attention. He stood up, intensely nervous. His mouth opened but he only gaped, searching for the first word.

"Goofy things are goin' on," he finally said.

The crowd nodded its agreement. "Hmmm-hmmm. I'll say. You said a mouthful."

"You know all about the fire from the morning paper," Jarvis went on. "They blame the Guild."

"Yeah. Right," said the crowd. "How come?"

"Or maybe you saw it on TV."

"Uh-huh. Right. Yep."

"Or heard it on the radio."

"Yeah, man. Yowsah. Yup-yup."

"The company is mad at us."

"No. Is that so? No kiddin'?"

"They think we set the fire."

"Us? Set the fire? Did we?"

"There's no proof," Jarvis said. "But you all know we've got some pretty wild members."

"You said it," said the crowd, and faces turned toward Bailey. "Wild men. Crazy guys. Nutballs."

"Just a minute," Irma said. "Are you accusing any of us of setting that fire?"

Jarvis ignored the question.

"My welcome doormat was stolen this morning," he said. "And our walkie-talkies were taken during the night. So was our bulletin board. Maybe more stuff. We don't know yet."

"Wow!" said the crowd. "How about that! That's the limit!"

"And I have here," said Jarvis, raising Smith's knife into the air, "a weapon that a gypsy is supposed to have used to try to kill one of our members."

"Zot!" said the crowd. "Murder? Kill? Ring-a-ding!"

"But this is no gypsy knife," Jarvis said.

"No? Hey! Are you sure?"

"It's an ordinary, regulation Boy Scout knife. I've had it investigated."

"Say. How about that! What d' ya know!"

"That doesn't mean we blame the Boy Scouts for the fire."

"No. Natch. Of course not."

"But it makes you kind of wonder."

"Yeah. Right. Wonder what?"

Jarvis began to speak with authority for the first time since he'd stood up.

"Why do you suppose those gypsies lived in that store anyway? Why didn't they move someplace else? And where'd they get all that money? And why were the guards around, not to mention the police? And how about that paper boy on the street selling papers like a goddamn maniac during it all, eh? Think about it. Why didn't the doctors make the gypsies stay in the hospital till the cops got there? And where is Putzina's corpse? And you think I don't know what stealing my welcome mat means? It means I'm next. Get it? Welcome. See the connection? Gypsies, knife, money, fire, guards, cops, paper boy, hospital, ink truck, snow and the welcome mat. Everything fits. Very, very neatly."

Jarvis sat down to silence. He was smiling. Adam Popkin immediately took the floor.

"The crux of the situation," Popkin began, "the only way to stop reprisals, is an apology to the company for what some of our members did last night."

The comment stunned Bailey. Apologize to the company? Irma frowned.

"With the help of Brother Jarvis, I've drafted such an apology. We have mimeographed copies for your approval."

As Popkin passed out copies to the crowd, Bailey marveled at his efficiency. The mimeograph machine hadn't worked in months. And the crowd in the room testified to a perseverance and persuasiveness that Jarvis did not possess. No one in the local really had that kind of talent. The tigers of wrath had their place, but it wasn't fixing mimeograph machines. A copy of the apology reached Bailey:

During the evening of the ink truck, we the undersigned acted in ways that encouraged violence and hatred, and we now recognize this was not in the best interests of brotherhood and we deeply regret it. We will henceforth work toward solutions through tranquil, le-

gal and nonviolent ways, for we know that the company
officials, just as much as we, want to end this strike and
thus enable everyone to work and live in peace and bles-
sedness.

"I must add," Popkin said, "that the company has re-
quested this apology, and unless it is given, they say they'll
press arson charges against several Guildsmen, myself in-
cluded, and further, will undertake a nationwide campaign
to blacken the Guild's good name and also to disinter all the
malicious myths that circulated about our esteemed founders,
about heroes of our earlier campaigns and about our wives,
our children and our dogs. Nothing will be sacred to the
company, should we not accede to its wishes."

"This is dumb," Irma said to Popkin. "I wouldn't sign this
for anything. Nuts to the company."

"You will not have to sign it, my good woman. The sign-
ers are to be Rosenthal and Bailey, who instigated the trouble.
The International Guild board of directors agrees with me
and Brother Jarvis that unless they sign the apology, their
memberships should be revoked. It remains for the membership of this local to sanction such a move."

"And what is the Guild supposed to get out of this?" Irma
asked.

"A return to sanity," Popkin said. "An establishment of
standards for future conduct."

"And we find out who's boss around here," Jarvis said,
hitting the table with his fist, lightly. "I call for a vote on this
right now. Those in favor?"

"Yea," said some of the chorus.

"No, no, no," said Irma.

Bailey said nothing.

"Carried," Jarvis called out.

"Is there any comment from Brother Bailey?" Popkin
asked.

Bailey shook his head.

"Brother Rosenthal will be expected to sign when we locate him," Popkin added, and at that the meeting broke up. The crowd moved toward the door, sliding around Bailey and Irma with wide clearance. Jarvis thrust the original type-script of the apology at Bailey.

"Stanley's waiting for this in his office," Jarvis said. "He wants it hand-carried over by you."

Bailey nodded and signed the apology. Jarvis smiled tri-umphantly and moved off.

"I don't understand why you're standing still for all this nonsense," Irma said.

"It was a democratic vote," Bailey said. "That's how they want it."

"You sound like that poopy old Socrates. I thought you had more sense."

"Let me remind you," Bailey said, "that when lightning strikes the ding-dong, the golly birds panic and wise men fly no kites."

"Oh, hell," Irma said.

The room was all but empty, the picket signs leaning against the wall, announcing their dog-eared message: ON STRIKE.

"What gets me," Irma said, "is that I told that slimy Pop-kin I liked his moustache."

"Don't let the slime get you," Bailey said. "Let me remind you, a baseball game often has nine innings."

"Okay, you jerk. Maybe you know what you're doing. But you look like a sad apple."

He leaned over and peered down the front of her flimsy blouse.

"That's the old Bailey," she said.

No one stopped Bailey as he walked past the three hired pickets and into the company building. The guard by the elevator watched as he pressed the button, and two female faces peered at him from the accounting-department picture window. He pressed the sixth-floor button, but the car stopped unaccountably at the fourth-floor advertising department and the door opened on a noisy, busy room. The department manager and workers near the door stopped work and stared with vacant faces until the door closed. He stepped out at the executive suite, met by the gaze of old Miss Bohen, the crone receptionist who had spent a lifetime with the company growing lip whiskers and chin curls, seeing her pores become craters. She was eighty, at least, but she fought her age with black hair dye. As her flesh fell away, her black dresses lengthened. Instant mummy, Bailey thought.

"I'm here to see Stanley," he told her, feeling no need to be more than civil.

"I know all about it," she said. Her breath smelled like hay. She dialed three numbers and said: "He's here," then hung up and stared at Bailey. A door opened and Miss Blue in a miniskirt came at Bailey, bobbing her charms.

"Mr. Bailey?"

"That's right."

She whirled around, and he followed her to an inner sanctum where he'd never been. They walked on a thick, beige carpet down a sunless corridor past knobless push doors. At Stanley's door she turned and winked at him.

"We're strangers, get it?" she whispered.

She held the door for Bailey. He brushed her outer edges as he stepped into the lair alone. Stanley, suntanned and fiftyish, tight-collared and gray-toupeed, a flea-sized mogul behind his great mahogany desk, smiled at Bailey and exuded the scent of a five-foot lilac. The anger Bailey once felt for

Stanley personally during contract negotiations had long faded, but now it seeped back.

"Where is your cohort Rosenthal, Bailey? The fellow who makes all the threats."

"I haven't seen him."

"Do you have the apology?"

"Here," Bailey said, tapping his pocket.

"You're such a bright fellow. You negotiated with such verve, and you wrote such a dandy column. It's a shame you waste your talent on the Guild."

"To each his own heaven. Or hell," Bailey said, sitting down beside Stanley's desk.

Stanley smirked, tapped his fingertips together. He worked amid plushness, surrounded himself not with newspaper memorabilia as did his peers on the company's high altar, for Stanley's concern was never with news, only with subterranean policy. Dominating the room was what Bailey therefore took to be either Stanley's own taste or a set of company totems: an antique stringed instrument on the wall behind his desk, an old china closet full of cut glassware, and two wall hangings that gave the office its tone. One was a framed propaganda poster from World War One that showed Madame Death with her breasts and much of her blue body exposed, holding a vulture on a chain and raising an overflowing cup of blood with one bony hand. "We fought in the open," the poster said, "Bubonic Plague, Yellow Fever, Tuberculosis. Now: Venereal Disease." The vulture was V.D.

"My father was a medic in the great war," Stanley said when he saw Bailey looking at the poster. "A martyr. He infected himself with gonorrhea for the sake of research." Stanley turned his face away, saddened, Bailey assumed, by the memory. Then Stanley turned back with a sly smile. "At least that's what he told Mommy."

The second hanging was an enormous, old-fashioned sampler that proclaimed: "To him who has no sense of pleas-

ure and no part in bodily pleasure, life is not worth having."
It credited Plato with the remark.

"That quote is cockeyed," Bailey said.

"Nonsense," said Stanley. "It's exact."

"It's not what he meant."

Stanley grinned.

"I get a kick out of making old man Plato a flesh pusher.
My father spoon-fed me his stuff before I learned how to wee-
wee straight. Doesn't it grab you here to give it to philosophers up the old gazoo?" He grabbed himself by the crotch.

"Let's get on with it," Bailey said, and tossed the apology
on Stanley's desk. "Is that what you expected?"

"Fine," Stanely said, reading it and pushing it back to
Bailey. "Read it out loud."

"It's written down and signed. It doesn't have to be read."

"I want to hear you read it."

"Jarvis and Popkin said nothing about reading it."

"I'd like to hear it read."

"I don't think so."

"Read it."

"No."

"You depress me, Bailey." Stanley walked across the room
and back. Not until he was inches away did Bailey remember
how Stanley's veneer faded in a close-up. His clothes didn't
quite fit, his fingernails were always a little bit dirty, his collar
a little bit soiled. He had once been fat, but now his jowls
wobbled like spaniel ears. He limped when he walked, a de-
fect from birth, some said. Others said his father crippled
him with a kick.

"This whole scene depresses me," Bailey said.

"The arrogance of you Guild people. You'll go to your
graves sneering at your betters, all puffed up with your stink-
ing self-glory."

Stanley abruptly calmed himself. He forced a smile.

"Let's not fight," he said. "Why not have a drink? Relax."
He buzzed, and Miss Blue came in.

"Drinks, please, Miss Blue, and have one yourself."

She fussed over the drinks at Stanley's antique liquor cabinet, then passed them out, jiggled across to an old mohair chair and sat down carelessly.

"You fellows think you're the only writers in the world,"
Stanley said, "but you know I've done a bit myself. I wrote a song, didn't I, Miss Blue?"

From his desk he took a box of Christmas cards and handed one to Bailey. "My private stock," he said.

On the front, surrounded by holly leaves, was a photo of Stanley in old-fashioned clothes, leafing through the *Police Gazette*, and beneath the photo Stanley's noel: "Happy Holi-diddle." Inside were two pages of sheet music, a parody of "Peggy O'Neill."

"Show him how it goes, Miss Blue."

She stood up, and in a little girl's voice unlike the deep, resonant moo sounds Bailey remembered from a few hours before, she sang:

> Peggy O'Neill
> Was a girl you could feel
> Any part,
> Any place,
> Any time . . .

The words grew filthy, and Miss Blue teased herself with her hands to render them more explicit. Then she shook herself and did a bump and a little-girl curtsy before sitting down to Stanley's polite applause. Again Bailey was sexed. But thoughts of the pacifier weakened his interest.

"That's the cutest tune, Stanley," Miss Blue said.

"You see, there's talent everywhere, Bailey. Miss Blue has the biggest talent in the company. I'm trying to get her into show business."

"She gets to you," Bailey admitted. Proud, Miss Blue wiggled.

"I'm glad to see you're relaxed," Stanley said. "It knots me up when people are tense. Why don't you unravel? Tell me about yourself. I don't want to be your enemy. Do you really think you can win this strike?"

"I don't have much of a meaning for win these days, but I know what lose means."

"It's gone to pieces, Bailey. You think we'll put up with stuff like last night?"

"You think we'll never make a breakthrough."

"Never," said Stanley, "is too long to talk about. Let's say I don't see it."

"Then why bargain with us?"

"It's something to do."

"I suppose this should discourage me."

"And it doesn't?"

"No."

"Bailey, you really depress me. I'm offering you a way out. A simple apology to show you're sincere, and I'll put you back to work with a fat raise. We'll all forget about the past. Is that asking so much? Is that cutting out your heart?"

Bailey giggled, then nodded. The drink Miss Blue had made was a double, and suddenly it reached him. Being in the enemy camp was reassuring. Stanley was no more of a threat to reason than he'd ever been. Still a pitchman for the company's medicine show, even with the same old pitch.

"Do you have a family?" he asked Bailey. But before Bailey could respond, Stanley babbled on.

"My mother was an honest-to-god genius on the lute." He pointed to the instrument on the wall. "Rare music from a rare person. She got it from her father. He made his money in land, furs, timber, oil and steel, but he never slipped up on his culture. He played a mean madrigal." Stanley waved his arms around the room. "All this stuff was my mother's. The furniture, the glasses." He looked back at the lute and pretended to strum it, but he only looked like a guitar player to Bailey.

"Mothers are wonderful, aren't they?"

"It's hard to overrate their function," Bailey said.

"You see, Bailey? It doesn't take much to be friendly. A little common ground, that's all. A thing as elementary as parents. Parents are important. Did you have parents, Miss Blue?"

"My father gave my mother nine new tires one Christmas," she said. "She put five on the car and four under the bed."

"She put four under the bed," Bailey repeated, creating an impact on Miss Blue. She pushed her lower lip at him.

"Why don't you forget that Guild stuff," Stanley said. "Come back to the company, and we'll have a great time. You'll get to congress a lot." He gestured with open hand toward Miss Blue.

"I'm afraid it's out of the question," Bailey said.

Stanley's tongue darted in and out of his mouth. The tendons in his neck tightened spastically.

"You say no?"

Bailey nodded.

"The first time I open my heart to one of you lousy cruds, and you say no?"

"You really hate us."

"My father was a hotshot union boss," Stanley said. "A penny-squeezing son of a bitch. He tormented my beautiful mother a million ways. Whenever she tried to practice her lute, he'd play his Al Jolson records. She'd cook chateaubriand, and he'd insist on fish-head soup. You want me to like unions? Kill me, I wouldn't eat fish-head soup. I got where I am without fish heads, or Al Jolson either. I spit on the Guild."

Bailey knew Stanley's moods from long hours at the negotiating table. He was near the edge, it was obvious. Bailey smiled, quietly, displaying even more control than he felt. Slowly he stared down Stanley and turned his own smile into a chuckle. He walked across the room sloshing his ice cubes, drawing Stanley's and Miss Blue's total attention, and poured himself a new drink. Casually, softly, he began to speak.

"Stanley," he said, "I spit on your spit."

He jiggled his ice cubes under Stanley's nose.

"I spit on your spit, because you don't know anything about the Guild. You never worked twenty years to teach yourself everything there was to know about how to do a thing. You never read all the books so that the only thing that surprised you anymore was your own imagination, and you never learned to value that, use it, wash and polish it until it was the shiniest imagination on the block. And you never put it to work and saw it work out your ears and your eyes and your mouth and your fingers and all your body situations. You never talked to people on doorsteps and deathbeds and in jails and got them to spill their guts, and you never learned how to talk to pool-room punks and professor punks or how to figure out how each was a punk and each wasn't. And you never learned how to con bishops and mayors and writers and whores and blacks and whites and spicks and dicks and loonies and goonies and all there was to con and deal and be with, for that's what the con is, to be with a man and have him know you know what he's all about and get him to tell you about his life and his loves and his faults, which is the trick, to get him to tell you where he's weakest. As a con man you're a joke, Stanley. You bring me in here to con me, and you don't even know where to begin. You never learned that trick, which is the basic tool, because it's not in you and never will be and nobody can put it in you. You'll never even know how much there is to know, because the trick is untranslatable and nontransferable. You learn it on days when the sun rises in your eyeballs. Stanley, you're a fig."

Stanley's darting tongue betrayed his agitation.

"A fig, eh? A fig. Well, don't you worry. My mother taught me to see through people. She knew about people, my mother did." He pulled Miss Blue to her feet, sat in her chair and yanked her onto his lap. "She gave me everything. Everything a mother could give. Even when I had polio at fifteen and couldn't make it to the joy house by myself, Mommy took me in a taxi and waited for me so I wouldn't lose out." He rubbed Miss Blue's left thigh, inside and out, with both hands.

"Stanley," Bailey said, "you're nothing but a screwy old symbiont. Didn't your mother ever give you a hint? Didn't your biologist ever tell you?"

Bailey laughed at his own idea, chromatic mockery to Stanley.

"I'll mother you," Stanley said as he pushed Miss Blue off his lap, "talking to my son that way."

"You poor old symbiont," Bailey said. "It's not even your fault."

"You call my baby a symbiont?" Stanley yelled. "I'll show you what my son thinks of the Guild." He dashed across the room to the liquor cabinet and pulled out a jar full of odd, slimy growths floating in liquid.

"Fungus," he said. "Pickled fungus. I keep it to remember what the Guild is. A filthy fungus. Here's what Stanley and Mommy think of the Guild." He threw the jar against the wall, shattering it. He leaped up and down on the fungus.

"Putrid parasite," he said, grinding it with heel and sole.

"Don't cut your tootie, honeypot," Miss Blue told him.

Bailey picked the apology off Stanley's desk, put it back in his pocket and left the office. Over Stanley's shoulder Miss Blue waved good-bye to him and winked. Miss Bohen thumbed her nose at him while he waited for the elevator.

Bailey walked out of the building and across the street to his car in the parking lot. His keys were gone from the ignition but he carried a second set. He pressed the starter button. Nothing happened. He got out and opened the hood, to find the motor gone.

"You the owner of this heap?" a lot attendant asked.

"I am."

"It's parked wrong. You gotta move it. It's takin' up three spots."

"I'd be glad to move it. Do you have my motor?" Bailey pointed under the hood. The attendant looked.

"We're not responsible for articles left in the car that get lost or stolen," he said.

Bailey retrieved his keys from the ignition switch, smiled cordially at the attendant and walked back to the Guild room.

Irma sat in her corner chair in the Guild room waiting for Bailey, telling herself it was right for him to apologize to Stanley. But no amount of reassurance, no amount of Bailey's addiction to the democratic principle, could prevent her from viewing his act as the most abject humiliation in the history of Bailey. But if she could not correct it, she could accept. She closed her eyes and thought of acceptance forms, and of herself signing them. In the corner of each form she signed she also wrote in script that no one could read: I really don't accept.

Jarvis answered the phone when it rang. Almost immediately Irma knew Rosenthal was calling, for Jarvis had glee in his voice as he recounted the decision of the membership.

"You've got personal problems?" Jarvis said. "The Guild is falling down and blowing up, and you want me to listen to your personal problems?"

Jarvis put the phone down and called Irma.

"He wants a shoulder to cry on," Jarvis said to her.

"You missed the show our leaders put on," Irma told Rosenthal. "Lucky you."

"Bailey signed the apology, I hear," he said.

"He did. Are you going to?"

"No. Not likely."

"I'm glad. Bailey shouldn't have either."

"I might have. I probably would have. But we had an invasion here. In the house. Vandals. Smith and his crowd, I suppose. No. I really couldn't apologize after this."

"What did they do? Are you hurt?"

"No, not hurt. You'd have to see it."

"Is it awful? Anything I can do?"

"Come and take a look and maybe something will suggest itself. Bring Bailey if you find him."

"I'll find him."

Minutes later when Bailey walked through the Guild room door, Irma was ready to scream at him, shame him, slap him, kick him for his stupidity, for his betrayal of all things human in the name of some empty principle. But she had no chance. He went straight to Jarvis and gave him the apology back, first scratching out his signature.

"Stanley is out of his tree," Bailey told Jarvis. "You can't apologize to a man who's out of his tree."

Jarvis stared at the apology, not comprehending. Irma could see how the neat little package he and Popkin had tied was coming undone. He looked at Bailey with dog eyes.

"That means you're suspended."

"I understand that," Bailey said.

"What a whangdoodle you turned out to be." Jarvis put his head down on the desk and stared sideways at the wall.

"Don't take it so hard," Bailey told him.

"We'll never get lunch privileges back now," Jarvis said.

"Call Popkin," Bailey said. "Tell him things didn't work out. He'll understand."

"No he won't," Jarvis said. "He'll yell at me."

"Yell back."

Jarvis raised his head.

"Would you go see Stanley again tomorrow?"

"No," Bailey said. "I'm afraid not," and Jarvis put his head down again.

"We've got to go see Rosenthal," Irma said to Bailey, slipping her arm into his. "He's got some serious problems."

"I should call Grace," Bailey said. "She doesn't know whether I'm dead or alive. I haven't been home since yesterday noon."

Irma let go of his arm, and he dialed his home number.

"Grace?"

"Is that you, you son of a bitch? You been with your whores all night? Don't think you can come back here and give me the clap." She hung up.

Bailey eased the receiver into its cradle and looked at Irma.

"Let's go," he said.

But he didn't move. He looked around the room at the empty space where the bulletin board used to be. He looked at his chair. He looked at the photograph of the first night of the strike. Irma thought she might weep, watching him. O departures! O wrenchings! But then she saw he was going to speak.

"Bailey says good-bye," he finally said. "Bailey stands here and thinks nostalgic thoughts. And then Bailey tells that spirit of the good old days: 'Spirit, you haven't got a hair on your ass if you think nostalgia will get Bailey.' "

He pulled Irma out the front door. Jarvis did not raise his head.

Rosenthal knew that he had done this himself. When you are in a war, even a guerrilla war, even a passive war of attrition, the enemy respects only force and he shows his respect with counterforce. Why shouldn't Rosenthal have expected this, and worse?

He swept the sawdust.

Rosenthal: Why are you having such elementary thoughts at this late point? You're not a bad sort, Rosenthal. You probably deserve better than this, even if you didn't expect it. You always wanted better for yourself and others at the smallest possible cost to anybody else. A reward for work done, no more. A just recompense. Room to live.

He swept the sawdust onto the grease that even in this freezing temperature had not congealed.

Does duty come to this?

His wife sobbed on into her second hour.

Grace once accused Bailey of being half-scared of everything. Half-scared: a likely truth: ascribable to himself even when it wasn't true. As long as there was a doubt in his head about what he did, Bailey could tell himself he was half-scared to carry it off. Self-punishment. Bailey knew Rosenthal had similar thoughts. Rosenthal called himself a duty-coward: Do the imposed duty, hide from freedom of choice. Relegate all doubts to the future.

Yet Bailey knew both he and Rosenthal did act, they acted with meaning, often with anger. Others saw the acts as hollow, but Bailey knew they were triumphs of a kind, an assertion of the unique self. It was why they both cultivated an image: Bailey and his cossack hat and green muffler; Rosenthal and his cape and Tyrolean feather. This is me, the image said back from the mirror. There was something honest about it. There was Rosenthal's aged convertible, his taste for

elegance. Rosenthal said it was how he fended off the malef-
icent forces, a flower in the seedy lapel of the spirit: No
matter what they take away from me, I've still got a little
class. But in himself Bailey saw that plus something else,
something that said: I'm one hell of a unique event in this
world. Anybody can see that from my image. That's why I
do what I do. That's why, right or wrong, half-scared, heroic
or cowardly, I'm me. What I do is right.

Justification for evil, Bailey thought.

He stood in Rosenthal's doorway with Irma, the door on
one hinge only. Rosenthal, sweeping the kitchen in his cape,
hat, gloves and rubbers, saw them. But he let the cold house
speak to them.

The wooden kitchen table lay in the corner in a dozen
pieces, sawed, then deeply gouged by hammer and chisel, or
an ax. All woodwork around doors and windows had been
ax-gouged, all windows broken. Broken china was piled beside the table. Kitchen chairs had become kindling wood.
Pots and pans had been hammered out of shape or punctured.
Walls were smeared with paint and all forms of grease available in the house: cooking oil, butter, lard, drippings, and
crankcase oil from the garage had been poured over all floors,
all furniture. Overstuffed furniture was sliced dozens of ways,
its stuffing strewn on top of the oil. Something like a sledgehammer blow had cracked the kitchen and bathroom sinks
and the bathtub. Similar blows had broken the plaster in
every wall. Food was emptied into a corner of the kitchen,
cans of beans and tomatoes on top of meat and rice and
cookies and flour and sugar and vinegar. All food was opened,
dumped on the pile and garbage emptied on top of it. Curtains
were shredded and rugs cut into zigzag pieces. The TV set
was smashed, all mirrors broken, dressers and beds sawed in
half or thirds, mattresses sliced and unstuffed, the wire of bed-
springs cut in dozens of places, all clothing smeared with
grease and paint, all jewelry bent, smashed or unstrung. Each

of Rosenthal's books had been ripped at least in half, covers torn off and floated in the bathtub mixture of water and grease. Windowshades, drapes, oil paintings were slashed.

"They also hung my wife's diaphragm on the pencil sharpener," Rosenthal said, "with a pencil stuck through it."

"We deserve it," Shirley Rosenthal said. She sobbed as she talked, the sobbing having worked its way up and almost out. A small, dark-haired woman with a pinched but pretty face, she sat on a fragment of mattress in the bedroom, wearing her coat, her legs wrapped in a blanket.

"It's p-p-punishment for p-p-pride," she said. "Ha!"

"Gypsy reprisal is what it is," Rosenthal said. "And you're stuttering."

"Of c-course I'm st-stuttering. God is against us. I've kn-known it for m-m-m-months. Everybody knows it."

"Who is everybody?"

"People. Just p-p-people. I was sitting at a drugstore counter and a w-w-woman next to me was t-t-tearing paper napkins into strips. I w-w-watched her awhile and she looked at me and threw the napkins in my f-f-face. 'You're no good,' she said. 'You w-w-wear three sweaters. You'll never be any g-good.' She knew. They all know."

Irma sat down by Shirley and held her hand.

"Those things happen to everybody," Irma said.

"No. It's G-g-god. He hates us."

"No, no," Irma said. "It's happened to me. I was walking along the street one day and a man I never saw before came up and hit me on the head with his umbrella and told me to move over to the other side of the street."

Shirley looked at Irma, studied her.

"You've got d-d-dark hair. He p-p-probably thought you were me."

The lost laughter of infancy was a phrase Bailey had read somewhere so long ago that he could not remember its source.

But he had read it at an impressionable moment, for it stayed in his mind. Bailey made up other phrases: the death of an innocent face. The corruption of adolescent wisdom.

"Stop sweeping, goddamn it. Stop sweeping," Bailey said. When he put the broom down, Rosenthal knew he would quit the Guild at last.

"I'm leaving the Guild," he said.

"Leaving me alone?" Irma asked. "You may not know, but they've suspended Bailey."

Rosenthal listened as Irma briefly recounted the events leading to the suspension. Now he didn't know what to do. As he listened, he realized that Bailey had been out of the Guild for months. He had been on his own since the day he quit as negotiator. He went through the motions, going along with an idea that no longer had any validity for him. But Bailey could live anywhere, under any flag, and it wouldn't change him. He would always be Bailey, nobody's servant.

Rosenthal picked up the broom. Work is a distraction.

When he put the broom down, Bailey knew Rosenthal would quit the Guild. He had to quit now, for it had at last come all the way home to him. Rosenthal was one of the few heroes in Bailey's life, and Bailey felt he knew precisely how Rosenthal would behave. He would exile himself to a place where there would be a minimum of companylike influence. He would devote himself to something with a dutiful concern that in time would become passionate. Bailey could not say what that would be, for Rosenthal could not say what it would be. But having found one world wanting, he would seek another one, a smaller one, as closely resembling the dream of the first one as possible.

But he would never recover from his wounds.

He would always be heroic.

When he saw Bailey staring at him after he picked up the broom again, Rosenthal stared back at Bailey. Something would always be possible for Bailey. He might even rebuild the Guild, stronger than it was even on the first night of the strike. He might even become a mythical figure in the Guild. Bailey was capable of great deeds. He was radical and talented, and for such men something good is always possible until they die. With himself, Rosenthal felt such possibility was remote. He did not accept it as a fact, but only sensed its truth. He also sensed that he had believed too long. In what? There was no what; because it was not an objective thing. It was his attitude toward all things. He did not resist elements foreign to himself. Bailey understood what to reject, what to keep. There was a chance for the salvation of such men. They kept themselves in a condition that always permitted something new to happen to them.

I tried too hard to get along.

I'm tired now.

Bailey is not as tired as I am.

Given the right frame of mind, Irma could cry over items in a mail-order catalog. Yet often when she cried she had an impulse to smile. For what moved her to tears was usually something so valuable that she had already experienced joy from it; and the smile would be the memory of that.

"I think we should clean this place up," she said. "I'll start on the mattress and the bedclothes. Bailey, why don't you use some of the boards to nail up the windows. And fix that damn swinging door."

To Irma, men who went through their lives saying only "I want" didn't really want at all. They were the men who professed love too quickly, who came too quickly, who gave gifts because they expected gifts. But they didn't "want" at all. They needed. They were addicted to the sop of every day. They had no grandeur like Bailey, like Rosenthal. So many people believed all work was holy, that one kind of work was as holy as the next. But that wasn't true at all. There were men who worked, and there were holy men who did holy work. Bailey and Rosenthal were holy men. God help them. They're going to die from such holiness.

If Bailey could have heard Irma think such thoughts, "Shit," he would have said.

Knowing the context, Irma would have called that a holy comment.

"You know we're pushovers," Bailey said.

"Creampuffs," said Rosenthal.

"Moderates," said Bailey, "always lose the revolution after they win it."

"We didn't win."

Bailey saw a black flower blossom in his mind. He stepped on it.

"I do believe I'll quit. I'll tidy things up for Jarvis before I do. But it's pointless to go on."

"Jarvis will miss your humility," Bailey said.

"My humility is a pose. Denying it is part of the pose. Mentioning the denial is another part. You should see that. I'd rather have your values."

Bailey grunted. Values. He had long ago contracted the disease of the open mind. So many unimportant things sat inside his brain alongside everything truly important, all claiming equal attention. He smiled that anyone could think this constituted a set of values.

"L-l-l-look at him laugh at you," Shirley Rosenthal said to her husband. She pointed at Bailey. "He's d-d-death, that's what he is."

When Bailey made no response, Rosenthal suspected guilt was taking him over. Possibly he'll think I'm bitter toward him too as a result of the fire and its consequences. He shouldn't have mentioned Bailey's part in the fire to Shirley. She didn't know how to read it. She couldn't link it to all that went before, both in the Guild and in Bailey.

Yet as Rosenthal looked at his destroyed home, he could not entirely blame an evolutionary cause. A single act brought this about, and as he had that thought, he felt anger deep within. All easy explanations, all the forgive-and-forget platitudes, all the brotherly tissue of commitment and resistance seemed like assuagements of a harsh truth.

Goddamn you, Bailey. Why did you do this to me?

He grabbed Bailey by the shoulder.

"She's not herself," he said. "Don't pay any attention."

"What she said isn't true," Irma said.

"Of course not," Rosenthal said.

The four of them worked through the evening, and by midnight the house was sealed off from the weather. Tables and certain chairs had been pieced together as if by blind, insane carpenters. Furniture had been broadly stitched and covered haphazardly with cloth of any sort, and the bed reconstituted. Irma bought food and cooked it, and Bailey repaired light fixtures. From neighbors and friends dishes and glasses were borrowed. Rosenthal went to the Salvation Army and bought two shirts for fifty cents and a blouse and skirt for Shirley for a dollar. Bailey promised clean socks, and Irma pledged underwear.

Something in Bailey wanted to take him away from the filthy destruction of Rosenthal's life, but a stronger force held him fast. He should have collapsed hours before, considering his physical low point, and he did not really understand why he hadn't. There truly are times, he thought, when the will does not betray the best part of us.

By two A.M. life in its essenials had been restored.

They entered Irma's apartment quietly at three o'clock and Bailey collapsed on the sofa. For the first time Irma saw the bandages on his ankles that Miss Blue had applied. When she asked Bailey about them he said they'd done it at the hospital. Irma said she didn't remember seeing them at the hospital. Bailey shrugged, closed his eyes.

"Do you want a drink?" she asked, and he nodded.

She fixed two bourbons on the rocks, then went to her bedroom to hang up her coat. She came out, still holding the coat.

"My mattress is gone," she said.

"Your mattress," Bailey said.

"Why would anybody take my mattress?"

"Maybe your sister sent it to the laundry?"

"My mattress is none of her business."

She went to Francie's room. Bailey heard low rumblings of speech.

"She thinks I'm drunk," Irma said. "She smelled the whiskey."

"Did they take your springs?"

"No, just the mattress."

"Well, gypsies have to sleep too."

"Not in my bed they don't."

"Buck up. There's still the couch." He squeezed himself closer to the back of the couch, patted the available space with his hand.

"My sister would be scandalized."

Bailey shrugged again and closed his eyes. He was thinking of how he could raise two thousand dollars to get Rosenthal back on his feet when Irma put the light out and lifted the half-finished drink out of his hand. In the matter of an instant he had a flash dream of his Uncle Melvin and his Uncle Melvin's money, riding along together on the back of a cat.

The dream passed, and he thought of it in a way which startled him. It had a reality that could not be contravened, could not be dismissed as something insubstantial. A man could act on dreams as he acted upon thought. A man could act upon delusions as he acted upon dreams. They would have only a private validity. No one would be able to accept them; but neither could anyone negate them. Bailey acted out of motives which no one seemed to understand or accept. His life was not a dream, not a delusion, only like them in result. He toyed with these notions, coming to no conclusion, for Irma curled her body around his, kissed his eyes and whispered into his ear: "Good night."

Bailey heard the door slam and felt Irma fly off the couch and away from him. Bailey blinked, saw her standing in the bathroom doorway talking to her sister, sister covered by housecoat, Irma's own roundness shining through the rear end of her negligee. The sisters screamed at each other in whispers Bailey could not understand. He turned his body toward the back of the sofa, closed his ears. The door slammed and Irma was again by his side.

"She's furious."

"You said she'd be scandalized."

"That's just a phrase. She's furious because I use mine and she doesn't use hers."

"Use your what?"

"My freedom."

"Oh ho."

Bailey and Irma waited until Francie had dressed and left before they arose fully to the new day. Irma felt this day would surely be the end of a complete phase of her life. With Bailey out of the Guild it would not be the same; not just the loss of that face or even of that spirit. It wasn't just the Bailey charisma, certainly not his big crotch that had pulled her back from the brink for so long. It was the Bailey vision. If

Bailey couldn't see it, then very probably it wasn't there. It was like a belief in oracles, in priests and philosophers, in anybody who has the word and tells it. Bailey the Jesus. Bailey the Buddha, Bailey the magician. To Irma.

They went together to Bailey's to collect a bit of his gear, a few shirts. Irma would stay outside. They saw the crowd on the stoop of his apartment house as they rounded the corner. Bailey edged into the mob, mostly children and a few women, and peered among shoulders and necks. He pushed into the center of it and disappeared. Then came the yelling, the screaming, the windmilling of arms, and the crowd broke. Children stepped back to watch. A woman clutching a shirt ran across the street. Bailey chased her and tugged the shirt away. Then he chased another woman with a pair of shoes and got them. The children scattered when he came back to the stoop. He bent over a pile of cartons, and as Irma approached she saw him holding a topless box half-full of trinkets: cufflinks, medals, money clips, tiepins, a pearl-handled jackknife, an Army patch, foreign coins.

"I don't even know what's missing," he said, staring into the box. "I'll probably never know."

Spilling out of the cartons were other Bailey belongings: underwear, ties, an Army fatigue jacket with corporal stripes, and papers: a chaotic strew of papers.

"Is it all yours?"

Bailey nodded. He stacked the papers without attention to orderly sequence and stuffed the contents of two boxes into two others and threw the empties on the sidewalk.

"What does it mean?" Irma asked.

"Grace. She was in that kind of mood."

"Maybe it was Smith. Maybe you ought to go up and see if Grace is all right."

"She's all right. See her in the window?"

Irma sat on the stoop by the boxes while Bailey went inside. In the apartment he found Grace still by the window, looking down at the street. She did not look up when he entered.

"Who's the floozy?"

Bailey didn't answer, didn't enter all the way, didn't close the door. He stood with his hand on the knob.

"You didn't have to throw the stuff on the stoop. I would have gotten it out."

"You would have gotten it out. You would have gotten it out."

"Has anybody been bothering you? Visitors? Phone calls?"

"So you're worried, eh? You know what you can do with your worry?"

"You can't reach me with that talk."

"Reach you, ha. Reach you, ha."

"Why don't you call your mother. Go down home for a few days until you get reorganized."

"Son of a bitch."

"I won't be coming back unless there's an emergency."

"Emergency. You won't be back unless there's an emergency. A fat lot of shit I give."

"You're swearing, Grace. You see? I think you should call your mother."

"Get out of here, whoremonger. You're pussy-mad, that's your problem."

Bailey stepped out and closed the door. Grace screamed as his right foot touched the first step.

"Baileeeeeeeeeeee."

He knew the tone: plaint. But there was really nothing to do, and his left foot touched the second step down.

Bailey studied the wreath of crepe beside the doorbell on his uncle's porch, wondering if it signified the old man's death, and if so, why he hadn't heard of it. He finally decided it was entirely possible not to have heard, since anything was possible lately. He pushed the bell.

"Oh, you," said his Aunt Rose. "Who told you?"

She opened the door and turned immediately away. He hadn't seen her in a year, perhaps more; couldn't even remember the last occasion. Was it a wake? A funeral? They were the only occasions for family gatherings in the last ten years. Rose always looked the same, with her tidy gray bun the size of a Parker House roll, her little unrouged lips, so tight, so neatly bloodless.

"Who is she?" Irma asked.

"My aunt. My uncle's sister. A sweet lady nut."

"She's crazy about you."

Bailey heard his aunt talking to herself as she rustled her skirts toward the kitchen. "Cats" was all he caught. And when he saw his Uncle Melvin in the dining room talking to a bald man in morning clothes he understood that the crepe must be for the only other resident of the house: Potato Flake. Aunt Rose, stirring a pot of chicken soup, raised her cheek for a kiss when Bailey leaned toward her. He introduced Irma as a friend from the Guild.

"Where's your wife?"

"We've kind of separated," Bailey said.

"I never thought much of roller skaters anyway."

"The cat died, I take it."

"Poisoned yesterday, and good riddance, I say. I know about cats. They smother sleeping infants. They tear out the eyeballs of corpses and eat them. What kind of pet is that to have around?"

"After all these years with that cat you can still ask such a question?"

"I'll ask it till I die. I know how evil cats are. I've read his books. Look here." She stopped stirring and picked up a book that lay open, face down, on the kitchen table. "Here's a woman," she said, tapping a page, "who taped up her sleeping husband's mouth after a red cat crawled out of it. Then when the cat couldn't get back inside, it disappeared and the husband turned into a blue mouse. What would the old man say to that?"

Bailey grieved for his aunt. She had lived in an everlasting pout since she discovered that her brother preferred his cat to her. Such estrangement began when the old man, a tug-boat captain and a widower, returned home from a river voyage to find that his daughter, her husband, their four children, plus his younger brother who worked as a short-order cook, had been blown up when the gas seeped into the house along an underground pipe and exploded, possibly at the flick of a light switch. Only the cat, which lost an eye in the blast, survived. The captain viewed the cat, a Siamese female, as the spiritual repository of his disintegrated loved ones. Insurance and a settlement from the gas company left him rich. He quit the river and moved into the old family homestead where Rose lived among the relics and memories of a bygone family. The old man devoted his days to stuffing Potato Flake with lobster and cream until its once svelte black-and-tan body turned into a silky butterball. He quit his Queen Putzina then too. For years she had met him at odd junctures along the river and sometimes rode the tug. But he abruptly put her out of his life along with the rest of the world.

"Was he always a little bit off?" Bailey asked his aunt. "I mean when he was a kid."

"Everybody in this family was a little off. Your grandfather used to throw boiled potatoes at trolley cars. Your grandmother wore the largest bustle in the city. She had a rear end like a turkey. Your Uncle Jack used to pull the beards of old Jews till he was damn near eighty. He took many a lickin' for it but it never stopped him. What else do you want to know?"

"Who poisoned the cat, was it you?"

"Don't think I didn't think about it. But no. He figures the Italian up the road did it."

Bailey left his aunt to her cooking and with Irma he went to see his uncle, only to find him still so engrossed with the bald man that he did not intrude. He wandered through the old house, so full of relics of the family history, and he yearned to know the secrets it might yield about his uncle and his other relatives whose lives had been lived in it. There was a picture of his Uncle Tim with a bicycle team, and Aunt Julia with a huge bosom and no waist at all; and a tintype of a man in a derby who was a relative beyond connection in this age. Even Melvin and Rose weren't sure who he was. Maybe a great-great-grandfather. Maybe a grand-uncle. Maybe a train robber or a copperhead or a canal digger.

In the old living room all the furniture fabrics had been shredded by Potato Flake, and one entire wall was given over to a bookcase full of cat books, from the most arcane lore on the cat in antiquity to modern picture books on famous Hollywood cats. The collection made Bailey conscious of the money the old man could spend on luxuries while Rosenthal, poor bastard, was destitute. Must get him some money. He tugged Irma, and they went back toward the large pine-paneled room where the old man was talking.

The room was full of cat paraphernalia: a table full of rubber mice of assorted sizes and colors, some of them fur-bearing, some of them bell-tailed; flea-powder jars and boxes of catnip balls, a fish-scented plastic fish dangling from a wire, a scratching board, a round, full-sized lemon-colored bed (Potato Flake's), a compartmentalized silver food dish, a silver-edged glass drinking bowl, a display case full of used ribbons, bells, collars, cat booties and angora sweaters that

Potato Flake had worn; and on the walls huge photographs of Potato Flake scratching, eating, running, sleeping, slapping the pendulous fish and staring into the camera.

The captain, in black suit and string tie, was still talking with the same chubby, bald and bumpy-skulled man. Bailey saw the cat at last, sitting at the far end of the room in a stagelike frame with salmon-colored satin backdrops. Bailey deduced that it was a side-loading animal coffin that allowed Potato Flake (and would have allowed a Great Dane) to sit regally in death. The cat looked relaxed. One might have expected it to step down from its silken perch and bite a mouse, claw a fish.

"Hello, Cappy," Bailey said to his uncle. "Sorry about the cat."

"A sad day," said the bald man, and he introduced himself as Mr. Toasty, a TV children's-show emcee who, Bailey recalled, had a compassion for animals that was unrivaled in North America.

"Tears aren't enough when you lose a pet," Irma said, shifting her gaze from the coffin to the old man. The captain stared back at her.

"By the Jesus," he said.

No one spoke, waiting for him to continue. But he didn't go on.

"I'm very sorry," Irma said. "We know how you must feel. It was a lovely animal."

"A severe blow," said Mr. Toasty.

"By the good goddamn Jesus mothers," said the captain. He clenched his fist and screwed up his face.

"Who would poison such a pet?" Mr. Toasty asked. "Only an evil person."

"I'll get him," the captain said. "By the beards of all shit-mongers, I'll gibble his guts. Eeeeeeyyyyooooeeeoooowww!"

He threw punches at the specter of his enemy. One, two, three and down. Then he kicked.

"Why don't we begin the service?" Mr. Toasty said.

"The service?" said Bailey.

Mr. Toasty nodded and took the old man's arm and led him to a seat at the center of a semicircle of chairs facing the coffin. He indicated chairs for Bailey and Irma and then went for Aunt Rose, who sat down, still in her apron. Mr. Toasty took a position to one side of the corpse.

"We see here the resting place of love," he began with great solemnity. "The soul of this sweet animal has taken with it into the place where good cats rest, all the love a man can give to an animal on this earth. Just look at this room. Did ever a body see evidence of greater love? God loves a soft, little lamb. God loves a furry, white bunny rabbit with a pink nose. But I sometimes think that most of all, God loves a pussycat. When I go to sleep at night I my very self count cats as they leap after tiny little white mice. And then when they catch those mice they petty-pet-pet them, ever so gently, and then they let them go. Then I always reward those nice, kind kitties by dreaming of a big dish of chicken livers and lobster tails for each one of them. Such wonderful, wonderful creatures, I sometimes think they're superior to human beings. I sometimes even go so far as to think that maybe, after all, God is a cat. Which of us could say different?"

A door slammed, and Bailey turned to see a large tiger cat swaggering across the room. It was half-bleached so that from midsection to tail it was splotchy white and from head to midsection the original gray-and-black mottle. Its tail had been recently cut to a nervous, scabby stump, its mouth was a malicious gap with teeth bared. Its back left leg was a wheel that spun as the other three legs moved, and its right ear was a green plastic thimble that twitched on its bloody ear stump as the cat advanced across the room on oily paws, leaving tracks.

Its irrational bravado and the depravity of its condition made it seem evil to Bailey, no matter how much a victim of others it unquestionably was, and he instantly knew its origin and the cause of Potato Flake's death. Smith. No doubt about it. Smith. Exploiter of his own mother's death. Inventor of the cow frame. Perverter of cats. Bailey leaped to the window and looked onto the porch for Smith or one of his cohorts, but saw no one. And when he turned back toward the cat he saw it advance toward Mr. Toasty and spring at his face. With an agility Bailey did not expect, Mr. Toasty veered to one side, grabbed a vase full of pussy willows from a stand beside the coffin and neatly clubbed the cat. The animal was stunned but recovered direction and came again at Mr. Toasty, who this time kicked it across the room, It arced past the Potato Flake photos, hit the wall and fell unconscious by the plastic fish. Mr. Toasty touched its carcass lightly with his toe, then leaned over and inspected its genital region.

"An unaltered animal," he advised the mourners. "The worst kind."

He picked it up by its stumpy tail and with its rear wheel spinning he carried it out of the room. Captain Melvin turned and spoke to his beloved Potato Flake.

"I'll get that cat-kicking son of a bitch," he told the corpse.

Bailey tried to talk to his uncle, but the old man would not listen. He was too concerned with carrying out his promise to the cat to be distracted; and when Mr. Toasty returned empty-handed, the old man was ready and went directly to him. He first rubbed the Toasty nose in a plate of Potato Flake's two-day-old poo, retrieved from a kitty-litter basket; then he put a foot on the surprised animal lover's chest and catapulted him across the room. Mr. Toasty rose with dignity, wiped his nose and left the house.

Winded, spent, the old man sat in his chair staring at the corpse of his cat. Bailey was saddened. Grief was grief no matter what caused it; and he felt strangeness too at what he was about to tell his uncle. He watched for evidence that they

still had something in common, but he could not find the look that would admit they were kin. The old man looked at him as if he were a stranger, welcome in the house but not privy to anything beyond cordiality. Bailey saw some of himself in this kind of behavior: the ability to dispense with something that had once been almost vital. The friends who had been close before the strike, but failed to see in it the same virtues Bailey found, were all but forgotten. The strike had created something so callous in him that he often thought he would make no more relationships that would last beyond the moment. Ties would bind as long as the moment lasted: an instant, or perhaps a year but no longer. And he would not grieve when the moment ended. It was desirable to get beyond sentimental attachments, beyond trouble, beyond love, to be equal even to death. He would like to be able to talk to death if it entered the room, make intellectual chitchat, crack macabre jokes with it. He was not far from such liberation. His life now was almost like a sealed bottle that nothing could touch. He lived in great intimacy with his dreams and his failures and he yearned for an end to emptiness but no longer expected one. He expected almost nothing from life but the next thing. And good or bad, it no longer seemed to matter. Rosenthal's wife may be right, Bailey thought; maybe you are death.

"Listen," Bailey said to the captain, "I know who killed your cat."

The old man squinted at him.

"And it wasn't one of your neighbors," Bailey said.

The old man sat up straight. Bailey talked then, nonstop. He explained who Smith was, that his name was really Seventh Elevator and that he was a gypsy. He explained the gypsy presence and its role in the strike. He explained the fire (without implicating himself) and Putzina's death and the vengeance Smith was taking on Guildsmen. He told the old

man how Smith and the gypsies had kidnapped and tortured
and cursed him, and how a kid named Skin tried to make an
arhat out of him. He skipped Miss Blue, since Irma was
already bottle-eyed listening to the story. He did not dwell
on anything until he came to Rosenthal and then he explained
with painstaking detail the total destruction of Rosenthal's
home and the hours it took merely to make it barely habitable
again. Finally he made his point: a request for two thousand
dollars that would help Rosenthal get started again. He came
back to the cat and vowed he would take his own vengeance
on Smith for all that had been done, including the murder of
the cat and the thrusting of the corrupted animal into the
midst of the funeral ceremony. When he finished he thought
of how little the old man really knew of the Guild and he
backtracked and talked of Rosenthal's commitment and of
Irma's role, and of himself and of the others who didn't last
so long, and of the year-long loyalty to a cause that provided
a common bond to its adherents, a deep kind of brotherhood.
Rosenthal, he told the old man, is one of the gentlest souls
on earth, a lionheart, the worthiest man he knew.

Uncle Melvin nodded his head and stroked his whiskers.
When Bailey finished he looked him in the eye for a few
silent seconds, then stood up and motioned for Bailey to follow. He went to the living room and rummaged in his roll-
top desk for an envelope and told Bailey to wait. Bailey sat
at the desk while the old man went upstairs. To his hoard,
Bailey assumed. Then he was back, and dropped the envelope
in Bailey's lap. He said only: "You ain't very smooth."

Bailey opened the envelope and found two sheets of sand-
paper.

"Are you leaving?" Aunt Rose asked Bailey.

"I think it's time."

"At least help him with the coffin. If you don't he'll probably give himself another hernia."

Bailey agreed to stay, and Rose relayed the information to her brother, who was already fussing with the coffin. Bailey helped him close it, and together they carried it to the old man's station wagon and slid it gently in through the tailgate. The old man climbed in beside it and sat down with his hand holding it steady.

"You drive," he told Bailey.

Irma and Rose got in and Bailey drove to the pet cemetery, guided by his uncle's directions. A guide at the cemetery office took them over a snowy road to the burial area and directed them to an open grave, one of many dug in the fall, and covered with tarpaulin and manufactured sod to await winter usage. The guide tried to help Bailey unload the coffin, but the old man pushed him away and with Bailey carried it to the grave. The guide pulled up the tarpaulin and kicked the ice and snow off it. Bailey and the old man knelt in the snow and lowered the coffin into the grave. Then, while the others watched, wondering what was next, the old man stood up and doffed his captain's cap and held it over his heart. He looked at everyone, demanding an absolute silence. And then he began to mumble his threnody, taking it beyond grief, beyond prayer:

By the hair and fat
from a phantom cat,
by the death and pains
of Siamese brains,
I swear to Bast
I'll live the last
to pum the drum
and skewer the one
who pized the bell
of the catsy sun,
who stole the sky
and dried the pool
and took the old man

for a fool.
Be-elzie zott bezumm bezoo.
O cat of mine,
O cat o'nine,
Be-elzie zott bezumm bezoo.

He fell to his knees and cried. The guide covered the grave
with the tarpaulin and rolled the manufactured grass on top
of it. Rose and Irma helped the old man to his feet and led
him weeping to the station wagon. Bailey drove. They were
halfway home when the captain spoke the first word of the
ride.

"Gypsies?" he said. "Gypsies? Did you mean any of that?"

"They've poisoned their enemies' animals for centuries,"
Bailey said. "They even used to use a special kind of poison
called drao that just might be traceable."

"Hard right rudder," the old man said. "We'll have an
autopsy."

Bailey turned the car around and drove back to the cemetery. He and the old man walked to the grave and stared
down at it in disbelief. It was a raw wound, the tarpaulin
and grass pulled back and the coffin obscenely smashed, and
empty. The old man stiffened, then spoke to the wind with
clenched teeth, pounding his hand with measured strokes of
his fist.

"By the balls of dirty Judas, I'll pay a fortune to get the
fiends who did this."

Even as he spoke, Bailey was in motion, leaping among the
tombstones incribed to "Fido" and "Faithful Tippie" and
"Tabby the Third." At the crest of the hill he looked in all
directions but saw no one. Then, moving at a great gallop
and with green muffler flying, he came down the hill, suffused
with the vision of banishing the old man's grief and restoring
Rosenthal's life in one swooping gesture. He grabbed his
uncle's arm and stowed him in the station wagon, where Irma
waited with bewildered look. Then he leaped behind the wheel

and with a frenzied gun of the motor he roared off into a brand-new possibility.

Smith was gone. The gypsies were gone from behind the burned building. Bailey's income from the Guild benefits was gone. Bailey's apartment, abandoned by Grace when she went to her mother, was gone. And for Bailey the Guild was gone too.

Solve the riddle or die was the ultimatum he had always lived under. And as he worked to solve the riddle, he also prepared to die. But he never conceived that the riddle would be taken from him.

He rented a room-and-a-half apartment and paid a month in advance out of a diminishing bank account. He called friends he hadn't talked to in a year or more. He asked them to help him find work.

His inability to help Rosenthal and his Uncle Melvin drove him ever deeper into the gloom of guilt.

(Bailey, halt!)

(One, two.)

EXTRA!

PIGS ARE WHERE YOU FIND THEM, OUTLAW DECIDES

SOUL IS A PORK CHOP, HE DISCOVERS

Within the soul, within the body social, there must be—if we are to experience long survival—a continuous "recurrence of birth" (palingenesia) to nullify the unremitting recurrences of death. For it is by means of our own victories, if we are not regenerated, that the work of Nemesis is wrought: doom breaks from the shell of our very virtue. Peace then is a snare; war is a snare; change is a snare; permanence is a snare. When our day is come for the victory of death, death closes in; there is nothing we can do, except be crucified—and resurrected; dismembered totally, and then reborn.

—JOSEPH CAMPBELL
The Hero with a Thousand Faces

He took a job in the State Library, menial work sorting and shelving books. On his first workday the head librarian gave him instructions and presented him with a wallet-sized copy of the library's essential dogma:

> A book improperly shelved is a lost book. A lost book might just as well not have been written. Worse, it is a promise unkept to users of the library, for it exists in our card catalog, but only as a man exists through having his name on a tombstone. Do not bury books. Shelve them properly.

Bailey stepped into the stacks elevator and began his descent. Down he went into the earth, one of the city's deepest points. He drew a breath of the dry air that filled the elevator cage and at bottom level stepped out into the burial vaults of the past. He was in a long concrete corridor with green metal racks everywhere. Small bulbs lighted the aisles near the elevators and illuminated the beginnings of dark passageways among the dusty shelves of knowledge.

A wagonload of books awaited him, as the librarian had promised; also a stack of bound volumes of old newspapers. These, more than anything else, aroused his curiosity, both from a professional viewpoint and because he felt he might trace something of himself through those old years. He shelved the books, then noted down stories that beguiled him from the old papers: Costigan's brass tools stolen from his shop; Alderman Wingate gives two-hour declamation on the anniversary of our independence; Miss Lavinia McQuade found at old Ale House with more young men acting as gallants than befits a young lady of prudent conduct; Lanahan rolls off roof and is believed to have sunstroke but is only drunk; squad of stragglers returns from war after hiding in mountains for one year after Appomattox.

He constructed personal equations out of brass tools, independence talk, gang bangs, drunkenness, blind allegiance to a dead cause. He felt he could take them all to heart. And his perusal of the crumbling old papers told him he could find a thousand more items like them and equate them too, proving that he was all the world, all the world was he. But he knew no more about himself than he did before he began.

Irma gained access to the stacks on the pretext of researching a thesis on immigrant stupidities from 1800 to 1850 and reported that Guild locals around the country, and also the liberal wing at International Guild headquarters, were calling Bailey, Rosenthal and Deek the Ink Truck Heroes. This was unofficial banter. The official line was to deplore what they did. Popkin and Jarvis had quickly rejected Deek's application for Guild membership on grounds of ineligibility, but Rosenthal forwarded it to Guild headquarters, suggesting honorary membership.

"Now Popkin and Jarvis don't know what to do," Irma said. "Deek's broken bones are too heroic to argue with."

"What about the ink truck?" Bailey asked. "Did it come back?"

"Yesterday afternoon."

"What did Jarvis and Popkin do?"

"They sent all the pickets home."

By the third day on the job the randomness of his rummage through time faded, and Bailey focused on individual subjects. The gypsies took on a fascination, and after poring over the old papers, historical accounts of the city and books of gypsy history and lore, he turned up a newspaper account from 1866, contained in a twelve-volume potpourri of historical data of the city and indexed under "Gypsie Event."

Two men gave information to the police yesterday that

a corn doctor who called himself Tercero Ascensor demonstrated a new corn medicine to John Muldowney and Michael Burns in the Dingle Bar. The pair removed their shoes and the doctor painted their feet with a sticky substance. While they waited for their feet to dry, the corn doctor took Muldowney's hat and Burns's coat and the shoes of both, and leaving his own tattered things on the floor he departed at such a rapid speed that the men with the sticky feet were unable to lay hands upon him. After hearing the man's description, Police Sergeant Cahill asserted that the man was surely a gypsie, very likely from the nomadic band that has camped at the south edge of the city for the past four days. A Spanish merchant on Fox Avenue advised Sergeant Cahill that Tercero Ascensor in Spanish translates as Third Elevator, which led the sergeant to proclaim that the name was surely a pseudonym.

Using Irma's notes on what the gypsies had said as they wailed and danced in the hospital corridor, Bailey discovered the words to be from the language of the Zincali gypsies of Spain. Their tongue had been systematized by an Englishman who lived among them in the early nineteenth century. "Meripen pa busne" Bailey found to mean "Death to the gentiles" and gentile meant any nongypsy. The gypsy chant translated:

Death to the gentiles, Holy God.
Dung for the gentiles, Holy God.
Cut off their genitals, Holy God.

And the words "querela nasula," which Mr. Joe had uttered at the close of the great gypsy curse, Bailey found to be a request that the evil eye of god be cast on the victim. But in spite of all this ominous knowledge, Bailey sensed that if there was a god, then he had certainly incurred divine favor by burning the building and indirectly causing the death of the old woman. It was never his intention to kill. And yet indirect disaster was god's favored style. By this reasoning Bailey felt he had performed an unpunishable, godlike deed.

At the end of a week in the library's silence Bailey saw precisely how imprisoned he was by his own history, his own psychological cell structure. He had often talked of mutation but never felt it possible. Yet you died from being unable to change. You believed profoundly in the stupidity of glory and perished from its absence. Otherness. You denied the power of whole areas of life that you found unworthy, and slowly they smothered you with their presence. Otherness. When Irma whispered to him on the way to the hospital: "Why did you run to that clubbing?" he had whispered back: "That's all there really is." Run to the glory of the club. Otherness. In Fobie's one night to break a depression he talked to a young woman with a virginal, unspoiled mouth, a benign, maiden-of-the-flowers smile, a face like an apple blossom. In his six-beer euphoria he delivered a monologue of hope to her based purely on intuition. The world was like her. There was no one in it who could not understand him; none who could reject him once his lucidity prevailed. It was like speaking to a beautiful day, and when he took her home he dared not touch her lest he break the spell. A week later he found she was an apprentice slut who had only wanted transportation from bar to door. She told his dreams to a crowd of scabs at the bar. When he confronted her she said to him: "Jerk, what do you want from me, kind words?"

Precisely. The grand folly of otherness.

But now, perceiving such folly, he resolved to kick the habit. The Guild was otherness: an unreal dream that had no possibility of being realized. It was hopelessness. It was a hideous, recurring death he would die no more. Newer, flashier and much more hopeful deaths in the possible world, in the world of here and now (touch it, taste it) awaited him. Retired hero, he had the right to choose his death.

So good-bye, old paint.

I'm out to find a horse of a different color.

Bailey was shelving books with their backs to the wall, pages facing out from the shelf, when Irma discovered what he was doing. She said nothing, turned their backs out, followed him as he worked. "A book improperly shelved is a book lost," he said aloud. She made a note of shelf areas where he was working, planning to return and reshelve the books properly. Bailey was ignoring the decimal system, putting biography on biology shelves, fiction under finance, drama under dogs. Somewhere his brain was functioning, but oddly. He spoke soundlessly to the darkness of the unused stacks. When the wagons were empty he returned repeatedly to the old newspaper files. Irma spent her days looking after him from afar.

From the rear of the stacks as Bailey stared into their darkness, a birdlike voice whose consciousness had been eavesdropping on Bailey's reverie, spoke squeaky words to him:

VOICE: As to the old way of life, Bailey old man, what will you do with it?

BAILEY: I'm glad you asked me that. What I plan to do is shred it, stomp it, beat it, cheat it, disembowel it, screw it to the wall and murder it at least once. Also I'll probably flay it, feed its drying pus lumps to the snakes, cremate it, bury it, canonize it, apotheosize it, blaspheme and deny it, unearth it and violate its remains. Then I'll prescribe its bones and dust for use as wolf bane, shoe polish, fertility reducer and suggest it to friends for combating toothache, menstrual pain, diaper rash, epilepsy, narcolepsy, psoriasis, satyriasis, impotence, acne and hot nuts. As an optional use, any sinews should make swell dental floss. When springtime comes I plan to grow it in a flowerpot, smoke its leaves, sniff its stalk, chew its roots and inject the leftover juice into my armpits as a permanent deodorant. I also have high hopes for it as a dandruff renewer.

VOICE: I suppose all this will help you discover something.

BAILEY: You bet. All secrets of the hidden past. The history of lost Guildsmen. The precise location of the golden seeds. How navels are formed. The purpose of the appendix and the mosquito. Plus certain truths about political, religious, artistic and racial causes. Nietzsche generalized that all good things approach their goals crookedly, and so for very crooked reasons I'll put his idea to the test.

VOICE: How do you think people will react when they see that you've discarded the old way?

BAILEY: They're sure to find it wonderful, sad, fitting, terrible, stupid, grotesque, absurd, egocentric, hilarious and meaningless. They'll pass the funeral home and shrug. They'll buy new iceboxes and toilet seats, new spectacles and trusses, new corsets and jocks, new toupees and contact lenses. The old way will lie in state, in repose, corrupting quietly as they pass. They won't cry.

VOICE: And while you're waiting for all this to happen?

BAILEY: I'm glad you asked me that. I plan to write a series of apparently incomprehensible columns to illustrate my apparently incomprehensible thought. You're welcome to read my first one if you like. I call it:

HEED GOKKI

Our men derived inadequate dignity and a coarsened suavity when their adversaries expected them to be equanimous to an inferior horse. The method, like that of the dead-fish fashion, turned increasingly to a pollution of the lakes. Swimmers objected from several of the wagons. Fishermen coiled their crystal sifters, excited beyond fear of Gokki, the great unknowable. Many of them refused to leave the bedrolls. But by nightfall the men had infiltrated into the area with consummate arrogance, encouraging the weary and the filthy to contain their hunger. No one wanted to be forced to eat the uneven ground. The great hordes moved their wheels to disengage. But be it rough hump or furrowing the bay leaves, whatever it would be—

the wagon tools and frying pans clanked throughout the night. Instincts slid from side to side among the group's elders, regardless of their allegiance.

Nevertheless, some hostile adolescents, as the mood continued around our fire, kept their places. Disorder prevailed, in and out of minds. The night chattering of the birds was followed by the silence of the young selves, drinking wildly, excitedly, soundlessly. One of the boys invited the fishermen to share.

No one expected Zorquila to do what he did. And when Magor leaped away from the fire as in the old days, emulating Gokki and thus in pursuit of lovely self, the youths touched each other—cautiously alert, spreading out, crying, loving it all because snapside around them was alive. Zorquila, squatting, grew angrier. I had seen him angry before, cooking barn swallows with his Lumbena pride in being young and new. The horses were impassive, like several dog faces. There was a constant threat of action. Magor's face whitened with tense dust at the newness while his whipsnaps and his pockmarks called endless attention to his ostentatious sucking of Gokki's peculiar (but inimitable) stoicism. He swaggered with several drops of gray liquid. Old. The same. Superiority bulged in his trouser pockets. It smelled of Gokki's whipping (that ritual) and it turned our stomachs. His smirk broadened, habit from jail, throwing a challenge to Zorquila and the others. Zorquila stood and drew his kespar. Then began the bundle wheeling and the shimbo throwing, the wrestling and the stomping. Contests were drawn up, over, between and across his gaping mouth. Children and young girls stared

from the wagon slits. All shifting pursuits waned
as the sun began to rise. The shimbos were pulled
out. Zorquila retrieved his kespar. Magor's blood
was gone. Gokki the unknowable had made his
message plain: Remain unchanged, perish.

VOICE: It's a problem.
BAILEY: We're all victims of our own matrix, that's the
problem; and it could be solved if there were
only a matrix mart. But since there isn't, certain
radical measures are called for. I've concluded
that the only way out is not only freedom from
history, but from future glory lusting as well.
Other men have rid themselves of the worst of
vices. They've plucked out their own eyes, cut
off their own hands, even become autocastrates
and submissive lobotomites to get beyond desire.
The Guild, after all, *is* eradicable. It's only an idea,
the climax of a particular, historical kind of behavior. One chooses to work as a Guildsman as one
chose knighthood or asceticism in the Middle Ages.
The quality of the man, of course, dictates the
achievement. Pigs don't have wings. Eagles don't
snuffle in garbage. And I do wonder about my
own niche, but without conclusion. All I can say
is that my steadfast illusions in this time have become far more compelling than most of my shifting
realities, and I'd like to take this opportunity to
curse all those who have helped me reach this in-
verted pinnacle.
VOICE: Beyond this cursing of your influences, how do
you plan to get rid of the future?
BAILEY: First I plan to move steadily forward into the
blackness, where I know I'm quite certain to perish.

But even as that final moment nears, I nevertheless feel pressed upon to pursue the light, follow the dream, chase the will-o'-the-wisp, trap the unicorn, capture the golden fleece, clutch the grail and in all ways solve the riddle of What, How and Why, which does not speak very well for my ability to wreak substantial change upon myself. Yet there I will be, perversely united at last with the filthy dogmatists who tell us all to visit Paris and find out for ourselves that there is no Eiffel Tower. And as I grow faint, as I curse my desiccating blood, my shriveling flesh and diminishing consciousness, I will see ahead at the center of the darkness the slavering jaws of the Monster of Infinite Eyes, and I will know my fate. But once inside the monster's maw, I plan to toss my last grenade into the depths of its large intestine, and when the blast sounds and the black blood flows out through the cavernous wound, I'll start to slide on that flowing river of life-giving grease, out past the scabless gap. And then I'll stand, bloodied up from tooth holes and digestive acids, I suppose; but if the plan works, bloody well cleansed as well. I'll stand, then, into one of those ruby days; one of those new and brilliantly ruby days; one of those arrival days. At least that's the plan.

"An incident of the cholera occurred in this city a few days since," Bailey read, "which for several reasons we think worth recording. Among the households which have been entered and stricken by the fatal disease was that of Mr. Peter Hangley, a worthy Irishman, who has long been employed by the commissioner of streets. His wife, a warm-hearted, motherly woman, was taken with the cholera and died and was buried Thursday last. Next, a lovely little daughter, seven years of age, was taken sick, and she too died. The father applied to Alderman Wingate for a coffin but for some cause its delivery was postponed for an hour or two. During this time Mr. Hangley returned home, and the supposed dead child stretched forth her arms with the exclamation, 'Oh, Father! I have been to Heaven, and it is a beautiful place!' After the surprise and the excitement, she gave a relation of what she had seen, as she expressed it, 'in Heaven.' She saw her mother taking care of little children, many of whom the mother called by name, and among them were the four children of Uncle Martin Hangley and three children of Uncle Chauncey Casey. 'Aunt Maymie is not there now,' said the child, 'but she will be tomorrow.'

" 'But,' said an older sister, 'it cannot be so, dearest, for there are but two of Uncle Chauncey's children dead.'

" 'Yes, I saw three of them in Heaven,' said the child, 'and dear Mother was taking care of them. All were dressed in white, all were very happy and playing. Oh, it was beautiful there. I shall go again Sunday next at four o'clock!'

"Mr. Peter Hangley informed Alderman Wingate that the child was not dead, and when the alderman, in company with Dr. Morrison, visited the house, the little girl told them the same story. And while they were present a message came from Uncle Chauncey giving information of the death of another Casey child and inviting the Hangleys to attend the funeral. . . ."

Bailey peered up from the 1832 newspaper, his eyes watering from the strain of reading the small and faded print. Pigs were coming slowly through the aisle toward him, snuffing the dry air of the stacks. Oink. One of them snuffed at his trouser leg. Oink, oinggg. The sound seemed a signal. Other pigs came into the aisle, two, four, eight. He climbed to the second shelf, above the level of their backs. More came, crowding in until the aisle was full. He could not step down now without stepping on slimy pig backs. He edged along the shelves, pushing the bound volumes gently to gain a foothold, holding the edge of a high, dusty shelf with his hands, straddling the pigs. At the end of the aisle when straddling was no longer possible, when jumping down was still impossible because the pigs had clogged the main aisle also, he went hand over hand along the end of the shelf to the next aisle, feet dangling. He found the next aisle full. Also the next. Oink. He moved to an aisle where only two pigs wandered and he leaped down and sprinted toward the darkened rear of the stacks, where he had heard the birdlike voice. Behind him he heard: Oinggg. He turned the corner away from pig voices, heard pig steps coming toward him. He ran into the total darkness of the stacks, beyond where he had ever gone. He felt for a switch but found none. He climbed the shelves to touch the bulb but found none. He moved into ever deeper darkness, imagining irrationally that he would soon be in a corner where exit would not be possible. Behind him, some distance now, he heard: Oingg. He was outdistancing them. They would not chase him into the darkness. But though they came no closer (he estimated there were hundreds), they did not leave. They stayed in the area of light. He, in darkness, was only vaguely certain of the way he had come. He had made so many turns that he could not say now where the elevators were. Surely he could not reach them without confronting the pigs, and this he had no urge to do. The pigs had run down cats and dogs in the street, trampled them, eaten them. Four thousand were loose in the city streets, increasing by a thousand a year. He knew this from the old newspaper accounts. It had been a Dutch privilege to let the hogs run, and the city council was careful how it impinged on such tradition. Debate continued in the council: Should the pigs roam and be allowed to eat the garbage in the street, or should they be penned? Pork fattened on street garbage was not good food, one councilman insisted. But doctors reported that hogs are the best scavengers, and their running loose is beneficial to the city. The hogs would shrivel if penned, and the swine were the food of the poor. Penning them would also inflict disease on the owners. No. Let's collect our garbage with men, not pigs, said one councilman. But the council defeated the confining motion 188 to eight. And so the pigs ran loose.

One slip, Bailey knew, a fall into the midst, and they would do the same to him as they did to the street garbage, to the dogs and the cats: trample him, devour his face. Blood would whet their fevers, and they would rip him out of his clothing, gnaw away his flesh, crack his bones with their teeth, lick up his blood.

He receded into a new corner and saw along the wall a line of light. He moved toward it, touched the wall, then a door, pushed it and stepped into what he took, because of the overcast, to be the waning light of the day. But he had lost track of time and could not be sure. The overcast was almost a fog, and the air had an acrid smell when he swallowed it. He had left his coat in the library, but he did not need it. The day was unseasonably warm, in the nineties, he guessed. Yet he could see no sun. He walked down a slight hill, and when he looked back he could no longer see the library, so shrouded in the pall of fog was the hill. He walked on a planked sidewalk and was swept backward by a stream of people coming at him from the city gate. He sidestepped and let them pass, counting about forty, all of them in a great hurry, none of them giving him more than a glance, all of them drifting away from one another as they moved farther from the gate. Their clothing was different from his own; the streets were dirt paths. When he saw a horse and rider coming toward him, rider with a white mask covering all of his face but eyes and forehead, he knew something had changed in his perception of events, that he was in a primitive stage of life. The faces of the people who had almost run him down with their haste were familiar to him, but he placed none of them. It seems, he thought, that I have done a clever thing in reaching this place.

"To where be you bound?" the masked horseman asked, coming close with muffled hoofbeats and reining his horse in front of Bailey.

"Why should I answer a man with a mask?"

"You do be answering, or go back from whence you came. And from where do you be coming?"

"From the library."

"An arrogant liar. Where did you get that uniform? To which army do you belong?"

"To none. I'm a civilian, going to the city."

"On what business?"

"None in particular. I'm a sightseer, I suppose."

"Twice a liar. The people are leaving the city in great numbers, and you come to see the sights? You will be watched. Take note of that."

As with the passing stream of faces, Bailey recognized something in the rider: voice, perhaps, or manner, or possibly the eyes. But he could connect the familiarity with no name.

"Get to the quarantine shelter," the rider told him. "The doctor will say whether you'll enter the city or not." The rider indicated a slanted-roof building ringed by a post-and-rail fence; then he turned his horse and rode back where he came. Bailey headed for the quarantine shelter, where a woman and a boy together, and one man alone, sat on wooden benches along the wall of an almost empty room. Bailey stood watching. A man wearing a mask like the rider raised his head above a wooden partition and told Bailey to sit down, then ducked back behind the partition. The woman and the boy looked at Bailey. The man alone kept his eyes on the ground.

"How long have you been here?" Bailey asked the woman.

"Three days."

"When will you leave?"

"When they let me. Some stay as much as a week. But they feed you all right, which is more'n you might get in the city, prices bein' what they are and the farmers scared to come in t' sell anything. Potatoes a dollar a bushel. Mind that, would you, when they used to sell for twenty-five cents."

"Why do they keep you here?"

"They want to see if you're sick with the cholera. They can usually tell in a few days."

"If you haven't got it, you'll surely get it here."

"You'll get it sure anywhere, is how I look at it," the woman said. "One of three that gets it dies. Sometimes more."

A man in a red hood and wearing gloves, boots and sweat-stained shirt and trousers approached Bailey and studied his eyes. He took off a glove and felt Bailey's forehead and wrists. He gave Bailey a drink of water and ordered him to drink it all, then sat and waited for Bailey to vomit. When Bailey did not, when he also replied negatively to inquiries about diarrhea and collapse and dryness of his body, the hooded man went once more behind the partition.

"All of us gets that," the woman said. "And some says he's not very particular where he checks the ladies for fever, though he was a gentleman with me."

The man alone stood and screamed: "I *must* get to the city!" He pounded the partition. "I *must* get to my family." He got no response.

"Poor man," the woman whispered to Bailey. "He doesn't know his family's dead. The ones here think he's coming down with it too. It's his second day here."

"Then why do they leave him with other people? Why not

put him with the ones who have it, instead of letting him contaminate others?"

"I do believe they have," the woman said.

Bailey stared at her. "You have it?"

"I do believe," she said.

"And the boy?"

"I do believe."

"Why didn't you go someplace else? Anyplace else?"

"I have no place to go. We left the city to go to my sister's funeral. I only live a little ways inside the gate, just me and the boy. But now I don't know as we'll get there."

She nodded her head, satisfied with having stated her condition. Bailey backed away, staring at her with fear rising in him. A white-masked guard on the tower above the gate hoisted his rifle to the ready position as Bailey moved out of the building and toward the gate. Bailey backtracked and waited beside the building until the guard looked away. Then he ran along the city wall until he found a place to climb it, well out of the guard's vision. On the road, running, he looked back to see the pall enshroud the guard's tower, the gate, the quarantine shelter, just as it had enveloped the library.

He heard hoofbeats behind him then and anticipated chase, the masked horseman; but a team of horses rose out of the mist, pulling a stagecoach. A lone driver, wearing a handkerchief around his mouth and nose, snapped his whip over the backs of the horses. The stage was empty as it rumbled toward the city.

Bailey reached the edge of the city at what seemed like an hour or two after daybreak. He walked past padlocked stores and shuttered houses, a jail with its door open, a blacksmith's, closed, an empty barber shop and a food market with the sign "No Food Today" in the window. On a pole he saw a handbill urging all citizens to be about at nine o'clock in the morning to burn tar in hopes of abating the cholera, which, said the notice, succumbed to heat and smoke. As Bailey neared the center of the city the pall thickened. He passed barrels of burning tar, smoke and fumes rising, but still he saw no people.

"Hello, come in," he heard, and turning saw a portly man with a droopy moustache and eyeglasses deep in the interior of a large general-merchandise store beckoning to him. Bailey entered but kept his distance from the man, who also kept his distance from Bailey, the lone customer. Testing him, Bailey moved forward past shelves of harness and candles, knives and bolts of cloth. The man backed up, talking as he moved.

"Welcome. We're open for business here, as you can see, one of the few stores in town with any gumption in days like these. You'll notice, I'm sure, that things are improving. Just yesterday we in the Merchants' Association drew up a manifesto stating our position and giving the latest conditions in the city, and as the president of the association I welcome you to our store. Please take a good look at our merchandise. Quality all. Other stores will be opening up later in the morning once the tar has been burned, but as you may have gathered, the tar burning is just a formality now. There is no more cholera in the city. We have it on good authority from several medical men that the plague is over. And so, good sir, it is time for the people to return to normal habits. We have confidence in the future of this city. Just last year a new spike factory established here. We've got a town on the move, I'll say, and we merchants have full confidence in the public. We have confidence in our medical men too. And our mayor. And our militia. Just because there are some people who still fear the plague is no reason for us to go out of business."

A pig brushed past Bailey's leg and wandered into the store. The store owner took a yardstick from a counter and chased it. He caught up with it near the door and struck it on the back several times. The pig ran squealing into the street.

"A nuisance, these pigs," the merchant said. "But as long as they're well ringed, it's easy enough to control them."

"You have no customers at all?"

"The frightened ones have left the city and the rest stay home. But they'll be back. The cholera is over. We have a manifesto."

The merchant grabbed his stomach and suddenly vomited. He stared with whitened face at Bailey, who backed out of the store and ran down the street, stopping short at the sight of a crowd of masked men destroying a building. Some were breaking windows with clubs, another was chopping off the door, another hurling lamps, books, chairs, dishes, clothing out of a third-story window. Down the stoop ran a Negro, and the masked men clubbed him as he ran their gauntlet; but he did not fall, and when he hit the street he ran swiftly into an alley, where no one chased him. A young white woman followed him through the gauntlet and took an equivalent clubbing, then ran toward Bailey. The masked men hurled stones at her, and one knocked her down. Bailey raised her up and helped her limp around a corner into the Black Bear Hotel. The desk was empty, the lobby empty. Bailey, seeking a place to hide, swept the woman into his cradling arms and ran up the stairs with her. He placed her on a bed in an empty room that looked down onto the street. He could see no one through the window, hear no movement in the building. He reconnoitered in the hallway and found a window near the back stairway that looked out to where the men were attacking the solitary house. One man ignited a torch from a barrel of burning tar and threw it into the hallway. Another tossed a torch through a window. Bailey went back to the room to find the girl unmoved, her lip bleeding slightly, her eyes following him.

"I think you're safe," Bailey said. "They're burning down the house."

"Everything I own."

"You're lucky you got out alive, from what I saw. Why did they stone you?"

"They said we were a nuisance."

"Who was a nuisance?"

"The ones who lived in the house. They said we were harlots."

"And the Negro?"

"A eunuch, an ex-slave. He gave sweet baths to people."

"Are you a harlot?"

"Women are harlots sometimes."

"Do men pay you?"

"I never took a penny."

"I don't understand why they stoned you."

"I gave them my hymen. They all saw my innocence trickle down my leg and stain the bed. They can't forgive me for that."

"I don't understand why they stoned you."

"They kissed me and touched me secretly and then went away."

"All of them?"

"They smelled the death of first love. Sweet love. And it was their fault. All I wanted was to be loved."

"I don't understand why they stoned you."

"They found my madness. One after the other of their organisms touched the center of my moon. But they only made a hollow noise, and then they hunted around with torture. Scales of light among the dripping lies. Broken flakes of flowers. It was marvelous sometimes, though."

"I don't understand why they stoned you."

"I distorted them. Their stars died out in my orchard. Then they had to comb the berries and eat the weeds. I was always their victim, lovely me."

"I don't understand anything you say."

"I am not sick, if that's what you think."

Bells clanged in the street, and a horse-drawn fire wagon raced by with buckets rattling. A second wagon carrying a treadle pump pulled up behind the first, its bell clanging at a different pitch. Bailey watched as the firemen rushed one another. He ran to the hallway window and saw the nuisance building in flames, the crowd of destroyers gone.

Back in the room the young woman had not moved, but she had licked the blood off her lip. Lying quietly with her long black skirt covering her ankles, her soiled white blouse buttoned at the neck and her arms crossed on her chest beneath a pink lace shawl, she presented no picture of harlotry to Bailey. He looked away from her, watched the two dozen firemen fight one another. Several were unconscious already.

"The firemen are fighting while the building burns," he said.

"They're rival companies," she said. "Forget them. Please don't treat me like a lady, now or ever. I don't deserve it. I don't like it."

"You really puzzle me," Bailey said.

"I'm glad they stoned me. I deserve whatever I get. And God, do I love it. I just love to be ravaged. They're overhauling the canal boats. They're cleaning them to get rid of the plague the way they cleaned up the open sewers and cleaned out the lake where we get our water. But they can't overhaul me. I'll always be this way. Even where you're going you can't help me."

"Where am I going?"

"To a place where you can't help me, or anybody but you."

"You don't know where I'm going. I don't even know myself."

"Why else did you pick me up in the street? Why else did you bring me here? Why else would you be dressed so funny? Why else would you be out without a mask? I know where you're going. Anybody could know, just looking at you."

"I don't understand anything you say."

"That doesn't matter. You once did, I'll bet. The main thing is to like me. Remember me fondly. Will you promise to do that?"

She sat up and extended her arms to Bailey. He could not

help but embrace such a plea, but he did not kiss her. He wanted no plague, no disease of the harlot. He patted her between the shoulderblades, comfortingly, and for the first time she smiled. He was tempted then to kiss her. He truly liked her. He would not have to pretend. She was quite beautiful, though there was in her eyes an age beyond the youth of her skin, and in her mouth a sensuality that had to have been born in her. But she had no harlot's sneer, no smile of fleshly wisdom. Her experience had not reached her face. Bailey kissed her cheek. He could not yield to her mouth.

While he held her he heard noises downstairs in the hotel. In the hallway he peered through the spindles of the hall banister and saw three men, one with a rifle and two with clubs, searching behind the desk and in sitting rooms and small alcoves off the main lobby. Bailey went for the girl, and holding her hand, led her down the back stairway. Together they rushed along the planks of the deserted sidewalk. The planks ended and slate sidewalks began as they entered the business district. Signs were larger, fancier.

"We'll be safe in church," the girl said. "Everybody will be there today. It's the penitential day."

She led him to a small, white-steepled church with a large, well-kept front lawn. A sign nailed to the church door advised that there would be no evening services during the remainder of the plague, that the City Council had canceled all evening meetings on grounds that the cholera did its worst work in the hours of darkness. Inside the church, as neat in its architecture and upkeep as was its exterior, hundreds of people were crowded into pews, listening to the tall young minister who stood on the dais with Bible open. Bailey ignored him at first but then a mention of the Book of Lamentations caught his attention with its relevance.

"Jerusalem hath grievously sinned," the minister read; "therefore is she become unstable. . . . Her filthiness is on her feet and she hath not remembered her end; she is wonderfully cast down, not having a comforter. The Lord is my portion, said my soul: therefore will I wait for him. The Lord is good to them that hope in him, to the soul that seeketh him. He shall put his mouth in the dust, if so be there may be hope. For the Lord will not cast off forever."

Bailey watched the people nod their heads in agreement. He gripped the hand of the strange girl he had protected, squeezed it in anger.

"We have seen the death wagons go by too often," said the young preacher. "We have seen mothers, wives and children die terribly. We have seen fathers and husbands ripped from their families. We do not know the cause. Some say it is intemperate habits, but we know that the temperate and the intemperate have died together. Some say it is from the indiscreet eating of unripe fruits, and this is the most logical of all, though some have died who were known to have eaten the fruits discreetly. Some say it is the immigrants belched up from the foul sewers of Europe who have brought us this scourge, and that may be true. Our people have stoned the canal boats to keep the immigrants away from our city. We wish the immigrants no evil. We just do not want the trouble they bring us. Our hospitals are full. Our schools and our arsenals have become sick bays, overflowing with the afflicted and the dying. The poorhouse can handle no more cases. The undertakers cannot properly bury all of our dead."

"Scourge me if you will," Bailey heard the girl say.

"Our sin is unknown to us," said the preacher, "but we know we have sinned."

"Stone me if you will," whispered the girl.

"Shut up," Bailey told her with a snarl. "Don't be stupid."

"But we have had two omens," said the preacher. "There was a halo around the sun this morning. And after yesterday's heavy rain a fisherman caught seven thousand suckers above the dam, enough for all of us in this time of scarcity. The scows towed in the fish this morning. God giveth and God taketh away."

"Your god is a bloody fiend," Bailey yelled to the preacher. But no one seemed to notice that Bailey had spoken. He wondered if he was invisible, now wondered about the reality of this moment. Was his fantasy wild again? He squeezed the girl's hand, felt the flesh and the bones within. He touched a man standing in front of him, and the man turned and looked at Bailey.

"You're all being cheated," Bailey yelled, but again no one seemed to hear.

"Draw my blood again if you will," the girl whispered.

"You're all insane," Bailey screamed. "Don't you know what the cholera is? Pen the pigs. Clean up your garbage. Your tar is polluting the sky."

"We must stop sinning," chanted the preacher. "We must stop, even though we know not what our sin is."

"You didn't sin," Bailey yelled. "You're just ignorant." He let go of the girl's hand and stepped into the center aisle. He walked forward and shook his fist at the preacher. "You're a madman, telling these people filthy lies. You know it's not their fault. Why don't you preach about ignorance?"

A vestryman came from a side aisle and struck Bailey on the head with a short, narrow plank. Bailey fell in the aisle, bleeding. The young woman came to his side, blotted his blood with her lacy shawl, and when he came to consciousness, she helped him out of the church.

"Thou hast covered in thy wrath," the preacher was saying, "and hast struck us: Thou hast killed and hast not spared. Thou hast set a cloud before thee, that our prayer may not pass through . . ."

"Liar," mumbled Bailey. "Filthy pig liar."

"Shhhh," said the girl. "Shhhh."

They walked toward the city's edge. He yielded to the pull of the girl's hand, holding her shawl to his head with his free hand to stop the bleeding. He heard, before he saw the source of it, a voice that belonged to the alderman. A voice with a wheeze and a wheedle. The girl led him to a clearing where he stood by a small coffin adorned with yellow and white wildflowers. The family, a father and two grown daughters, looked at the coffin with tearless eyes while the alderman spoke with head bowed. The father was smiling. Bailey did not know where he was, but the woman reassured him he was still in the city, in a meadow where the dead without status were being buried; for the cemetery was full. Over the hill, she said, the immigrants were camped: those who had come on canal boats and had nowhere else to go. The canal had its terminus in the city, so the immigrants could go no farther. The plague had closed off the river to steamboat traffic, and the stagecoaches would not carry such rabble. Their improvised shanty town was a last-resort move by the city fathers.

"I'm no immigrant," Bailey said. "I was born here." But even as he said it he felt its irrelevance echoing. And even if he had been born in this city, he knew nothing of it in this condition.

"This beautiful child," said the alderman, "had no will to live, but preferred to return to her mother. She was bright, like her father, and beautiful, like her mother. She learned her faith well and understood Heaven is a far better place."

"This is a silly man," Bailey told the girl. "A politician who talks like the preacher."

"Her story of seeing her mother in Heaven," said the alderman, "draws largely upon believing capacity. But he would be a bold man who should say dogmatically that it is not true. There are many things which cannot be explained but much that is not easy to deny. On the other hand, we must confess that her story was never properly authenticated. So there you are."

The smiling man spoke up: "I was sorry when my good wife died. I was sorry when my first child died en route over the sea from Ireland. I was sorry when my second child died of the cholera and I was sorry today when this beautiful child died of it too. But I am sorry no longer. Though I still have two children, I know they are happy in this world, and I am not. I long only to be with my good wife and my beautiful children. I ask the good God to take me to Heaven with my family." He smiled brightly.

"He's a cheap quitter," Bailey said. "His kids are better off without him, a punk like that."

Bailey felt nauseous. He wondered if it was from the blow on the head, or from what he was seeing. Or was it the plague?

"We almost had no coffin for this dear child," the alderman said. "Coffins are at a premium, as I'm sure none of us has to be told. But I saw to it that the City Council had one made especially for this rare little creature. I could not bear the idea of her lying in a common grave with no protection from the earth. Just the thought of worms crawling in and out of her eye sockets disturbed me greatly."

"He's mad," Bailey said. "You don't say that sort of thing at a child's funeral. Is there anybody who isn't mad?"

"We found the wood down behind the wheel works," the alderman continued. "You may note that it is not a conventional coffin that the child lies in. It has no sharp edges. We used curved wood. It is the only oval coffin I've ever seen. A fitting thing for a unique, well-rounded child."

"I'm quite sick," Bailey told the girl. "I must lie down someplace."

"You have the look about you," she said. "I've seen it often. It's a devilish pallor. Your blood is drying out."

Bailey looked toward the cemetery. A great oak tree shaded where he stood. Sunlight, the first he'd noticed, came through its leaves and dappled the child's coffin and his own feet. The girl pointed up the bright, green hill toward where the tombstones formed a jagged ridge.

"The immigrant camps are beyond that hill," she said. "They'd take you in there. They have nothing to fear. They'll either die or they won't, but they have no escape."

"You've never gotten it," Bailey said.

"No, I guess I have very wet blood."

"Go with me."

"No, I couldn't go in there. There's things even I can't do. I'd take you home with me, but I have no home anymore. You must lie down and get fresh, ripe fruit. Don't wash. Husband your strength."

"You may notice," said the alderman, "that there are real, square-headed nails in this coffin, and not the improvised wooden pegs that have been used lately. The lid is secure, you can all be sure of that. Your City Council, under my prompting, appropriated funds to send to the wire and nail works beyond the town limits for a special-priority order. No snakes, no rabbits, no rats, no gophers will eat holes in this child's pink and lovely flesh."

Bailey looked at the young woman beside him and felt a profound sadness. He handed her back her blood-covered shawl and she threw it around her shoulders as if it were not soiled. He touched her lips with his hands, touched her soft black hair, ran his hand over her neck and shoulders and drew her close. He kissed her lips this time, unafraid, for she could contaminate no one. She was the beautiful, innocent harlot of his dreams: tough, selfless, accepting: O Lord, I am not worthy. Ah, but she was worthy. And even as she kissed him, even as she prepared to leave him, even when she was gone, she would be with him. The lovely purity of the ravaged virgin, the bleeding hymen, the unconquerable face. She would be his bride.

He walked away from her, up the hill toward the ridge, his nausea growing. Hundreds of huts of rough lumber and logs had been thrown up at irregular angles along the slope and laid across with wood scraps, pieces of tin and tree bark. Some were only lean-tos. And a few people were lying under trees or in the shade of large bushes with no overhead protection at all. As he passed them, Bailey saw that a few had their mouths permanently gapped, their fingers permanently clawed, their pockets slit open.

All eyes watched him walk through the tombstones and into the shanty village. Black flags were posted in front of some shanties. Since no one he had ever known would voluntarily admit they were sick to the death, Bailey assumed that even at this level a kind of order prevailed, a majority rule that segregated the quick from the walking dead. It seemed certain that this was a wistful segregation. The future of this impromptu village was total doom.

Bailey saw a drunken man in rags, bottle in hand, sitting with his back against a tree. He smiled at Bailey and waved the bottle. Bailey approached, only to see the man looking beyond him to another man in rags, equally drunk and also with a bottle in his fist. The drunks converged and offered Bailey a drink. He refused, emulating nausea, which the men took to be a spasm, and sadness came over their eyes. But Bailey smiled, and they tipped up their bottles and grinned at him.

"What do you do here?" he asked them.

"We get the cholera," said one.

"Where do you get the whiskey?"

"Some makes it, some buys it, some steals it, some gets it as work rations. And all as can drinks it."

"Do you live under the tree?"

"Except when it rains. Then we go in with the dyin' bastards."

"How long have you been here?"

"Months, I guess it is. I lost the track of how many they be."

"Neither of you has the cholera. Does whiskey keep it off?"

"Whiskey keeps everything off," one answered, and the other agreed.

"Do people ever leave here?"

"Leave?" One man laughed. "There's no boats."

"Who brought you here?" the other man asked Bailey.

"I came on my own," he said, and the two drunks looked in wonderment at each other.

"Hey all," one of them called out in a loud voice, "here's one come without a shove."

Heads peered out of huts, and sick men under the lean-tos sat up to gawk at Bailey, who stood in bewilderment, looking from face to face. Women gathered around, holding children. People walked up and touched him. Men made a circle, and all stared silently at the wonder of Bailey. In the profound silence Bailey understood their awe. It would be momentary. In the moment beyond, they would resent him, not as an enemy but as some odd statuary to be befouled at will. Then, too, there would be a few who would clean off the statue, keep it shined for future awe-seekers.

"Why did you come here?" a woman asked him.

"I have a need to open my pores," he said.

"Three cheers for open pores," a drunk called out.

The crowd cheered, and a man thrust a bottle into Bailey's hand. He drank. When he tipped the bottle down, the crowd was dispersing. He was alone again.

"I need a place to sleep," he called out to no one in particular.

The man who gave him the bottle turned and pointed toward a ramshackle shelter of red tin and charred boards at the end of a path. Bailey nodded his thanks at the man and headed for the shelter. Once inside on the soft earth, he finished the whiskey. It seared his throat and set him coughing. But his nausea waned as he fell on his back, and with his head throbbing from the blow at church, he fell into a profound sleep in which no dreams were possible.

Bailey sensed that he had been awake for a long period of time without realizing it. He made a cursory inspection of his body, found that his shoes were off and that his toenails had grown to extraordinary lengths. His hair had grown over his ears. He had a small beard. His fingernails were as long as his toenails, and had curved. His big toenail had grown long and curved at its sides. His fingernails had curved not at their sides, but under his fingers like claws, like the nails of a dog who walks only on carpet. He attempted to draw conclusions from the difference between the manner in which his big toenail had grown and the manner in which his middle fingernail had grown. He assumed that the claw theory was relevant for the hands of man, but not for his feet: that prehensility was a forgotten trait in the lower extremities, but not in the upper. After reaching this conclusion, he felt at ease and did not think of anything for some time.

At length he felt his hair, long over his ears, and he spent an uncertain period calculating its growth rate between haircuts, and how long it had been since the last haircut. But since he could not calculate how long he had been in the city (it seemed only a day, but he sensed it was longer), there was no meaningful way of estimating time previous. All periods he could recall seemed imprecise, as if one measured time in abstractions such as: some, too much, excruciatingly long, just enough, inadequate and a bit more, please. He concentrated on the age of his clothing, but all he could say was that it was not new, not terribly old. He thought of looking outside the place where he was, but he had not yet looked around inside, and so he did look and saw walls, and the absence of sunlight and sky. He conceived then of turning around, and when he did he saw a doorway with light shining through its cracks. He tried to determine whether the light was straight or slanted or curving and judged it to be straight and felt that at last he had reached a conclusion, but one of dubious value. He looked away from the light to see whether anything else might yield a conclusion, and he found his shoes. He studied them for an indefinite period of time before deciding that they belonged on his feet. He felt greatly satisfied with this conclusion, for one could think about it, whereas the straightness of light did not lead to any new avenues of perception. He saw that his toenails had grown straight out like points. Surely they would not have grown so pointy inside the shoes. They might not have grown at all without the sunlight. And he concluded: Perhaps sunlight nourishes growth. He wondered whether he should go where there was more sunlight.

More sunlight. He considered that notion.

Yes, there were places with more sunlight: yet another conclusion. He felt very pleased. It was indeed a certainty that there were such places.

He turned around and pushed at the door. It did not readily open, and so he gave it a violent kick. Dried flakes of time fluttered out of his hands onto the ground.

EXTRA!

FAMINE CAN BE FUN BOARDWALKER TELLS FRIENDS

AND NECESSITY TURNS OUT TO BE A MOTHER

Now all the truth is out,
Be secret and take defeat
From any brazen throat,
For how can you compete,
Being honour bred, with one
Who, were it proved he lies,
Were neither shamed in his own
Nor in his neighbour's eyes?
Bred to a harder thing
Than Triumph, turn away
And like a laughing string
Whereupon mad fingers play
Amid a place of stone,
Be secret and exult,
Because of all things known
That is most difficult.

—WILLIAM BUTLER YEATS
"To a Friend Whose Work Has Come to Nothing"

"**B**ailey."

When he looked up from the small fragments of the old newspaper that had fallen to the floor he saw Irma at the edge of the aisle. He smiled warmly, stared dumbly.

"I'm here," she said.

"There you are," he said. He did not move.

"Well, come and sit."

He responded to that by pushing the bound volume back into its niche on the shelf and walking with Irma to the table near the elevator.

"I don't like it here," she said. "Every word you say goes right up the elevator shaft."

"Okay," Bailey said, but he didn't move.

Irma grabbed his hand and pulled him back toward the large work table at the rear of the stacks. It was covered with dusty cartons of records, indexed and covered with newspaper to keep the dust off. But there is nothing to keep the dust off the newspaper, Bailey thought, looking at the cartons. The dust falls like the dew.

"My undertaker friend," Irma said, hanging up her coat and sitting down in a chair beside one of the book carts, "is spreading the word that I'm the Guild's concubine."

Bailey looked at Irma, thinking: Love is Irma's vocation. He felt the need to respond to her remarks, though he preferred to look at her as a specimen of value.

"Why would he say that?"

"He knew about you coming home with me."

I. Going home with Irma.

"I'm not the whole Guild."

"Francie must have given him some hot ideas about me."

Hot Irma. True or false?

"True or false?"

"I'm no little Miss Muffet, you know. I never was. I didn't sit on *my* tuffet all my life."

Irma's hot career.

"You never did tell me all your secrets."

"You never asked. You always behave as if you met me the day before yesterday."

Sweet hot Irma. Bailey smiled in his daze, enjoying. He was not dead. He was not going to die. He felt like a discoverer knowing this. Who would care? Of course you're not going to die, they'd say. Ah. He listened to Irma, hearing her recounting her old trouble. It reached him as if through brilliant sunlight. The sounds of Irma were too bright. They hurt his eyes. She was recounting a tissue of crazy events. Irma the lovely victim: married young, divorced, fell in love and got pregnant, aborted that to spite her lover, who wanted to be sure he left a child somewhere in the world, then cheated on Irma and so she dumped his dream. Then she had a son, a love child, out of guilt, who was born and swiftly died. Irma went back with her husband; then again to her cheating lover. Then Bailey came along, and when that broke off she dallied with assorted Guildsmen to pass the hours; then the love child's father again; then the undertaker, then back to Bailey. She nodded glumly at her chronology.

"Sometimes," she said, "I think I'm just a nostalgic screw unit."

Bailey was smiling when he realized that the brilliance was becoming comfortable. He was acclimatizing. Not dead, Bailey. You won't die of sunlight either. He could look forever at Irma. Though she was thirty-four, people would take her for twenty-seven. Sweetface. Twenty-seven unless they took note of the telltale furrows above her nose, which bespoke not only age but an anxious soliloquy, years long. But not dead, Irma. Not dead of your trouble. Bailey could listen to it and not be saddened, for the victimization of Irma was the strengthening of Irma. Toughness in trouble. If he were to paint Irma, Bailey would make her a naked love goddess, wearing only butterfly wings and brass knuckles.

"Francie walked out," she said. "This morning. She said she didn't want people getting the idea she was everybody's too. What a sister."

Sister, trouble, undertaker, trouble.

"Some fiancé you had, too."

"I was pretty dumb to take up with a dud like that guy, wasn't I?"

"Something you needed, I suppose."

"Damn, Bailey. Damn, damn, damn, damn, damn."

Her voice went up on the last syllable. Then she stood and paced by the table. Making policy decisions, Bailey thought. She sat down and smoked, and he sensed she was poking her breasts at him across the table. They seemed to send out messages: Stroke us. But this was not a conventional call to arms. Irma was changing, complexifying and in crisis. Beware of women in crisis, Bailey. They're like flypaper. Even if you tear yourself away you leave a wing in their stickiness. Irma was lovable, all right. The loveliest of all lovely, perpetual innocents. Are you ready for that, Bailey?

But as she looked at him with all of her things, he reached out and stroked her left one, softly, as you might pet a goose that would hiss and bite if the pet were imperfect. Irma took his hand and kissed it and put it back on the left. Her hair fell in that soft, black diagonal across her forehead. Her eyes glistened, but it wasn't tears in the making.

"Am I a whore, Bailey? A nymph? An easy make? Tell me the truth, is it wrong to like it?"

The question was melancholy, also provocative, and Bailey moved his free hand toward her right one, working both in the quasi-circular motion that he remembered soldiers calling tuning-in-Berlin during the war years. Irma smiled through wondering eyes.

"Lovely cupcake," Bailey said.

"I'm no cupcake. Some men liked me for my mind. Did you know that?"

Bailey worked in silence, and the question passed.

"Am I opening Pandora's box a little wider every time? What's next for me? A do-it-yourself kit?"

"Maybe," he said. "But that's a long way down the ladder."

"Hold me up, Bailey. Every way."

They stood and kissed, and Bailey thought: Time to crank up the machinery. He raised her skirt while he kissed her, but then broke away. Bailey wants full view of one of his great pleasures—Irma's body being freed of its covers. Her great globy breasts, sweet cushions, pushed out of her brassiere as he lifted her sweater over her head. She unhooked her skirt and stepped out of it daintily, then tugged at his zipper. She whipped it out then and pounced on it, smothering it with kisses like a new arrival at a family reunion. Bailey let her work for a few minutes, then stood her up and pulled down her half-slip, which was tattered at the edges, its lace crumbling from too many washings.

"Couldn't that undertaker afford to buy you a new slip?"

"He never saw anything but the outer layer. I told you he was a dud. He liked to do it in the dark."

"Maybe he liked to think of you as a corpse."

"That's a rotten thing to say. I wonder why I never thought of it."

Bailey was squatted down, untangling her slip from her high heels when she grabbed the back of his head and pulled his face into her garter belt.

"Hurry," she said. "Hurry."

He stood and undid her bra, and her bulby diamonds took their natural position, obscuring the rest of the world.

"Nibble one, nibble two. Upsy, upsy."

"Get on with it," Irma advised, and at that moment she succeeded in undoing belt and top button, making him suddenly trouserless, then shortsless. Then she was back at him, dealing with his varied crevices.

"You won't let me at it," he told her.

She stood up then, still holding on. He looped her out of her pants and gained access at last, her charcoal-gray stockings and garter belt with its faded flowers remaining in place.

"Would it mean anything to you," she asked, "if I said I loved you with all my heart?"

"It'd mean something," he said, sending a finger in search of her magic button.

"It'd be true," she said, beginning to undulate.

"Would it also be true for any members of your nostalgia squad?"

"I don't think so. Not anymore."

"You don't think so."

"Eeeeeeeaaagh. That's right."

"Did anybody ever tell you what a fickle woman you are?"

"Sometimes I think nobody was really made for monogamy."

"Ooo-ooo there," Bailey said. "Careful."

"Bite me, Bailey. Long and easy."

"Bite you?"

"However it's done. I always wanted to see what it was like."

"And nobody ever did it for you?"

"I never asked."

Bailey did what he could.

"How's that?" he inquired.

"More."

No more, Bailey thought. Continence is no longer my strong suit. He whipped her heavy coat off the book rack and doubled it on top of a wagon loaded with philosophy books to be shelved. He pillowed her head with her skirt, and he laid her down on the wagon. Then, climbing to the second shelf of a stack in one aisle to gain proper angulation, he split the loveliest breach he'd ever known.

"Yaggghhh," she said, and then she started the cart moving, kicking off from whichever shelf her foot touched. They zigzagged past Plato and Aristotle, Spinoza and Descartes, Schopenhauer and Sartre, and Bailey's last vision was of Emerson, the transcendentalist.

"I don't give a goddamn what you think, Bailey. I love you with everything. Heart, soul and cunny."

Bailey could not say whether it was the sentiment, the antique word or merely the action, but something triggered the machine and his great bolt of love syrup carried Irma's abjectly honest profession of love back into herself with quick, sweet requitement.

"Now the pain is gone," she said.

"Irma," Bailey said, "I love you dearly. And it keeps getting different."

They smooched then, Bailey reveling in his discovery, Irma in her ease. A nice day at last, Bailey thought. A day without losers.

Things seemed unfinished to Bailey when he came up from the stacks. He walked in the daylight of the cold and clear late afternoon, full of odd compulsions that no longer seemed to have anything to do with the Guild, the strike, the company. He felt no rancor toward company people or gypsies. Outrage had faded. Revenge had no foothold in him. He had revenged himself so many times, always uselessly. It was another power ploy: eye for eye, wound for wound. I am greater. I have the final say. I. That was always the crucial turn. Follow that path and you slid to the center of the maze where the all-devouring monster waited with open jaws. And he had beaten that monster. He was done with useless argument.

Yet the compulsion to act remained, for everything in the clarity of daylight seemed unfinished. Seeing Skin, for one. The image of Skin crying at Miss Blue's after his failure as a subversive nagged Bailey. A man with that kind of intensity might be worth saving. Possibly he was mad, or neurotically addicted to self-defeating games. But his striving seemed genuine, and Bailey felt kinship with any debauchery of the spirit after intense failure: grotesque self-indulgence until the cloud passes.

He knew only the general neighborhood where Skin's apartment was located: a slum. He approached it at the close of the workday, stores and offices letting out, the slum trade just beginning. White men in cars circulated through the largely Negro neighborhood, questing for cocktail-hour poon. Bailey quizzed bartenders and store clerks about Skin but learned nothing. But he found the block and after several tries found also the hallway where he'd fallen among Skin's garbage. He knocked and Stephanie answered and stared at him, not sullen, not hostile, only blank.

"I'm looking for Skin."

"He's not here."

"Is he around? In the neighborhood?"

"Who wants to know?"

"I'm Bailey. Don't you remember?"

"No."

"I was here the night of the fire. We talked. You asked if I wanted to fickydick."

"Why don't you just say plain what you want. Come on."

"No, I want to see Skin."

"He's not here no more."

"Isn't he in town?"

"What do you want with Skin? Who are you, mister?"

"How could you forget me? I was tied up with wire, right in your apartment."

"Lotsa people been in my apartment. I just ain't about to remember 'em all."

"Forget that, then. Where's Skin?"

"He's dead. Just dead."

"Dead."

"Hung himself."

"Agggh."

"Tied a rope around the radiator and hung himself out the window. Little kids found him, the wind just blowin' him easy. Just easy."

Bailey shook his head.

"Look, you comin' in or not? I got no time for yakety strangers."

"No," Bailey said. "I won't be coming in." He remembered she cleaned his fingers in the barn, that he called her an angel. Now she looked at him with dead eyes and a slack mouth, and Bailey thought: another one of the very suddenly dead.

"Cheep-cheep," she said in a bird squeak, and closed the door.

Bailey took a bus uptown to where Deek lived and found

him alone in the living room watching a quiz show on television. Deek hobbled to the door to let Bailey in, then hobbled
back and elevated his plaster-cast on a footstool.

"Another couple of weeks I'll be rid of this."

"I should have come to see you before," Bailey said, "but
things went crazy."

"Sure. I know how it is."

"I understand they put you in for honorary membership."

"So I hear. That was nice of them."

"You took a beating for the Guild. That was courageous."

"I didn't know what I was doing."

"Very few heroes ever have. Those who survive get medals."

"I'm out of it now."

"Out?"

"The Guild really isn't my cup of tea. It's too vague for
me. I've taken a fancy to writing for television. Lot of money
in commercials. Maybe learn something about movies. Plenty
of action in the movies these days."

"Ah."

"You're not pleased."

"Pleased, not pleased, that's not my place."

"You know what the Bible says," Deek said, avoiding
Bailey's eyes. "Many are called but few are chosen."

"I never bought that," Bailey said.

"You never bought it?"

"Anyway, I hope you get well soon."

"Young bones knit fast, the doctor said."

"Variously," Bailey said, and he went out the door leaving
a half-formed word in Deek's mouth. As he went down the
steps Bailey heard the clomp of Deek's plaster-legged hobble,
and from the doorway the young man cried out: "Who the
hell are you, anyway?"

He knew something had changed when his Aunt Rose
answered the bell and looked at him with an odd grin that
had no mirth in it.

"What happened?"

"He's in bed. He's been there six days now. Doesn't say a word."

"He's not sick?"

"He eats a little but he won't get out of bed. The cat came too, only I didn't dare tell him. It came in the mail, wrapped in a plastic bag and in just awful shape."

"Are you sure it was the same cat?"

"I'd know that cat anywhere, even if it was just bones."

"What'd you do with it?"

"I burned it. You don't suppose I'd leave it around for him to see."

Bailey went upstairs to his uncle's room. He found the old man lying on his side, looking out the window at the cold, gray day. He had a vision of him sitting upright in the coffin, like a cat might.

"Hello, Cappy. I just came by to see how things were going."

The old man said nothing. Bailey sat down and looked at his face without speaking. His aunt was right. The face betrayed no illness, just grief. Bailey had no intention of trying to talk him out of his grief. He just watched, silently, for twenty minutes while the old man stared out the window. Then he patted him on the shoulder and left.

Now life had a flat quality about it as he walked the streets. The evening was coming on, its darkness blotting out sectors of what was real. Buildings fell into mutilating shadows, streets divided into the abysses of dark and light. Nothing was right, not his uncle, not Deek; and Skin dead of malevolent profundity. Bailey had no wish to bring life down to an either/or principle: join or die. But all pressures indicated that direction. The problem was that there was no longer anything to join. Except Irma's flesh. Starvation diet of love-alone. He called Rosenthal and found the phone disconnected. He walked to the Guild room and found it locked. He tried his key, discovered the lock had been changed, peered through the window at his chair. Someone had moved it, newspapers a foot deep on its seat. He called Irma.

"I've been looking all over hell for you," she told him. "You didn't say you were leaving the library early."

"The Guild room is locked."

"Don't you think I know it? I'm sure that's Popkin's work."

"Where did Jarvis go?"

"He's home. I called him but he said he couldn't talk and hung up. He's addled, the poor simp."

"We'll go see him."

When he reached the corner by Jarvis' house Irma was waiting, her hands in a muff he'd never known her to carry. What he felt toward her made him feel comfortable at last on this bleak day. He wanted to go over all the absurd things they'd all gone through, separately or together, and explain that they had no explanation, that they were fixed in time and space and stood only for whatever meaning he, or anyone else, cared to give them. It seemed like a wonderful notion to explore with someone who could understand; and it seemed like a palliative truth that conclusively proved the falsity of all paranoid philosophies. Paranoiacs would be instantly converted to peace by this truth. It seemed the very edge of titanic revelation, and it exhilarated Bailey. But then the ideas began to cloud over. Possibly it was not revelation. Possibly it was just another lie or another delusion and means that we're dead. Or that we have become sterile. Or mutants. The consummation of a wish: dream sundered, hope exploded. Another kind of death.

Irma pulled one hand out of the muff and let him look inside. In her other hand, the muff hiding it, she held an antique pistol.

"Take it," she told him.

"For what?"

"It's my grandfather's old railroad pistol. He gave it to me and Francie when he died so we'd have some protection."

"I don't want it."

"Listen. Something's definitely wrong. I called Jarvis back and he said not to come over, that it wouldn't be wise. But he wouldn't say what it meant and he sounded spooky. So take the pistol."

"But I don't want to shoot Jarvis or anybody else either."

"What if somebody shoots at you? What've you got, a sheet-metal chest?"

Bailey smiled and guided Irma's hand back into her muff. The streetlights came on and Bailey smiled. As they walked up the steps of Jarvis' house, scar tissue grew on Bailey's sores. He clenched his fist, opened it, clenched it again. In the bright light on Jarvis' porch he squeezed the tendons in his wrist, felt the pulse of his own life. His action seemed vital, then willfully symbolic, then comic. He laughed at this.

"What's the joke?" Irma asked.

Unable to answer, Bailey brought his laughter to a logical conclusion.

Jarvis and his dog greeted them. Jarvis wore a yellow shirt with sleeves rolled below the elbows, meticulously creased black trousers and highly polished black shoes with pointed toes and Cuban heels. Bailey noticed that the black wart on Jarvis' chin had been camouflaged with a round nickel-sized bandage and his hair slicked with tonic that gave an alcoholically sweet smell.

"I see you're all sharped up," Bailey said.

"Popkin said we were all slobs. What do you want from me?"

"We wondered where you went."

"I'm here. Here at home. Any more questions?" He held the door ajar, but not enough for it to be an invitation to enter.

"Where is old Popkin?"

"Around somewhere. Here and there."

"Why is the Guild room locked?" Irma asked.

"Who wants to know? What is this, the third degree?"

"Why is it locked, Jarvis?" Bailey said flatly.

"Popkin said we deserved a rest. He'll open it when he comes back from wherever he went."

"Do you believe that?"

"I believe what I'm told."

"What if I told you I'd smash your skull open and scoop out your brains for bird food unless you told us the truth? Would you believe that?"

"I can see you're on edge," Jarvis said. He opened the door for them. "Let me take your coats."

Jarvis' dog, a dalmatian, sat down when Jarvis carried the coats to a hall closet. But then the dog yelped and stood up. He tried to sit, yelped again and remained standing.

"That's what my wife and her gang did to him. His testicles are all swollen. And that really hurts."

Jarvis led them to his basement playroom and directed Bailey to a low rocker. He sat himself on a high barstool and suggested Irma sit in a far corner and keep out of the conversation. Irma shrugged and kept her hands inside her muff. Jarvis leaped off the barstool and made the drinks.

"Why didn't you want us to come here?" Bailey asked him.

"I'm glad you came. Glad."

"Is that so? You seem unusually nervous."

"Having visitors does that."

"You have a lot of visitors?"

"Sometimes my wife comes by for a towel. But you've never been here. You really don't know me at all."

"I suppose it's possible to think of it that way."

"It's silly to think you know somebody you just work with."

"Sometimes the part illuminates the whole."

"You intellectual bastards always think you're so goddamn smart."

"That's not very civil, Jarvis."

"You snotty sonsabitches think you can drive me crazy."

The dalmatian yelped, rose, sat, yelped again. Jarvis passed out the drinks in silence, then sat down. Bailey sipped his drink, which was heavy on the Scotch.

"How ya doin'?" Jarvis asked, smiling. "How's it been goin'?"

"Oddly," said Bailey.

"Here's to it," Jarvis said, raising his glass. "To all of us." When Irma and Bailey didn't toast, Jarvis looked hurt.

"You don't like my whiskey?"

Bailey sipped it and shrugged.

"What I want to know is what happened to the Guild room."

"Here's to happy times," Jarvis said. "Happy, happy."

"What are you hiding, Jarvis?"

"I'm not a bad guy. But I get terrible headaches. I always got them, but lately they're worse."

"You should see a doctor. A neurologist or a neuro-surgeon."

"Don't tell me what to do." He stood up, furious. "You smart babies know the names of all the specialists. A good old family doctor is good enough for me."

"You're too touchy to talk to," Bailey said, standing up.

"Don't leave," Jarvis said. "I want to show you something."

He left the playroom and ran up the stairs two at a time. He was back quickly with a large book.

"Look this over," he said. "It's my pride and joy."

Bailey flipped through the book, a fifteen-dollar volume of photos showing an Australian golf professional named Barley Boy Benson instructing the reader in the use of golf clubs. The book was autographed by someone named Fred J. Selby with the notation: "To Jarvis, with best regards for better golf and all sorts of other improvement." Bailey hunted for Selby's name among the book's credits and found him to be the layout artist. Bailey was still turning pages when Jarvis bounced in with four volumes of *Speedwriting Self-Taught* and dumped them in Bailey's lap.

"I went through all these," he said.

On top of them he put a wooden shield-shaped plaque inscribed on its lacquered brass front: "To Claude Jarvis, this American Legion School Award for the year 1939, for demonstrating those outstanding qualities of scholarship, leadership and gymnastic ability that have made this nation great."

"I got that for graduation from P.S. 28. You see what it says?" He pointed to the word "leadership." "Now what do you think of old Jarvis, eh?"

"Frankly," Bailey said, "I don't know what to think."

"You're not impressed, eh?"

From his wallet he took a yellowed newspaper clipping of a head-and-shoulders photo of W. C. Fields.

"My father told him to go to hell once in a Third Avenue bar back in nineteen-thirty-three when nobody had a dime. My father was a tough baby, and you better believe that. He took no shit from nobody."

Jarvis was trembling, and Bailey noticed his arms for the first time. They were puffy, as were the lymph-gland areas of his throat. His wrists and the backs of his hands were also white and puffy, as if a fluid had inflated them. Yet Jarvis did not look fat to Bailey; merely bloated, puncturable. He held the Fields clipping in front of Bailey's face long after Bailey had stopped looking at it.

"Nothing impresses you, does it, Bailey?"

"It's interesting the way you revere your father. Nice."

"He was a giant in his time. A giant."

"I take it he's dead."

"Who knows where the hell he is?"

"What ails you, Jarvis? Get to the point."

"What's your rush? What are you, in a big rush?"

"I'm trying to figure it out."

"You tell me I stink, and you're trying to figure it out."

"I never said you stank."

"I saw you whispering to people at the meeting. What am I, a deefy?"

"I never said you stank at the meeting."

"I suppose nobody told you anything about my wife either, and that you never passed it along to anybody else."

"You told me all I know. The first you mentioned her was the night she borrowed the dog."

"Right. And you blabbed it all over."

"You're wrong, Jarvis. I told no one. Why should I?"

"I sicked the cops on her anyway, so what the hell. I told them what she was doing. I warned her to quit makin' those movies. I saw them. I watched them through the window the night she took the dog and gave him the crabs. He never had the crabs before. He got them from her and her mixed friends. They were ruining my dog on me, but they won't do it no more. I was a hell of a lot smarter than she gave me credit for. She didn't even want me to go into the chicken game when we got married. But I sent myself through correspondence school running that game. Twenty-five bucks if you could pull the half-cut head off a chicken with one yank. Ten bucks if it took two, and a five if the heads were droopers others had a go at. I learned algebra and advanced spelling on that dough, but after a while I couldn't stand the stink of chicken blood. And I was fed up being out in the country with all them apple-knockers and shit kickers. That's when I got on at the newspaper. I worked up from copy boy to assistant-Thursday-night news editor. Not bad, eh? I know what you reporters think of copy-desk guys, but I'll tell you this, fella," and he raised his middle finger in front of Bailey's nose, "you're nothing but an electronic-age Barney Google, you and your neurosurgeons and psychiatrists and all the tranquilizers that blow you up like a hog's bladder. I'll tell you right now, you'll never get back in the Guild."

"I have no intention of getting back in."

"No intention my petunia. You couldn't get laid in Omaha. You're no more gonna get back than Barney Google. What do you take me for, eh? Goo-goo-googly? Eh? Eh?"

"Get the coats, Irma."

"Don't leave," Jarvis yelled. He fell on his knees, groveling at Bailey's shoes. "Please don't leave."

"You should get help."

Jarvis looked up at Irma, who had both hands in her muff.

"You and your knockers," he said to her. His face was astream with tears.

"You're in ghastly shape, Jarvis," Irma told him.

"It's all over," he said with a great sigh. "The strike's all over."

"Who said so?" Bailey asked.

Jarvis took an envelope from his shirt pocket and handed it to Bailey, then broke into a mighty sob. The dalmatian stood, sat, gave a yelp. The envelope was addressed to Jarvis at the Guild room. Bailey took a stiff, engraved announcement card from the envelope and read:

You Are Cordially Invited to Attend
an
END OF THE STRIKE PARTY

To celebrate the occasion of the meeting of minds of management and labor, and on said occasion to partake of cocktails, dinner and a special Scandinavian entertainment.

The invitation was signed by Stanley and directed the invited guest to an address Bailey knew to be Stanley's home.

"I'm not sure I totally understand this," Bailey said to Jarvis, who was on the floor, still awash in tears.

"He's mocking us," Jarvis said. "I didn't know he'd do this."

"So let him mock. It wouldn't be the first time."

"You don't get it," Jarvis said. "He invited all of us along with company people."

"Is that why you're all upset? Forget it, Jar. It means nothing. One side can't simply declare the war over."

Jarvis broke into a new cataclysm of sobbing, wetting the floor with his tears. He pounded his forehead on the floor as he cried.

"What is it, Jarvis? What's got you?"

"There's a cover letter with it," he said, amid snivels.

"Cover letter?"

Jarvis pounded his head until blood began to stream from his forehead. Bailey and Irma watched in silence. Then Bailey grabbed Jarvis and leaned him against the wall.

"The letter says the Guild agrees the strike is over," Jarvis said, exhausted, gasping. "Popkin signed for the International, and I signed as president of the local." Then Jarvis' face collapsed into babyish grief. Bailey let go of him, and he fell between his own knees. Irma and Bailey looked at one another in silence; then they started up the steps. Jarvis grabbed Irma's ankle with one hand.

"I love the Guild," he said. "I love Bailey. I love you too, Irma, not to mention Rosenthal. I always loved everybody and everything. You won't believe this, but it's true. It's a deep fondness for all creation."

Irma pulled her leg away, and Jarvis lost his balance and fell forward on his chin. He lay flat and pounded the floor with his fist and cried uncontrollably. The dalmatian licked his ear, sat, yelped, rose.

When Bailey first stepped aboard the ancient trolley, clad in the formless robes of his hopeless faith (not a conventional faith, of course; religion was his ho-ho; but he enjoyed the hair-shirt quality of the robe's inner lining, enjoyed its itch, its tickle), he saw Irma and Rosenthal sitting apart from each other, facing front, riding in silence, and he was comforted. He would have company on his pilgrimage. The three of them would ride to the stop at Our Lady of the Aberration. There they would all get off and wait for the nun with no face to escort them to the quadrangle, where they would watch the inmates joining with God and other exalted social powers, having their aberrations whipped out of them at the stocks and the pillory. Along the walls of the courtyard, monks and other disciples of omnipotence would be kneeling, having grown to be part of the brick walls and floor of the quadrangle, their knees, shoulders and elbows an extension of the inanimate clay, a perfect union of busy and lethargic molecules. The monks' and disciples' faces would have grown wild with brambles. The sun would make their eyes glisten, and their hair would turn green with soft rains, while the winter snows cracked their bones and the winds eroded them like rocks into sand. The three visitors would watch these things from the walls of the institution, and Rosenthal would, of necessity, wear a funny hat that would signify his Jewishness. Nuns would thus be careful not to utter Christian phrases in his presence. The three would watch the proceedings without comment for several months, unmoving, transfixed by their awareness of the external and internal forces of a vocation. Punishment would greatly exceed the misdeeds performed while the aberrations had run free in the inmates. Prayer for their salvation would greatly exceed its need. The men and women in the stocks, at the pillory, would, in lucid moments, comprehend their own natures, but around them the behavior of others would contribute to personal confusion.

The relevance of torture and prayer to the deepest part of their natures would be apparent to all but themselves. At the conclusion of their time at the institution, which would be at the moment of the hauling away of the first dead inmate in a donkey cart, Rosenthal, Irma and Bailey would once again board the trolley and continue riding separately. As the trolley approached the cliff, Bailey would climb out the window, stand atop the moving car, and with instinctive timing, dive into the dry rocks below, assured that great waves would break deeply on the rocks before he struck his head.

Bailey walked toward the newspaper plant, Irma tucked away in her apartment. He drifted, feeling less concern for the dying Guild than he had ever felt, yet stung by his own failure to truly mark the earth with his signature. Then, as he approached the plant his eyes seemed to trick him. Was that another ink truck parked in front of the plant? No people now, no headlights, no traffic, no snow. But it was a truck. He stopped, took stock of his drive. Would he slip beneath the truck now if he could? Would he somehow, come what may, find a way to color the earth with the ink, a way to bleed the tank of its bloody blackness? He judged himself, stood quietly and wondered: Do I have the strength? The perseverance? Am I prepared for another clubbing? He walked slowly and cautiously to the corner, certain that he would act, fearful of being premature. The truck, he saw, had a flat front-left tire. Then he saw that it was different from the other ink truck. He read the lettering: not an ink truck at all. An oil truck. No driver, no guards, probably no oil, cargo already deposited. But perhaps not. He could investigate, spill what oil was left. But on what whiteness? The snow had gone gray: slushed and sooted. Optimum reduced one notch. And as he thought of it, spilling oil was very unlike spilling ink. Absence of ebony. Difference in consistency. Reduction in indelibility. Oh, no. No greaser, Bailey. He hawked an oyster of phlegm, arced it toward the oil truck. Ebony is the color of my true love's hair.

He walked across the street to the burned building, stared at the remains of his deed: charred wood, broken shingles, nothing where something had been. Part of a chair stuck up from the remains. Bailey tugged it free, a backless seat with uneven legs, scorched and blistered. He sat. He studied the embers. And around him the power of his thought slowly disintegrated the exterior universe.

"Okay there, bud."

Bailey heard this but didn't turn.

"Okay, bud. You hear me?"

Bailey turned to see a company guard. New man. Mutual unacquaintance.

"You can't sit here."

"Why not?"

"You been here all night, they tell me."

"I bother nobody."

"We don't like loiterers, transients, vagrants, indigents, insolvents or bums."

"I'm none of those. I'm on strike."

"Strike? The strike's all over."

"Not quite."

"You see any pickets around anyplace?"

"Wouldn't you call me a picket?"

"They pulled all the pickets off."

"Nobody pulled me off."

"I think you better get movin'."

"And I think you're out of order. Call a cop. See if he'll arrest a picket."

"Pickets got to keep walkin'."

"Then I'll walk. First up, then down."

"We'll check you out, buddy boy. We'll check out that snotty nose of yours."

Bailey stood up from the chair and stretched, then walked up and down in front of the burned house. The guard crossed the street and entered the company building. By the clock in the company lunchroom Bailey saw it was eight-thirty. The morning was warm, almost springlike, a thaw. He walked the stiffness out of his legs, the cold out of his feet. He did not need gloves, and his throat was not cold with the collar unbuttoned. He watched the bosses arrive, the ex-Guildsmen, the scabs. He did not hate them, or fear them, or need anything about them. Yet they all judged him. His resentment of this, his unformed yearning to alter that judgment, disturbed him. And beyond that he was growing hungry. He kept walking; that was the important thing; and soon the hunger seemed unimportant. There would be time to eat later; now he would just walk and wait for what he felt was going to happen, what surely must happen.

By lunchtime company people in twos and threes were watching Bailey. None spoke, none came near him. He walked without a picket sign, talking, gesturing to no one. By one o'clock company windows were dotted with faces. The faces would appear, see that he was still walking, then recede to be replaced by other faces.

At two o'clock Jarvis turned the corner and came toward Bailey with obvious purpose. He seemed neater to Bailey without his overshoes and muffler, his hat on top of his head instead of smothering his ears; sartorial mutation: a slob in adversity, in defeat a dude.

"I'd like to know what you're doing," Jarvis said.

"I'm walking up and down."

"What for?"

"I'm not sure."

"We're not picketing out here anymore."

"It's a good place to picket, though, Jar."

"We don't think so."

"Who's we?"

"The Guild."

"That lets me out. I'm not in the Guild."

"Then why the heck are you picketing?"

"Because I'm on strike."

"You can't picket if you're not in the Guild."

"Are you in the Guild, Jarvis?"

"Of course."

"Then why aren't you picketing?"

"Popkin says you shouldn't picket. He's really out of sorts."

"Who's Popkin?"

"Come on. You know who Popkin is. He's from Guild headquarters."

"I'm not in the Guild, I tell you."

"Popkin says he's near a settlement with the company, and you'll only mess it all up."

"What are the terms of the settlement?"

"He won't tell me."

"As a Guildsman, don't you feel left out?"

"I'll ask him again. But meantime what'll I tell him you're doing out here?"

"Tell him I'm walking up and down."

By four o'clock workers on the company truck dock began calling out to Bailey: "Quittin' time . . . strike's over . . . pickets go home. . . ." He stopped and stared at them. They stood amid a few bundles of newspaper wrapped with wire, undistributed morning editions. The dock was otherwise empty, all trucks on the street, and the young paper boys an audience for the mockery of Bailey by the workers.

"Are you nuts?" one worker yelled.

Bailey stared back at the men, who fell silent. The smiles died on the newsboys' faces. "Aaaaaaah," said one worker after a long, silent interlude; and he turned away. Others milled about, and the newsboys talked to one another. Bailey resumed walking until Irma arrived.

"What in the world are you up to?"

"I'm walking up and down."

"Popkin just reopened the Guild room, and he's got Jarvis running around like a dog with distemper. I've never seen anything like it."

"Popkin has a way with Jarvis."

"He had to cancel his press conference. He was going to announce a settlement until you screwed it all up."

"If you see Popkin, tell him if he calls a press conference so will I. If he and Stanley can privately declare this strike settled, I can declare it unsettled, just as privately."

"Have you been here all night long?"

"Since I left you."

"I'll bet you haven't eaten."

"I'm not hungry now. I was this morning."

"I'll go get you a sandwich."

"No, don't do that."

"Why not?"

"I don't want to eat."

"Is this part of the plan?"

"I don't know. I've been thinking odd things."

"Don't be a jerk. All it'll get you is an empty stomach."

"You could be right."

"I'll go down to Fobie's and get you a roast-beef sandwich and coffee."

"No."

Irma was sitting on the backless chair watching Bailey walk when Rosenthal arrived at five o'clock, hat jaunty, no cape.

"The word's around that you've started a strike of your own."

"Is that what they're saying? I'd say it was still everybody's strike."

"You're crazy, of course."

"I didn't expect you to fight me. Above all."

"You're out of the Guild. I'm out. I thought we'd finally gotten some sense."

"Fuck sense."

"Ah."

"We never needed the Guild. It was always just a name we called ourselves."

"Sure. Do you want me to walk with you awhile?"

"You've got other problems. A house to fix. A nervous wife. I don't want to complicate anybody's life anymore."

"I'll walk awhile."

"He's not eating, you know," Irma told Rosenthal.

Bailey shrugged when Rosenthal looked at him.

"A kamikaze?"

"Not quite in that league," Bailey said.

"It's a great idea," Rosenthal said. "I wonder why none of us ever thought of it before."

"We didn't have to," Bailey said, as Rosenthal fell in beside him and walked in step with him toward the corner.

By seven o'clock a small crowd was rooted at the corner, watching Bailey, Irma and Rosenthal from a distance of half a block. Four guards had joined the company's outside patrol, six altogether now, all sitting in two cars parked in the company lot. The lights of Fobie's beer signs came on. In an upstairs window of the company a uniform guard stood in silhouette against the dim light of a hallway. A taxi pulled up in front of the three strikers and Deek got out, on crutches. He left the taxi door open behind him and the driver waited.

"I heard you were up to something," Deek said. "My old man says all the company wheels are spinning. They can't figure it out."

"Same old strike," Bailey said.

"But with a twist," said Deek. "I always underestimate the Guild."

"You can't really underestimate the Guild," Irma said.

"Is it true none of you ate all day?"

"Just him," Irma said, slapping Bailey's shoulder. "He's the one with the stomach that doesn't bark back at its master."

"I brought three sandwiches," Deek said. "I thought you'd all run out of money." He leaned on his crutches and fumbled in his pocket for the plastic-wrapped sandwiches. He offered them to Bailey, who shook his head.

"I'll take them," Irma said. "We're hungry, even if he isn't." She gave two to Rosenthal, kept one.

"I don't get it," Deek said.

"He thinks he's on a hunger strike, that's all," Irma said. "And poor soul, he probably is."

"I didn't mean to yell at you yesterday," Deek told Bailey.

"Now don't get reverential," Irma said. "You'll make him nervous and he might eat something."

They all stood then without anything obvious to say. Bailey smiled and walked toward the corner. A policeman stood apart from the small crowd now, a new addition.

"I think I'll stick around awhile and watch what happens," Deek said. He paid the taxi and sent it away.

"Be my guest," Irma said and gave Deek the backless chair. Rosenthal took a bite of the sandwich and Irma turned up her collar against the cold that was beginning to point out that this was not really spring at all, but genuine February.

"If they see you eating," Deek told Rosenthal, "that crowd'll think Bailey's eating too."

Rosenthal stuffed the sandwich in his pocket. The lump in his mouth felt like a pool ball. He chewed secretly and swallowed suddenly.

"You catch on quick," Irma told Deek, studying his face, noting all over again how gorgeous he was.

"Where will you sleep?" Irma asked Bailey.

"I've been wondering about that."

"This is the wrong time of the year for a hunger strike," Rosenthal said. "Nobody stays out in the cold to watch. And without a crowd you've got no witnesses. And therefore no credibility."

"What do you do if it snows?" Deek asked.

"Or dips below zero?" Irma added.

"Those are problems," Bailey said.

"Don't be so goddamn cavalier," Irma told him. "What the hell are we supposed to do while you fly off your branch after this thing? Sit around and watch your blood coagulate into red ice cubes? You don't even have a used match to keep warm by."

"And you didn't drink anything today either," Rosenthal said.

"Dusty ice cubes," Irma said.

"Do we know anybody with a tent?" Bailey wondered. "A tent might stave off some of the elements, keep out a little bit of wind."

"I had a pup tent I stole from the Army," Rosenthal said, "but the rats ate it."

"My father's got a tent," Deek said. "He used it on fishing trips until he got allergic to fish. It's rolled up in our cellar. If you come with me," he said to Rosenthal, "we can get it. There's a kerosene lantern and a cot too."

"God really does watch out for sparrows," Irma said. "Not to mention cuckoos."

With help, Bailey pitched the tent in the vacant lot beside the burned building. Then he sat on the cot, keeping the tent flap open so he was visible to the crowd at the corner. Rosenthal expressed his concern to the policeman that Bailey be protected from public nuisances and from possible attacks by vindictive guards or company loyalists. The word of Bailey's actions had spread and as Rosenthal talked to the officer two cars stopped in front of the tent. Their occupants watched a few minutes, then moved on. The policeman gave Rosenthal bored and perfunctory assurance that he would maintain law and order. At eleven o'clock Rosenthal sent Irma and Deek home and went to Fobie's. He ate the half-eaten sandwich, then the whole one, plus four whiskeys. The crowd in Fobie's talked of nothing but Bailey: what a madman, idiot, jerk, creep, nut, fool and stoop. But with big balls. A scab raised doubts about his not eating but Rosenthal stared him down and the scab changed the subject. When Rosenthal returned to the tent Bailey was under the blanket with the lantern burning, his arms outside the blanket, his face in full view, asleep. Rosenthal sat on the backless chair and waited for three A.M., when Deek would spell him. At seven A.M. Irma would take over.

Walking through the snowstorm with a compelling but vague purpose, Bailey arrived late at the trolley stop. A hero wearing the Great Medal was waiting with a cap of snow and a bottle of brandy. "Bailey's the name," Bailey told the hero, so he wouldn't be embarrassed by not knowing. But the hero knew, shook his hand, clapped him on the back. "Lazarus wasn't worth a doodley squat after the big boy revived him," the hero said. "He was used to being dead, and there he was famous, just for being alive like everybody else. It killed him, you know. He could never live up to living just to live up to living and so on." Bailey and the hero then boarded the trolley, which was packed with inquisitive passengers who rubbernecked in the aisles to get a look at the hero and the newcomer. The two sat together at the front and Bailey shook hands with another bemedaled hero, heavily clothed, dignified and riding backward. "He's putting on the Vercingetorix suit this year," the first hero told the second one. "Being crucified or buried alive isn't as nasty as it's cracked up to be," said the second hero. "But can you imagine being trampled to death by crickets?" Bailey's impulse at that moment was to swing from strap to strap to show how apelike he could be. But instead he took a long drink of brandy. "Vercingetorix was a good sport about it, all right," said the second hero. "Hope you'll weather it." Then the two heroes toasted Bailey, each raising the bottle in turn, in salute, then staring at him with sorrowful eyes. Bailey sat quite still, sweating and trembling.

Bailey stepped off the trolley alone and entered the house of the triumphal figure, gray-haired nobleman of the indomitable spirit. He passed through the kitchen, where middle-aged maids and chefs in starched black-and-white aprons prepared dinner. The smell of cooking produced an appetite in him that nagged. On a table near the stove stood a giant grasshopper, its body half again the size of Bailey's head. Upon scrutiny it proved to be a great vegetable, akin in texture to a carrot. It had been scraped by the maids and like a peeled potato was turning gray from exposure. Bailey, smelling its hideous raw odor, happily left the monster and walked toward the enormous front room, its walls lined with books and adorned with honors, its furniture covered by soft purple cushions. Before he spoke to the nobleman, noises drew Bailey out the front door to the street, where a crowd of frantic youths carrying unintelligible banners talked of strikes, of economic and social revolution, but in mixed tongues. They clamored to make their meanings clear to each other and to Bailey, but he caught none of it and after an hour or more he returned to the nobleman's living room. Dinner was being served in a formal manner on an antique dining-room table that gleamed with polished silver, elegant china and a great silver bowl out of which the nobleman filled the soup plates. The grasshopper had been sliced into small pieces, all of which Bailey devoured. He told the nobleman that without a doubt it was the most delicious soup he had ever eaten and that he regretted staying in the street so long when such a delicacy as this awaited him. The nobleman's wife said this pleased them greatly and that most guests spat the soup onto the rug after the first mouthful. Bailey ate it piggishly, enjoying his own eccentric taste.

He awoke making slavering, hungry sounds with his mouth, which embarrassed him when he realized what he was doing. He sat up into the dawn, finding Irma asleep on the chair, leaning against the edge of the tent, cocooned in slacks, coat, blanket and head wrapper. And he loved her. He crouched low and edged past her and walked to the corner in the warm morning. He counted the hours since he'd eaten anything: sixty: a full day with nothing eaten even before he'd begun to consider the hunger strike, then a day and a half on the line. He already felt freakish. The mass of people would mock him. With the main strike all but forgotten by the public, little heeded by the press, abandoned even by the men who once were Guildsmen, a hunger strike seemed essentially a personal statement. Yet as he considered this, it seemed the only recourse left to him once a collective statement was made impossible. Would he hunger even to the threshold of death? Was this passivity, this abnegation, the statement he wanted to make? The more he thought of it the more absurd abnegation became. But how more absurd would abnegation begun, then abandoned, be?

By the afternoon of the second day the crowds were again gathering, watching, thinning to a few, then fattening again, the majority young people. Deek stood on the corner and talked with them, orating periodically on the purpose of Bailey's strike, as Deek understood it. The purpose, he said, was to destroy all that the company stood for, overthrow the Establishment and all its traditions, uproot false values and impose genuine values, to develop a truly humane relationship between management and labor, master and slave, capitalist and radical, Gog, Magog and the heavenly host, ins and outs, haves and have-nots, good and evil, rich guys and cheapskates, smart guys and dopes, cats and mice, artist and philistine, angel and devil, fink and funk, hump and lump, sump and dump, bump and frump. People failed to understand the mockery of Stanley inherent in Deek's comments, the hero worship of Bailey, or the free-form language patterns. People failed to understand that Deek was beginning to render his own message, not Bailey's. People failed to understand that Deek was truly of the opinion that he was serving Bailey's best interests when in fact he was distorting Bailey's ideas, serving his own interests, gaining status with his peers. Girls in the crowd sought to mother him, inquired about his broken leg and autographed his cast. Young men asked where he went to school, where he worked. All wanted to know how he knew Bailey. Deek was able to provide endless anecdotal remarks to satisfy the hunger of everyone. When he ran out of facts, he watched Bailey, and his imagination was stirred. He lied eloquently for the cause.

At four o'clock a television news crew arrived at the corner. They photographed the crowd, then Bailey walking. Then they photographed the tent, and only when the shooting was well along did a newsman approach Bailey for an interview. Bailey stood in front of the tent and answered readily, but with weariness in his tone.

"Our viewers are curious what you're doing, Mr. Bailey."

"I'm walking up and down here."

"Why, may we ask?"

"Because they won't let me sit still."

"Who won't?"

"The guards, the police, the law, the American concept of success, the power, the glory."

"I'd like to get a bit more specific. Are you on a hunger strike right this minute?"

"I haven't eaten in about sixty-eight hours."

"Would you say this constituted a hunger strike?"

"Not worth mentioning yet. I'm just a hungry striker at this point."

"Do you plan to eat today or tomorrow?"

"Probably not."

"What would make you eat?"

"I suppose if I got really hungry."

"Guild spokesmen say what you're doing has nothing whatever to do with the Guild strike."

"I'd say it's got something to do with it."

"How long do you plan to hold out here?"

"Until it stops serving a purpose."

"What purpose is that?"

"Hard to say. Subliminal, actually. But also it's in a useful tradition. Preserves the mood while we wait for insight."

"Into what?"

"The purpose of the strike."

"Now, as I get this, you're striking to find out why you're striking. Is that it?"

"More or less."

"Do you expect any outside support?"

"I have three friends who spend time with me."

"Is that all?"

"I think it's rather a lot."

"But can you really hope to change the course of events with this kind of approach?"

"Change the course of events? Not likely. And I think something's gone wrong with this interview."

"Wrong?"

"It's flat. Would you mind starting over?"

"The same questions, you mean?"

"Precisely."

"This is very odd. But would you, again, tell our viewers what you're doing here?"

"In terms of the Chinese autograph?"

"Chinese autograph?"

"Or about going over the hill to blueberry? Or under the bridge to greenswill?"

"Are you trying to confuse our viewers, Mr. Bailey?"

"Bullfighters and portrait painters confuse one another with similar names. Everybody bakes pretty calico muffins neatly, or breaks up the sidewalk, depending on whether or not they can work the oven."

"Mr. Bailey, ladies and gentlemen, is now uttering nonsense as we interrogate him here."

"Touching the piano keys," Bailey said, smiling at the camera, "the snorer gorged himself on gorgon juice and sweet williams from under the window seed. Gorgon porgon. Friend to all the world. Sweet violence. Sweeter than all neuroses. And everybody in the pool together crying oil, mud, slime, shit and grease."

"Thank you, Mr. Bailey."

Bailey stepped off the trolley at the corner where emaciated emissaries would take him to see Alderman Terence MacSwiney, Lord Mayor of Cork. They led him through deserted streets, into the subway entrance and across wobbly boards that spanned the platforms on either side of the long-unused tracks. MacSwiney, his stomach wide between his thighs, sat in a high-backed chair wearing a felt skullcap that l..d been cut into a kind of crown. He munched apples and cheese, popped chocolate candies into his mouth and drank stout drawn from a monstrous barrel by a short assistant in green elf shoes, a refinement Bailey found excessive.

"Nothing I can do," Bailey began, "can have even the slightest meaning compared to your great deed."

Bailey felt stupid complimenting the man. It was evident he neither needed nor desired the admiration of others.

"What I mean to say," Bailey went on, "is that by comparison to you I'm a cheap pretender." MacSwiney gave no notice that Bailey was in his presence. He continued to munch and drink.

"I am utterly without purpose," Bailey continued. "Nothing can give clear meaning to the acts I perform, and yet the absence of a cause doesn't stop me."

"Slainte," said MacSwiney, and he took a long draught.

"Thank you, sir. But saints shouldn't toast mortals any more than mortals should worship saints. I think mutual respect is the proper condition. But I do appreciate your toast and hope you enjoy my admiration."

"Are you out for seventy-five days to beat my record?"

"Not at all. I have no wish to die for the cause."

"Then either the cause is unworthy or you are."

"I've always suspected both."

"You're just one of those play actors," MacSwiney said.

"Possibly. But I feel I'd act truly, given the chance."

"How would you act truly?"

"I can't begin to say. But I have faith I'll recognize the opportunity when it arises."

"My advice to you, young man," MacSwiney said, moving backward through the concrete wall with barrel and elf, "is very simple. Try very hard to . . ."

The weather turned cold on the fourth day and Bailey wrapped himself in a blanket as he walked. Stanley, wearing derby hat and Chesterfield overcoat with a yellow rose pinned to the lapel, arrived during the noon hour, flanked by guards and followed by newsmen and photographers. Stanley carried a small box under his arm, which he took in both hands as he greeted Bailey.

"I bring you a little luncheon music," Stanley said.

"You're more than kind," said Bailey.

Stanley lifted the lid on the box and chimelike music played. Bailey recognized the strains of "My time is your time, your time is my time . . ." The newsmen smiled and Bailey knew a reaction was expected of him. Without it, Stanley would win the skirmish through irony alone.

"I'm not a difficult man," Stanley said. "I want you to know you're perfectly welcome to keep your tent pitched on company property until Saturday at six P.M., the hour of my party. You've received an invitation, I trust."

"No," said Bailey. "But then I haven't been getting mail here."

"I'll be disappointed if you don't come," said Stanley. "Also if my guards have to tear down your tent. I hate to be disagreeable."

Bailey listened solemnly. Slowly he saddened. The corners of his mouth turned down. His eyes squinted. His lips parted in a bawl. He fell to his knees, grabbed Stanley's hand and clasped it in his own. He looked up imploringly.

"Please, Massuh Stanley, don' hurt this chile no mo'."

Photographers snapped the scene wildly. As guards pulled him off Stanley, Bailey leaped up and in a deep-throated, Jolsonesque voice he sang, gesticulating with all the melodrama of minstrelsy:

They always, always pick on me,
They never, ever let me be,
I'm so very lonesome, awfully sad,
It's a long time since I've been glad,
But I know what I'll do by and by,
I'll eat some worms and then I'll die,
And when I'm gone you wait and see,
They'll all be sorry that they picked on me.

He finished on bended knee, then leaped around like a crazed gorilla, scratching himself under the armpits with loose-jointed arms, hopping on both feet, then rocking on one foot, then the other, ape fashion, his jaw thrust into a prognathous, simian gape. He made ape sounds for the newsmen:

"Ugga ugga ooga ugga, eee-eee-eee." The photographers climbed over one another to record Bailey's performance, which had drawn the largest crowd of the strike to the periphery of his tent area. Finished, Bailey reassumed his solemnity. He picked his blanket up from where he'd thrown it and wrapped it around his shoulders.

"Stanley," he said, "I can't tell you what a continuing inspiration you are to me." He walked through the crowd to the corner. By the time he returned, Stanley, the guards and the newsmen were gone.

Stanley permitted no news of the confrontation to appear in the company newspaper. But competing papers printed pictures and amusing texts, and the TV news shows all showed Bailey's song and dance to their viewers. One effect was unexpected. By mid-evening, four ex-Guildsmen who had dropped out of the strike months before had formed a small picket line against the company, across the street from Bailey's tent.

By noon of the next day the picket line numbered ten. Bailey knew them all, not all personal friends of the past, but all reasonable, commonsense men who had left the Guild fight for survival reasons. Eight of the ten had gone on to other jobs, but two still worked for the company, and their jobs would either terminate or be jeopardized by this action. Bailey shook hands with all the men. They congratulated him. The two admitted their time with the company was about over anyway and that they were acting out of shame for early defection. One already had a new job lined up.

A disc jockey took up Bailey's fight, and his teen-age listeners gathered at the corner after school to cheer a hero. They sang high-school and college anthems and rock tunes to keep their own interest high. A peanut vendor set up shop in his pushcart on the corner and on his second day sold hastily and crudely painted Bailey Balloons on the side. Television and radio stations touched on hour-to-hour developments. The teen-agers sang a chant: "Bailey's Hungry," which as Bailey listened to it took on the properties of a foreign phrase. He heard it as Bale Esungri, Bay Lesungri, Bailee Sungree. As the young people chanted, Bailey began to twitch his arm and leg muscles to their rhythm. Soon he forgot his hunger; and twitching at full speed to the now mystical phrase, he relished the tempo and the ambiguity of what seemed to be his deepest truth.

The sixth day turned furiously cold. The weatherman predicted subzero weather for the evening. Bailey had weakened, the turning point being his song and dance, which sapped his reserve strength. He walked less, especially as it grew colder, and spent more time lying down in the tent. It was the last day he would have the tent, and he faced the impossible problem of surviving outdoor in killing weather, without food, without shelter and in a seriously weakened condition. It seemed incredible to him, as he fought the pains in his stomach, that MacSwiney had lived for seventy-four days without food, even if the British did put glucose in his water without his knowledge. It seemed incredible that professional hunger strikers fasted even forty days and forty nights.

As it began to snow Bailey saw Smith arriving and he equated the two. Walking with Smith were the two men in fedoras whom Bailey remembered from the hospital: Clubber Reilly and Fats Morelli, whose father came to America from Naples with two barrels of olive oil. They moved among the pickets, staring at each man on the line. Smith wore total black: a peaked cap, like a gas-station attendant might wear, black boots, black turtleneck sweater, tight-fitting black hip-length jacket, black gloves, dark glasses and still in his ear, the gold earring.

"Worms," Smith said from the curbstone, where he stood watching Reilly and Morelli moving among the pickets. "Nothing but worms."

The henchmen grunted and laughed.

"A can of worms," Morelli said.

"A bag of worms," said Reilly.

"Worms on parade," Smith said.

Reilly bumped a picket off the sidewalk. Then Morelli did the same. The picketers resumed their place, ignoring the assaults. From across the street Deek, sitting watch with Bailey, heard Smith's voice and recognized it. Bailey saw the gypsy intrusion but kept walking, knowing himself incapable of giving physical aid to the picketers. Never in his life had he felt so weak, so helpless. The cold was inside him now, the blanket useless in such temperatures. As he turned to walk back to his tent he saw Smith and henchmen crossing the street toward him. He stopped by Deek's chair, the snow falling heavily, already a white veneer on the street.

"Worms," said Smith. "More worms over here."

"Going out there is no other," Bailey said. "Returning there is no trace. That's an old saying, Smith. Have you considered the possibility of leaving no trace?"

"Don't waste words on that bird," Deek said, and he swung one of his crutches like a scythe, hitting Smith at the back of the knees and sending him to a kneeling position. Deek jabbed the crutch into Smith's stomach, raised it quickly and ripped Smith's lip and nose. Smith fell back, stunned, as Reilly and Morelli moved in on Deek and beat him with blackjack and fists. The corner policeman came running as Bailey grabbed Morelli's throat and threw him into the gutter. The policeman pulled Reilly off the unconscious Deek, whose head was split and bleeding. Smith rose sluggishly, his mouth running with blood. In that instant, conscious that this was total disaster, the collapse of all plans, the ruin of hope, Bailey looked past Smith's shoulder to see the ink truck backing slowly into the driveway.

When Bailey reached the point called Penultimo Trolley, he started walking alone on the boardwalk. He walked past old men whose lips and noses had turned blue from the thinness of the air. He walked past dudes and dappers who tipped the hotdog-stand clerk with twenty-dollar bills. He walked past the cringers, the clever women with sweet hair, the home-grown midgets and the professional nix-nucklers. The board-walk began to climb a hill after that and walking became difficult. Bailey wheezed, tempted by the rollercoaster and the merry-go-round. But he pushed on upgrade past the reviewing stand, where the judges with stopwatches clocked his time. He was faltering badly, he knew. They smiled knowingly as he passed and he caught each of their faint clickings as they drew their mathematical borders around him.

At the famine pound he saw children enter carrying the corpse of a playmate on a crude stretcher made of giraffe leg bones and stitched mouse hide. A janitor of the pound yanked a bawling infant out of the arms of a woman who had sat down on the road and died. The janitor stepped over a bony dead man who stared into the sun, and he placed the infant on a window ledge away from the dogs that ran loose, eating the dead. A child with a huge head, swollen belly and cracked skin spoke to Bailey from beside a fire where his mother was cooking a meal of leaves and bark.

"What is the relationship of art to life?" the child asked.

Bailey's eyes exploded and his blood boiled. His tongue fell into the dust and when he tried to pick it up his fingers separated at every joint. He stood upright and walked forward to meet the imperceptibly advancing black cloud of locusts.

Conscious of more blood, more guilt, of the central core of himself that demanded sacrificial offerings, that conspired against peace, sanity and the sweet beauty of resignation, Bailey ran past the policeman who was handcuffing bodies in the street. He leaped onto the runningboard of the old truck, yanked open the door and stunned the driver with a back-handed chop to the windpipe. He grabbed the key from the ignition switch and took a quick look at the dashboard for dials and switches that would simplify his task; but he understood none of them. Out then, door slammed, keys thrown into vacant lot, he fell to his stomach and rolled under the truck, coming face up to the heavy black rubber hose that ran from the underbelly to the back end of the tank. He reached for it, burning his wrist on the muffler. He pulled the hose and it gave, inches. A foot. He tugged, and it gave another foot. And another. Hands scrambled after his clothing, trying to pull him. He kicked at them and pulled furiously at the hose, which gave a bit more on its spool. A club struck his left knee. He pulled, raised his right leg into the hose's U-shape now, pressed with all his waning strength. And the hose loosened, end in sight, uncaught from the notch that held it. He grabbed the nozzle, twisted it, saw the ink come: a dribble, then a trickle. A club struck his arm, his right ankle; a hand grabbed his hair and pulled. He fixed his eyes on the end of the hose to see the gushing, then felt himself moving away from it, being pulled backward by the collar of his coat. No gushing came. The trickle became a dribble, then droplets. The hose and the ink had blackened his hands, stained his coat, his trousers, but most of it had fallen onto the ground, onto the new snow in which he had rolled, which he had packed. He wrenched his head sideways for a last glance before the hands had him entirely out from under the truck, and he saw that small puddle of ink breaking already, coursing through the new snow in tiny rivulets toward the gutter, toward the sewer. He gave no resistance then as the guards hauled him to his feet, jammed him against the back of the truck. And as a club rammed deep into his empty belly, as a fist flattened his nose, as he felt himself falling forward, he could not help breaking into a soundless, private, utterly internal but inescapably joyous giggle.

EXTRA!

ROWDY IS OUSTED AS LAST TROLLEY GOES CLANG, CLANG

AND THE BOON IS ON THE SPOON

If he says, What's going on? and you say, How do you mean? Where? And he says, Why, all over. Then tell him, Sam, I want you to know I don't know any more about it than you do. By God, Sam, I know less. Believe me, if you mean the trouble, if you mean people with money and others without and people with time and others without and others with good liquor and others without and others with fine places to sleep and others without, believe me I don't understand it. If you mean, even, one man and one woman, together, married or not married or in love or not in love, let me apologize. If I've given the impression that I'm one who knows or one who would be apt to know, I didn't mean to. I don't know. I can't make head or tail of it.

—WILLIAM SAROYAN
"For My Part I'll Smoke a Good Ten Cent Cigar"

Having reached an end to noxiousness, Bailey raised his head above the unconscious level. Success sat on his chest, a female dwarf with button ears. He felt more pain. Always pain. They always, always pick on me. He thought of Deek's bloodied head. They always, always pick on Deek. Smith's bloodied face. Smith had his bad days too. Irma nowhere in the room. Blue room. Blue for boys. Surrounded by old elegance. A moneyed nook. It's all over now Baby Blue. Ah, true, Baby Blue, ah, true. There is an ending to endings also, a climax to climaxes. If he sat up, something else would begin. A new adventure? A dream? His head ached even as he budged it. But he must move on, mustn't he? All that is human, said Gibbon, must retrograde if it does not advance. Good advice. But, said Aesop, never trust the advice of a man in difficulties. In that case, Bailey wondered, should I continue to listen to myself?

Rosenthal found his wife, Shirley, sitting in the bathroom on the side of their cracked bathtub, naked but dry, the tub filled up to the crack with clean water. "I love a hot bath," Shirley told her husband. He put his fingers in the water and found it cold. When he told her he was going to the party she slid into the tub and soaped her elbows and knees. When Rosenthal turned on the hot water for her she cried. To calm her he said he would take her to the party.

Irma spent an hour calling hospitals, the police, besieging guards, company operators, invoking saints, virgins, ethics, mystical holiness, common decency and human tears for a scrap of information leading to the whereabouts of the victim, the principal, the umbilical connection, the vaginal scream suppressor, the hero, the giant, the maniacal moloch of love.

Stanley, having lent digital aid to Miss Blue in her needful moment, washed his hands to the wrist line, dried them on a pink towel embroidered with rosebuds in the shape of an *S*, clipped a white carnation from an arrangement beneath the mirror next to his bedroom door and pinned it to his lapel. He huffed up his chest, shrugged up his shoulderpads, glanced back at the momentarily spent Blue sadness and descended to inquire about the food, the wine.

By request of Stanley, Clubber Reilly approached the party, driving his five-year-old Volkswagen, still chagrined by the three hours spent in jail and by the need for having bail posted by a company attorney whose disapproval of the case could not have been more obvious, and wondering: Wasn't it my duty to break that punk's head?

Fats Morelli, sitting beside Reilly, bailed simultaneously by the unsmiling barrister, touched his throat where Bailey's fingers had pressed, winced at the swollen, sensitive flesh, considered the kind of revenge he would take on his clownish attacker. But wondering then whether a man starved for six days and still so powerful could be easily taken, Morelli began thinking in terms of a two-man revenge squad.

Miss Bohen, standing before her mirror, slipped into her best black dress, a solemn number with a tiny, lacy collar. The dress fell over her pipelike body like a cover on a birdcage. She powdered her face, dabbed pale rouge on her protruding cheekbones, added a false bun to her thinning, coal-black hair, screwed into her earlobes the cultured-pearl earrings purchased for her at Bloomingdale's in 1939 by her third cousin from Elmira whom she met in New York for purposes of visiting the World's Fair and which also proved to be the only assignation she ever had, dabbed perfume behind her ears and on the front of her dress at the approximate spot where her breasts, had she any, would have come together, stepped one step back from the mirror and smiled.

Deek was shaken awake, opened his eyes to see a nurse, a pretty vision, telling him he must stay awake, not lapse into a coma, that he must be observed for twelve hours since he might have a brain concussion. But he grew immediately restive, thinking of the action, of Bailey in action, of the action-packed challenge of Stanley. Rest? Immobility? Peace? Time enough for that in decrepitude. He smiled at the pretty vision. He looked around the elegant room. Yellow room. Door there. Antique chair in antique corner. Antique etchings in antique frames. Antique linen on antique bed. He breathed old air, connived how to leap out of the past and into the pretty present. "What time does the party start?" he asked. "Sssshhhhh," said the pretty nurse.

Three scabs who since the strike began had risen to positions as editors, all in company with their wives, all in formal dinner clothes, backed out of a suburban garage. The suburban news editor was driving. As he backed into the street he ran over a suburban cat.

Popkin, his long face contoured with crags and fjords, sat on his rented rowing machine in his hotel room, trying to gauge the precise time from his wristwatch without interrupting his rowing, his fixed regimen: four hundred strokes, plus, today, ten, adding slowly to his muscles. Soon to be five hundred, then seven hundred, then with a gross chest and pulsating biceps, a strutting figure, an attraction. Personal magnetism lies in your desire to improve yourself. Shed ten years from your life. Add six inches to your chest expansion in three months. Lose your paunch. Popkin would eat no bread, no potatoes, should they be served at the party.

Smith, if he sat up quickly or jarred his head, would bleed again from the nose, and so he lay very still on his cot in his room over Stanley's garage, disturbed not so much over his injury, his lost blood, his ignominious flattening by a man on crutches, but by what the flattening, plus the failure to disrupt the picket line (grown to fifteen following the intrusion) would mean to his new and compelling aspiration: to become personal bodyguard to Stanley. Smith saw Stanley as chief buttress against the wave of evil that was sweeping the city, its people, its churches, its movies, its birds. Inured to ordinary fear, Smith found this anxiety strange, and profoundly disturbing.

Stephanie wondered what it was a man like Stanley saw in a girl like herself. She was surprised when Smith told her Stanley wanted her at the party and she decided he must like swarthy women. She'd heard of his many mistresses. She put on her lowest-cut blouse, debated whether to wear underwear, decided she would, rather than appear too forward.

The publisher, the assistant publisher, the general manager, the advertising manager, the circulation manager and the chief bookkeeper, knowing the opinion their wives had of Stanley's parties, sent regrets that they could not attend his gala evening. One pleaded illness, four previous engagements, the sixth excessive weekend work. All the executives placed great faith in Stanley's capabilities, his handling of the long strike having established for them the depth of his understanding of social complexities.

The phone call from Miss Blue did for the captain what no amount of withdrawal, self-pity or cheering talk by others could do: It got him out of bed. Miss Blue conveyed Stanley's good wishes for the captain's health, prosperity and long life, extended an invitation to the party, and announced that as an animal lover himself, Stanley hoped the captain would accept the gift of a six-week-old cat, since Stanley understood that the captain's cat had recently passed away. Paid such attention by strangers, the old man found the invitation irresistible. His sister Rose refused to go, explaining: "The next time I leave this house it's feet first." Her grisly outlook cheered the captain, who felt youthful by comparison. As he dressed he tried to recall his last social engagement.

Jarvis considered his future, should the strike truly be over. He could not go back to the company, having once sent out feelers and discovered that he wasn't wanted, not even as a defector. Popkin said there were no openings in the super-structure of the Guild, but he promised to get Jarvis a job. Popkin sounded sincere, but Jarvis grew pervasively sad. He could weep for the absence of justice in life. A man who worked as hard as he'd worked. And when he thought of the party he thought of having to face Bailey. And Rosenthal. And Irma. Not to mention Stanley, whom he feared, and Popkin, who merely by being neat and organized intimidated Jarvis. Popkin even scared Jarvis' dog.

Deek's nurse sat by his bed, holding his hand away from her leg, which it kept stroking at the smooth underside of her white-stockinged knee. Had he not had a probable concussion, had his illness been more external, less vital, she would have been less restrained, for the patient was virile and attractive. To pass the time she played hand games with Deek and told him hospital stories. Her first story was about the man who bled to death on the operating table. Then she told him about the man with pus in his eye and how he'd waited too long to treat it and by that time there was no point in operating. Also she mentioned the night everybody forgot to give a patient anesthesia when he was operated on for throat cancer. "We all talked about it," the nurse said.

The television commentator who had interviewed Bailey completed his broadcast on the show-cause order that had been handed to the pickets in front of the company. The order

cited each picket by name and ordered him to appear in
Supreme Court the next morning to show cause why he should
not be enjoined from picketing in light of the agreement between company and Guild which ended all known disputes
the company had with any formally organized or ad hoc
group known to exist in the city, state or nation. The pickets
were told the order would be dropped should they disperse,
which they did. And when the commentator left the studio
to cover the strike-settling party at Stanley's house, he felt
his workday was at an end and that what happened on this
festive night would happen for good or ill and not as news;
for, after all, the central figure in the strike was Bailey, who
was probably certifiably mad. And Bailey's madness had been
neutralized, his news story consummated, and further cover-
age better left to historians or Sunday-supplement specialists.

Miss Blue, alone on the bed, felt the fire being kindled deep
in her pubic hearth. Less than half an hour had passed
since last it had been smothered. She was weary of smothering
it herself. She tried to put the fire out of her mind. She thought
of her mother. She always got her letters back from her
mother, unopened. And her birthday gift to her mother, a
year's supply of depilatory, had been refused only yesterday.
So earlier in the day she had battered down her pride and
called her mother on the phone. "You don't do anything right
anymore," her mother told her. "You don't seem to have any
feelings, carrying on with that old man, making a spectacle of
yourself." Downstairs the guests were beginning to arrive.
Miss Blue's hand moved toward her natural center.

Grace Bailey was met at the railroad station by a company
guard who drove Stanley's private limousine. She had come
back because Stanley said he would pay her two hundred
dollars if she did, and had wired her fifty as a token of good
faith. But also she leaped at the chance to show Bailey that
she had finally caught his stupid pooka. She held a small,

plastic-topped animal carrier on her lap as the car moved through traffic.

Three junior executives from the advertising, circulation and business departments, with their wives, were the first to arrive. Stanley embraced all the women and patted them on the lower portion of the small of their backs. He shook hands with one of the men and told him his fly was open, "which augurs well for our party," Stanley added. He then hugged the other two juniors simultaneously, one arm around the waist of each. The affection embarrassed the young men, though they did not protest, for Stanley was their senior and it would have been unseemly to even hint that he could not do precisely as he chose. It was their first party at Stanley's house.

Irma arrived breathless, fearing the worst. She brushed past the guard at the door and walked to the living room, where Stanley stood amid the gathering throng: the young executives and scabs, Popkin at Grace's elbow, Smith by himself in a Louis Quinze chaise lounge. Irma, with cheeks reddened by cold and panic, still in her coat and hat, barked at Stanley: "Is he here?"

"Haven't you been able to find him?" Stanley said quietly.

"Is he here or isn't he?"

"You're very upset."

"Never mind me. Where's Bailey?"

"The last I heard he was upstairs sleeping."

"Oh, Jesus," she said, wheezing. The frenzy left her. She sat on a sofa and took off her hat. When she eventually looked around the room at the people, she was instantly bored. She was cooling but emptying. Now that Bailey was found she could think again of her own condition. The strike was over, all purpose gone from her days. She could devote herself to Bailey, and would, gladly, lovingly. But what would Bailey do? More than ever before, his purpose was voided. When she heard about his attack on the ink truck she understood his hunger strike. Did he understand it himself? She wasn't sure. He was so honest with himself that he thought secondary motives were as golden as primary. That was why he brought all his strength to whatever he did. Oh, Bailey, you dumb bunny. Not every venture deserves your whole bleeding heart.

Irma began to weep for half a dozen reasons.

Bailey knew the strike was not quite over, that Stanley had something in mind besides magnanimity and sociality. Stanley possessed a heightened sense of irony and it was this that Bailey expected to see him exercise by means of the party. Having endured an agonizing week, Bailey had small concern for ironic development. Irony was a fetching but effete weapon. Given the nature of most enemies, Bailey felt irony suffered by comparison to the chain mace.

Stanley knocked and entered the room where his guards had carried the unconscious Bailey.

"Time to get up and join the party," Stanley said.

Bailey only looked at him.

"Are you able to sit up and take nourishment, or has your stomach shriveled?"

"I already ate four knuckles and a billy club."

"Yes, I regret that. But then the guards couldn't leave you there under that truck, could they? You do bring out the worst in my guards."

"You've got your cordial manner on. Is this party for real?"

"It's been in preparation all week."

"You won't club me when I step out the door?"

"Tut-tut, Bailey. Do you take me for a barbarian? To do that in my own home?"

"I wouldn't be surprised if your home turned out to be a Nazi rocket base."

"Crude skeptics, all you newspaper people. Come along now, the lady wants to see you. Your friend Irma."

"Irma."

Stanley smiled like a congenial old grandpap. Bailey, comfortable in bed for the first time in a week, warm for the first time in a week, tried to resist being reciprocally pleasant. But strength was lacking. And need. The strike was lost, the hunger strike over, the ink truck assaulted and its contents indelibly on his hands. What jot or tittle might a joust with Stanley add to the events? He breathed easily and returned Stanley's smile.

"Send her up."

Stanley backed out, gently closed the door.

Irma fell on the bed, threw her arm over Bailey's chest and kissed him with a wet face.

"I always think you're dead," she said.

"And I never am."

"Isn't that nice? And I'm not dead either."

"We're both not dead."

"I don't know why you're not dead, the things you do."

"The timid mongoose will never liquefy the cobra."

"Never mind with the wisdom."

"Actions improve on speech anyway, wouldn't you say?"

"Yes. I would. Yes. Yes now, and oh! That's a lovely action now. Oh yes, oh my. Lovely. Oh!"

By the time Bailey and Irma came down the stairs, all the guests had arrived. And all noted Bailey's entrance. Rosenthal thought he looked weakened, but still strong. Shirley Rosenthal resented all eyes being turned toward him, always him. Stanley smiled, anticipating the surprises he had in store for Bailey and others. Clubber Reilly appraised Bailey's stature in light of Morelli's attack plan, decided it was not worth all that trouble. Morelli's anger intensified at the sight of Bailey. Miss Bohen wondered how such a trade-union clod like Bailey ever got so much attention. Deek studied the way Bailey carried himself. The scab copy editors grew nervous: One inhaled deeply, one lit a cigarette and one cracked his knuckles. Their wives, seeing Bailey for the first time, picked him apart with their eyes to discover what it was that made their husbands resent him so fiercely. Popkin debated whether to shake hands with Bailey or ignore him. Smith could not understand why Stanley invited the evil maniac to dinner. Stephanie smiled at Bailey, trying to remember who he was. Captain Melvin, having heard of Bailey's hunger strike only in the past fifteen minutes, looked at his nephew with new puzzlement, unable to say why he liked him better than he had ever liked any of his relatives. Jarvis slithered alongside the grandfather clock and peered around it at Bailey through narrowed eyes that would not have to admit that they met his glance, should he look Jarvis' way. Deek's nurse, conditioned to admire Bailey after listening to Deek praise him, found his looks odd but unexceptional, and a little peaked; certainly not what a hero should look like. The TV commentator sensed the tension that Bailey brought into the room and regretted not having his cameraman with him, just in case Bailey's madness should erupt anew. Miss Blue was the first to touch Bailey, shake his hand. Grace Bailey glanced from Bailey to the animal carrier in the corner, fought the impulse to run to it, shove it up in front of his face and laugh until she busted. The three junior executives looked upon Bailey with contempt: One snorted, one sneered and snuffed out a cigarette, and one, after glimpsing Bailey, immediately cast his glance elsewhere lest he somehow be thought to be interested in what Bailey said or did. Their wives, seeing Bailey for the first time, picked him apart with their eyes to discover what it was that made their husbands express such haughty contempt for him. Irma, one step behind Bailey, saw all the eyes upon him, felt like his queen.

Two waiters moved through the crowd with trays of martinis and highballs. A third waiter took orders from those who wanted neither. The guests spilled out of the main parlor into the huge library with its great oak tables, its mullioned windows, its walls lined with the Britannica, with law books and what seemed to be the complete works of every literary figure who wrote books in sets suitable for leather binding. The room had a mustiness about it, an unused eeriness that Bailey sensed despite the prevailing gaiety of the gathering. Nothing on the tables seemed meant for use, or even human touch. Vases were without flowers, magazine racks without magazines. There were no ashtrays.

"Your house has all the warmth of a museum," Bailey told Stanley.

"It's the way Mommy wanted it. I inherited her money on condition everything stay just as it was when she was alive. She felt if I started changing the furniture around that pretty soon I'd buy new stuff. And then I'd forget the things I associate with the old stuff. And her. An inspector comes in every week to measure the distance between chairs and tables. She had the house diagrammed, piece by piece, before she died."

"Won't all the people going around touching things jeopardize your inheritance?"

"I'll straighten up tomorrow."

"You could break a screwy will like that."

"My mother understood love, Bailey. You think I'd go against her last wish?"

"No, I suppose not. Not you."

Irma pulled Bailey away and through the crowd.

"This is obscene, us being here like this, behaving like nothing's happened. Instead of being so damn pleasant, I ought to spit in his eye. And his mother's too if I knew where they buried her."

"Let me remind you," Bailey said. "The cheetah plays Ping-Pong while the mockingbird challenges the clam."

"I never thought of it that way," Irma said.

"Yesterday," a scab wife was saying, "I couldn't get organized all day long. I was just as confused when I went home at night as I was when I got up in the morning. It's a great feeling."

"A cow fell on my cousin," said a junior-executive wife, "and broke twenty-six of his bones, including his collar one."

"Tonight," said a scab editor, "we ran over a cat."

"What did you say?" Captain Melvin asked.

"I said we ran over a cat."

"Did you hurt it?"

"Squished the hell right out of it."

"You sacrilegious rectum rat," the captain said, "you'll regret that foul deed." He leaped on top of the scab and began to choke him. Morelli and Reilly pulled him off.

"Over at the bank," a junior executive said, "they told me they found narcotics in the safe deposit boxes. About once a year they find a fetus."

Miss Bohen edged through the crowd, finally reached Stanley and whispered in his ear: "I was unfaithful to you last night. I dreamed I was ravished by a boa constrictor who belonged to the union." Stanley, without turning, surreptitiously rubbed Miss Bohen's right leg, a stick.

Smith, growing drunk, cast a gesture that encompassed all the books in the library. "There aren't any books in this room that are right," he said. "That picture is wrong. And that one. And that chair. The world is dying. People are sick and rotten. Evil is taking over. Take a look at those plants." Smith took off his shirt.

Grace Bailey broke through the crowd that encircled her, ran to the corner and grabbed the animal carrier. Holding it in front of Bailey, she yanked off its cloth cover and said only: "Hah!" Bailey stared at the carrier, looked inside it.

"What am I supposed to see?"

"You know what you see. Your goddamn pooka."

Bailey looked again, carefully.

"That's not my pooka," he said.

Popkin, holding Shirley Rosenthal's hand, told her how much he thought of her husband, how brave he was, how loyal.

The nurse felt Deek's hand nearing a vital region. She was tempted to stand up from his lap and pull down her skirt, but she resisted the temptation. She told Deek the story of the man who had his mouth and chin removed.

Stephanie leaned forward slightly to give the TV commentator a better view. Clubber Reilly made a muscle for a scab wife. Fats Morelli saw Reilly in action, did the same for an executive wife.

"Hello," Miss Blue said.

"Hello," said Rosenthal.

Jarvis, alone under a bunch of Renoir flowers, wondered which conversation he should try to break into.

Stanley smiled, sensing all was well.

At dinner by candlelight a wave of servants brought endless amounts of food to the table, giving the guests multiple choice. Stanley inspected each dish and then like a train dispatcher, announced it by name: Alexandra Consommé, Caesar Salad,

Oysters à la Rockefeller, Artichokes Knickerbocker, Asparagus à la Pompadour, Roast Capon Alexandre Dumas, Filet of Beef Garibaldi, Turkey Galantine à la Paderewski. "And especially for our hunger striker," he said, "Irish colcannon, O'Brien potatoes, Mulligan hash."

The heat in the room was unnatural. Stanley suggested loosening collars, necklines, taking off shirts. To put the guests at ease, he opened his own shirt down the front. Miss Blue doffed her blouse as people began to sweat perceptibly. A servant unveiled a sixteen-millimeter movie projector as Stanley explained: "A little diversion to help your digestion." Then the servant projected a crude Popeye cartoon. Popeye, en route to woo Olive Oyl, finds her in bed with Wimpy. Disconsolate for a moment, he finally leaps in with them.

"Boop-boop," said Miss Blue as it ended. "Wasn't that knobby?" She took off her skirt. The junior executive beside her took off his tie and shirt. Across the table his piqued wife, next to shirtless Morelli, took off her dress.

A second film was begun, the story of a burglary of a woman's apartment. Two men in masks enter and terrorize the woman at gunpoint. One forces her to disrobe. They ogle her. She tries to charm them, succeeds. They take off their masks, then their trousers. Soon everyone is occupied, partly on, partly off the bed. The woman, who looks Latin, smiles at the camera to show how pleased she is that she was able to charm her intruders, then returns her face to the one who was using it.

Captain Melvin turned away from the film to see Miss Bohen stepping out of her dress. The sight stunned him. When she saw him watching she grabbed his hand.

"Holy piss jars," he said as Miss Bohen flung herself onto his lap.

Other impromptu couples broke away from unfinished meals and began cavorting on sofas and overstuffed chairs. Shirley Rosenthal hit Smith with a wine bottle when he tried to handle her. Stephanie popped out of her blouse, and Jarvis, beside her, fell off his chair. Miss Blue, the first to be naked, her tattoos covered with flesh-colored makeup, turned on the phonograph and twirled about the room in waltz time.

Bailey had eaten nothing. The part of him that had fasted willingly wanted the fast to continue. The food looked and smelled succulent, delicious; temptation for the most discriminating gourmet. Bailey's stomach rumbled as it hadn't rumbled in weeks, juices roiling, the visual turning loose the visceral. Yet he could not make the leap into willful eating. He looked at Irma, at the Rosenthals, who were still at table along with an executive wife, and Stanley. Their eyes were all glazed with a contentment of the body, an obvious numbing of some control center of the brain. Bailey, clearheaded, felt removed from all possibility of abandonment to sensual pleasure. The reveling in food, he felt, was as orgiastic as the frolic on the sacrosanct furniture.

"You're not participating, Bailey," said Stanley. "You're not playing. You're not even eating. I'm disappointed."

"You're a perfect host, don't blame yourself."

Stanley smiled and mopped sweat on his hairless chest with his rose-embroidered napkin. He sniffed the wine, sipped it.

"Your wife seems to be enjoying herself," he said.

Bailey turned to see Grace dancing erotically with Popkin.

"Grace has the capacity for a good time," Bailey said.

"I think the whole thing is disgusting," Shirley Rosenthal said.

"I'm with you," Irma said.

"Likewise," said the executive wife.

Rosenthal stared at the executive wife. When she became conscious of this she stared back.

"Would you care to dance?" Stanley asked Irma.

"Go cut your throat," Irma said.

"Why don't *we* then," he said to Shirley. He stood and

touched her shoulder. "Do the host a favor. Strike's over, you know."

"You're an incredible louse," Shirley told him. But Bailey saw a smile around her lips, waiting to break. Rosenthal touched hands with the executive wife. Bailey saw Irma staring across the room at Deek, who was entwined with the half-dressed nurse. Bailey snapped his fingers, and Irma blinked, looked at him, then went back to looking at Deek.

When Bailey went over to his Uncle Melvin and suggested politely that the old man go home instead of risking a heart attack by such vigorous behavior and was told to mind his own pints and quarts, and when he suggested to Irma that it was impolite for her to sit on the sofa and stare into Deek's eyes as he made love to his nurse, and was ignored, Bailey knew that what was happening had been induced. And since he alone was in possession of his senses, he understood Stanley had drugged the food, or the wine: a little grass, perhaps; or a dash of hash; or some mild acid. And so he knew he could do nothing about it except avoid eating or drinking anything, and thereby avoid putting himself in Stanley's hands. Since both food and drink had probably been modified, he would have no meaningful communication with friend or enemy, for they would eat and drink until they fell, or went home. So he sat alone at the table, watching the interplay of the unshackled. He faulted no one, ugly as it all seemed to him. He felt like a beneficent deity: aloof, perceptive of the nature of frailty. He sensed that he knew at last how ascetics used hunger to induce mystical experience. He looked about the room with a lofty view of the passionate explosion. He listened to the moans of rapture. He closed his eyes, bowed his head, wiped away thoughts as they rushed into his mind, cut off their heads before they could sprout into ideas or visions. He wanted to blanch his brain, let in the whiteness that illuminates, the peace that calms the heart. He felt nearer than ever to the arhat Skin had wanted him to be. He pictured himself as he thought he looked and became aware of his folded arms, crossed ankles.

Priestly crisscrossings.

Sanctimonious son of a bitch.

He uncrossed his ankles, unfolded his arms, opened his eyes, raised his head. He tore a roll in two, a Potato Water Feather Roll, Stanley had announced, and buttered it. He bit into its softness, and his tongue came back to life. He tasted the Alexandra Consommé: tepid but delicious. He tasted the wine: exquisite. Stanley watched with a gloating eye. Bailey raised the glass.

"Up your symbiosis," Bailey said and drained the wine.

Stanley rolled to the floor, laughing, kicking his legs high in glee. Bailey poured more wine, then saw Smith sitting across from him, shirtless, wearing a wig and beard that made him look like Jesus. Bailey ate in silence for a few minutes, occasionally raising his head to see Smith staring at him.

"Jesus is a bald gypsy," Bailey said, and he snatched the wig from Smith and threw it across the room. Stanley laughed in unrestrained whoops. Smith retrieved the wig and sat down again at the table. He picked up a knife.

"You really want to look like Jesus?" Bailey asked.

"None of your business if I do."

"Don't talk like a kid, Smith. If you're going to be Jesus, be Jesus. Don't talk like a kid. Jesus wasn't a kid. Jesus was never a kid. Even when he was a kid he wasn't a kid. And he never needed a knife. Where the hell do you get off making up like Jesus?"

"Bailey," Irma said, sitting down beside him. She said it soothingly.

"He's got no right being Jesus, a bum like him."

"Forget it," Irma said. "Here. Have a Potato Water Feather Roll."

"I already had a Potato Water Feather Roll."

"Have another. Live it up."

"I note you've been living it up, eyeball-wise." He took the roll from her. "Woman," he added, "is often the bread of man."

"Oh boy."

"In the construction of the human sandwich, woman is also generally the butter half. Man, you might say, is the meat."

"Baloney," Irma said.

Through the room there suddenly came the ominous wail of a siren. A police car? A fire engine? An ambulance? A raid? Bailey turned to see the orgy mob righting itself, tucking in its shirts, covering up its viewables. Stanley, heaving his chest in superior mirth, lifted the arm of the record player and the siren stopped. Had Stanley learned from Skin? Vice versa?

"No need to be formal," Stanley said. "But the party must move along. The celebration continues now into the health phase." He swallowed some wine and resettled himself at the head of the table. Slowly the guests drifted back to their places, to the cold food and half-empty glasses, to a Bailey glazed with the flush of nourishment in his blood, alcohol in his brain and Stanley's secret substance attacking the center of his inhibitory structure. Bailey greeted the returnees with heart and spirit, but said nothing.

For some guests the drug was wearing off, and as it did they looked around to see who was looking at them. A scab wife began putting on her dress but halfway through said "The hell with it" and took it off again.

Stanley ordered all wine glasses refilled and then stood to make a toast. "I have noted," he began, "that some of you are more inhibited than others. You there, pretty lady," and he motioned to Shirley Rosenthal with his glass, "are far from the city of joy. You can't participate. How sad. But I have a remedy for such sadness. Dr. Stanley knows the answers. Won't you listen to him? Follow him? Give him your allegiance? Dr. Stanley showed you the beginning, won't you let him show you the rest of the way?"

Bailey had never seen Stanley so serious. He seemed evangelistic, a man in possession of a great truth whose weight compels its revelation to multitudes.

"You are all here tonight," he continued, "because the company's behavior in the strike was directed by a man who understands the need for direct action, who will not shirk from violence when violence is called for, who is not a milksop humanist stricken to immobility by conscience when survival is the order of the day, who is not . . ."

He paused.

"But why, my friends, my guests, my erstwhile opponents, why should you care what I am not? It is what I am, what the company is, what a man like Smith here is, that has made the difference in events. Our mandate is clear, and it would be a simple matter for such overwhelming victors to view the losers as a cargo of outcasts, a battery of rabble. But that would assume, oh so very wrongly, that the company has no heart. But look—here we huddle in the heat of this room, and by now you must have noted that it is growing hotter and hotter, in much the same way the caveman probably huddled beside the fire in times of storm and stress, huddled with strangers or even men he presumed yesterday to be his enemy. Under the human roof there can be no lasting enemies. Reconciliation, my friends, is the order of the day. Love thy neighbor, that is the call of the Christian. Joy to the world, that is the anthem of the Christs of every age. And so I offer you here tonight, my very good friends, an abundance of love, a very mountain of joy from the bottom of the company's enormous heart."

Stanley raised his glass, then drank. All but Bailey, Irma and the Rosenthals drank with him. When everyone was finished toasting, Bailey drank. He was drinking too much and he knew it. The wine was reaching him and Stanley's drug was alienating his body from his mind. Still, he could think clearly, without dizziness, and knew this was all he needed to remain the equal of Stanley.

"You are all suffering," Stanley said, "and I ask you to let me palliate that suffering. You are all afraid, and I ask that you let me give you courage. You are all confused, and I ask that you let me bring clarity to your days. Miss Blue, O lovely dove, will you lead us to the house of health, the high altar of joy? Will you do that for us, Miss Blue?"

"Boop-boop," Miss Blue said with a heavenly smile, and moving away from the table, naked but for her high heels, she opened a door off the dining room and waited for people to follow. Miss Bohen was the first, followed by the captain, then Stephanie and a scab wife and Smith and on and on until all were moving through the door. Stanley's troupe of servants came out of the kitchen, unbuttoning and loosening their clothes as they came, and followed the guests.

"Should we join the healthy ones?" Irma said.

"Either that or admit we can't face it."

"He's up to no good." Her eyes followed Deek and the nurse as they left the table.

"Magic," said Bailey, "is in the hat of the magician," and when he and Irma stood up the table was at last empty.

They moved out of the old house and along a shoveled sidewalk toward a small wooden building standing at the edge of a garden. The heat as they entered the building took away their breath. People were removing more of their clothing as Miss Blue coaxed them into total nudity, the only way, she said, to let the body breathe in such heat. She told them to hang their clothing in an anteroom. In the large central room a stove and hot rocks gave off the intense, dry heat.

"Should we strip?" Irma asked.

"When in Rome."

"I've still got our ace in the hole," she said, and she opened her purse to again let Bailey see the antique pistol.

He smiled but wasn't sure his face moved. He felt paralyzed, though he was not, for he could move his legs, pull himself out of his clothing, hang it on a hook. Yet time seemed at half-speed. That others were as drugged as he became clear when he looked at the naked multitude, their faces stiff with smiles, moving with exaggerated slowness. Stanley stood on an elevated wooden platform that like the floor was slatted for drainage. Beside him an old woman servant in a leather apron, but otherwise unclothed, poured two dipperfuls of water over the rocks, creating new steam. From the rear she seemed other than human to Bailey with her fold after fold of black and purple skin, so stretched that with the flesh gone from under it it hung on her backside and thighs like dead matter.

Stanley told the crowd to sit on the benches and platforms and enjoy their sweat. They could do little else in the unbearable heat. Steam condensed on bodies, people collapsed, gasped for air. Then servants opened two doors and a rush of frigid air, barely cool to the mob, eased the tension and froze each man and woman for an instant into a tableau Bailey suddenly felt the urge to paint: Popkin, hairless, and Morelli, apelike with hair; one of Stanley's maids with only one breast and beside her an Old Mother Hubbard's pair hanging to the waist like overstuffed satchels; a chickenbreasted scab with a long, dangling prong, and an executive's beer-bellied vat with an almost invisible faucet under its great curve; a hump growing out of a gray-haired executive wife's back, and Reilly beside her, standing crookedly, wearing a high shoe on his club foot; Miss Bohen, so thin her shoulderblades took wing; and on other women, freckled bosoms, veins like blue spaghetti, dimpled rears, parted, coiffed and flying pubes. And Stephanie with rouged nipples. Some men had womanly sags to their chests, knobby navels, hairy backs, boils and cultured muscles. Some women had pimples, face-lift scars, stretch marks. And an executive wife wore a lavender-gray merkin. Stanley displayed tattooed foreskin, and blond wives proved out with lampblack crotches. There were women with oiled skin, surgical scars, acne and Man Tan, men with scarlet splotches, warts, wens, moles, birthmarks and blister flakes.

Bailey saw the servants gathering in a semicircle, holding hands. Gradually they moved across the room like a flowering maypole ballet, encircling the vagrant guests, holding them in bounds with smiling faces, silently manipulating the weakened, sweating and drugged crowd into what seemed the beginning of a game. Soon all were inside the semicircle, backed against log walls. A few asked: What's this? What's it all about? But the protest mechanism was fogged by the drug. The servants said nothing. They smiled and gradually began to push until the guests were all in motion, shoulder to shoulder, hip to hip, immobilized like canned things, lubricated by their own sweat, swaying, swaying, back and forth, waves in a bottle.

Bailey looked beside him into the eyes of his wife, whose breasts floated between them, and saw the beginning of terror. Anger at Stanley rose in his throat. As he was about to speak

Grace shrieked hysterically, shriek upon shriek. The shoving increased in force, arms were raised, elbows shoved into ribs. It seemed the beginning of violence and Bailey could only think: all of this erupting out of Stanley's mind, all this a configuration that in an instant would be memorable as nightmare or imagined paroxysm, that lacked logic, reality. But the violence failed from the crowd's weakness. The rage rose into a crescendo of screams and cries, then ebbed into moments of containment, then near silence. The servants smiled, swayed. And in the midst of motion flesh became flesh in a new and primal way, although Bailey guessed that disorders adrift on imagined seas of flesh would anchor themselves in some on this night.

Bailey heard one man cry out "inhuman" and another cry out "beasts" and another plead weakly on behalf of his heart condition. On the platform Miss Blue swayed in time with the tidal motion of the crowd, eyes closed, immersed in ecstatic flood. "Flesh and skin," she cried, "flesh and skin. Stanley makes our joy begin."

Bailey saw the chickenbreasted scab giving all of his attention to the maid with one breast as she leaned against him, part of the servant chain. Bailey looked for other opportunism but found none so flagrant. He saw only heads bobbing on the swamp of flesh. Grace had moved like flotsam back into the depth of the crowd, and Irma came into view little more than an arm's length away yet with half a dozen bodies between them.

"Are you all right?" he called when he caught her eye. She gave him a resigned tilt of the head and raised her purse for him to see. He smiled, his life ever more absurd, ever richer from her antic strength. Irma: ready to shoot somebody, anybody. For what? For love.

Deek came into view, leaning on his nurse and one crutch. Then Rosenthal, arms around Shirley at shoulder level, holding her away from whatever quicksand, yelled to Bailey:

"Don't let go!" The captain, face puzzled but smiling, gave Bailey a wink.

Bailey tried to stand motionless, turning to avoid elbows, hands, hips when he could, giving the steamy surge his side instead of his belly or his back, trying to hold dominion over the spot where his feet touched the hot slats. He held his head aloft, at times on tiptoe, and became conscious of the aloofness that this betrayed: a foolish faith: They cannot reach me if I don't falter. But without dignity, hadn't he already been reached? I shouldn't have let them divest me of that, he thought. He tried to think in glory terms, always an antidote, but could muster nothing that would stay in his mind. Only Stanley stayed, standing on the platform, wearing a pigtail, his skin a brilliant yellow, his eyes Orientally cast: Fu Manchu incarnate, yellow peril reading Oriental warnings to the swaying crowd in incantatory tone:

"I spit in the cottage cheese of your father. I untimely pluck your mother's lotus blossoms. I wet on your aunt's blanket. I color your children's milk. I run your dog through the soil pipe. I befoul your wife with warm fatback. I put borax in your rice bowl, rubber bands in your tobacco, ticks on your cat. I shatter your grandmother's reading spectacles. I glue together the dentures of your sleeping grandfather. But I never hurt you."

Stanley strapped a metal box on his back and came down from the platform wearing a football helmet and padded jock-strap. In his hand he carried a long rod connected by wire to the metal box. When his rod touched a scab wife, who had collapsed on the shoulder of a servant, she straightened and smiled.

"Are you awake my dear?"

"I'm a chaste woman."

"I'm sure you are. And do you prize your chastity?"

"Oh, indeed."

"And is that why you stand before me naked as a fish-worm?"

"I didn't want to be the only one dressed for dinner."

"Excellent plan. But conformity befouls us all. Sweet dreams, madam."

He drew a circle on her stomach with the rod. When complete, the circle fell to the floor. The woman tried frantically to retrieve it but when she bent over, her entrails slipped out. She pushed them back in with her hand, tried to pick up her stomach with her toes. As it slithered out of her grasp a fox terrier ran off with it.

Stanley moved along to Popkin, touched his hairless chest with the rod, which Bailey now understood to be a cattle prod. Popkin shivered and smiled.

"Had any trouble at home?" Stanley asked.

"Once," said Popkin.

"Tell us about it."

"I found my wife in bed with a fellow with a lot of hair."

"What did you do?"

"I got horny."

"Wonderful," Stanley said. He stung Popkin's chest a dozen times with the device and long yellow hairs sprouted. Amazed, Popkin pleaded for more. Stanley touched him again and again and more hair sprouted like cornsilk. In seconds it had grown a foot. Stephanie, beside him, began to braid it as Stanley moved on to Clubber Reilly and Fats Morelli. He touched Reilly, who yelped; then Morelli, who squealed.

"Will you give two quarts of blood to the company?" Stanley asked Reilly.

"If I give two quarts I'll die."

"That's not the point. Will you give or won't you?"

"I'd like to a lot, but I don't think so."

"A conciliatory answer, said Stanley. "And you, Morelli, will you donate one of your testicles to our Ball Bank?"

"Not me. I need all my strength."

"Another understandable refusal. But, gentlemen, your answers are without magic. Step out please."

"We can't move."

"Squeeze downward and crawl between the legs."

The men obeyed Stanley. When they emerged on hands and knees a servant tied them together with rope. Stanley chased them up the stairs to the platform, touching their nakedness with the prod to keep them moving. Once up, two more servants grabbed them and threw them on top of the hot stones, where they exploded with faint pops like penny firecrackers. Bailey croaked a protest, but none came.

He heard Grace shriek again, then saw her slither up from the mob like a worm of toothpaste and crawl, kick and scratch her way across the heads of the crowd, clutching at hair and shoulders, gouging flesh with her nails and drawing blood, swimming on a sea of bodies. Almost to the edge of the mob she went limp. Stanley drew the prod along her thigh and levitated her. She floated outward at the tip of the prod; then when Stanley withdrew it she fell to the floor. Stanley laughed. Bailey craned to see Grace but saw only a thousand fragments, like the dusty clay of a shattered Etruscan wine jar.

Stanley stepped over it and touched Smith on the forehead, stunning him like a cow struck with a sledgehammer. "Now here," he said, "is a fellow with a center. He makes no pretense at morality or love. He is the tyrant supreme, from crib to coffin, the total self. And here is a man," he said, turning to Bailey and jabbing Bailey's stomach with the prod (Bailey felt the hand of omnipotence punch him in the solar plexus; breath left him; he was puny), "whose cry is death before dishonor. And yet he has committed arson, he has stolen, lied, calumniated me and my associates, abandoned his wife, committed violence on strangers who sought only to work for their daily bread. Who knows what other black deeds he can claim? I find them incompatible, these two men, this disciple of enlightened self-interest and this pawn of private grace. Let gladiatorial combat engage them. What say you?"

The mob sent up a cheer and thumbed-up Stanley's idea.

His prod curled around Bailey's neck, drew him out of the crowd magnetically, then lifted Smith out the same way. Smith smiled and said hello to Bailey. Bailey's hostility toward him fled and he tried to return the smile but could not; then was glad he could not. Glopping it up again, Bailey. The loser's pattern again, Bailey: that all-embracing allegiance to anybody who gives the proper signal. Victim of the open mind again, Bailey: When all things matter, nothing matters and single goals go awash in a sargasso of weed, muck and clutter. Here was the handle that made him usable, like the bathroom plunger that is dipped in and out of corruption or stands at dry attention in a corner until the works clog and further use is called for. Utilitarian Bailey. Enough corruption now, Bailey.

"I can see," said Stanley, "that these sluggards need a little push."

He tore off his pigtail and football helmet and pulled on a wolf's head, then ran howling up the platform stairs. He rose to the ceiling like a helium balloon and from there uttered soft wolf curses that could not be understood but whose meaning could not be misread. Smith looked up at Stanley and smiled, enjoying the curses. Bailey touched Smith's shoulder, and as he turned, Bailey swung, his fist a bag of feathers grazing Smith's chin, a wet sponge. Smith's smile faded, and he moved with slow, dancing movements toward Bailey. Bailey threw a left, and the horseshoe in the feathers clipped Smith's wooden chin. Crack, went the punch, and Bailey followed through, ending like a southpaw pitcher after the pitch. He fell forward in a slow-motion skydive and skidded along the floor into Irma's lovely leg. Sliding home. He could hear hallways of laughter, stomping and whistling on the roof. All the world was light and cool and the thing he had hit was gone and forgotten and only Irma was in his eye, his life. He touched her skin and laughed. He righted himself. For agelong minutes he sat and saw nothing but Irma, knowing neither where he was nor where he'd been. He heard Stanley's voice, saw him with lute in hand sitting on the platform, singing. "An old Elizabethan lyric my Mommy taught me," he explained. And he sang: "Keep the rabble randy and they'll never ask for candy . . ." When he finished he spoke to the crowd in oratorical tone: " . . . lonely souls who need contact . . . who die thirsting for the touch of a kind hand on their secret parts . . . false substitutes for joy . . . joy worship aroused in your groins . . . spell of togetherness . . . washed away shame . . . joy will roll the wheels over your filthy enemy . . . horrid blackness of your old fears . . . no such thing as filth . . . no such thing as evil . . . glory be to joy!"

Then Bailey passed into a valley of wider consciousness, heard Stanley again talking, but mockingly now. He saw Stanley standing over the supine Smith with prod pointed at Smith's belly.

". . . because you told me to wear it," Smith was saying.

"How could a mere man like me tell Jesus what to do? How could Jesus let somebody knock him down?"

"Quit saying I'm Jesus," Smith said. "I'm an American."

Stanley touched him with the prod. Smith squealed and wriggled backward, was shocked flat, wriggled again, was shocked again.

"Tell us, Mr. Jesus, how do you like your joy?"

But Smith couldn't talk. His mouth lay open, his eyes globes of animal terror. As he began to lose control of his bladder Stanley pressed the prod against his crotch. Smith slithered helplessly away, leaving a trail of water. It was then that Bailey grabbed Irma's pistol. Fully conscious, as he heard the first scream, that he was dooming Irma as well as himself, he squeezed the trigger.

When all else fails there is always another failure. As the hammer snapped, the ancient pistol exploded in Bailey's hand, destroying only the mood, shocking his bones and searing his flesh. Guards leaped on him and in minutes he, Irma and Smith were dragged to the front door and thrown into the frigid night. Some moments later their clothes came cascading after them. Still aflame from the hellish heat of the room, they scarcely felt the cold. They dressed on the steps under the light of the entranceway, Smith still in his wig and beard. He tagged along as Bailey and Irma walked through the parking lot.

"Give a fellow a lift?" he asked.

"Delighted," Bailey said. But then he remembered he had no car. He held Irma's arm and they walked toward the trolley stop.

"Why did you change your name, Smith?" Bailey asked. "Do you always sell out to the highest bidder?"

"Do you like girls or just girls' mattresses?" Irma asked him. But Smith gave no answer until they had all boarded the trolley.

"I'm all alone," he said. He explained he couldn't control the other gypsies after he'd yielded to Stanley in the barn. Stephanie went off with Skin and never came back, and then one night while Smith was out of the trailer, Mr. Joe, Tonya and Pito drove off and left him.

"I had to put all my trust in Stanley," Smith said with some bitterness in his eyes.

Bailey studied the little man, whose head was again bald. The wig pocketed? Perhaps. Bailey wondered how he could ever have felt that this sad little man was totally evil. Smith began to make small, sobby noises.

"Don't feel bad," Bailey told him. "You've just ruined your gypsy talent, that's all. You're corrupt, not evil."

"I don't know how to get along with people," Smith said.

He slid to the floor, drawing the attention of the motorman, whose hat, Bailey noticed, looked oddly like a Pilgrim bonnet. "Is he drunk?" the motorman asked. "No drunks allowed in the New World."

"He's just corrupt," Bailey said.

"We need that type," said the motorman.

Bailey picked Smith up and set him straight in the seat. Smith recalled for them how he'd lived in a secret room behind a coal bin for eight years to avoid the draft during and after World War Two. Putzina cared for him, and Stephanie, his cousin, soothed him sexually. A rat bite infected him, and he lost his hair. The darkness weakened his sight so that he assumed the Army would reject him. Putzina took him to the draft board when he at last came up into the world, and the examiners rejected him as unfit, even before the eye test.

"I could've done that years before," he said.

"You've had an ugly life," Bailey said. "I'm sorry for you."

"Misericordia," Smith said, and then, smiling ecstatically, he wet his pants.

The motorman saw this and left his throttle. He booted Smith and sent him sprawling. Bailey took advantage of the moment, grabbed Irma's hand, and together they leaped off the moving trolley and ran home through the tall grass in slow motion.

Bailey's room and a half seemed cell-like as a prospect, so they went to Irma's apartment and fell on Francie's bed in weary sleep. The doorbell wakened him, but not Irma. Two men dressed in black, with white shirts and four-in-hand black ties, stood at the door smiling at him.

"We're looking for a room," one said, a man with a round, open face. He looked like a coin to Bailey.

"Did you ask the superintendent?"

They both nodded and smiled.

"What did he tell you?"

"He said there weren't any."

"That sounds conclusive as hell."

They said nothing, merely smiled.

"Try the apartment house across the street," Bailey said.

They smiled but didn't move. Their hats sat straight on their heads. It was obvious to Bailey they didn't know how to wear hats. He waited for them to react to his suggestion. They only smiled.

"I'm Elder Wimple," said the coin-faced man. "And this is Elder Biscomb."

Bailey smiled. His turn.

"Do you know anything about the Mormon religion?"

"Not much," Bailey said, unable to concentrate on anything but his overwhelming desire to sleep.

Elder Wimple took a book from his coat, the Book of Mormon, he explained, translated from golden plates by Joseph Smith. Were they selling it? Well, fifty cents, but that wasn't the point. Mormonism was the point. The elder began reading to Bailey of Jesus, things written a hundred years before Jesus was born, written by a prophet in America who prefigured the miracles, the agonies of Christ.

"I'm not a religious person," Bailey said.

Elder Wimple read on.

"I don't believe in that," Bailey interrupted. "You're wasting your time on me. It sounds nice, but I don't believe in that or anything else. God is strictly possibility with me. Possibility, that's all."

Elder Wimple closed his book, and he and Elder Biscomb smiled at Bailey.

"Remember that we were here and gave the word of Christ, and that you received it," Elder Wimple said. They went down the hall smiling at one another. Bailey fell back into bed thinking: Everybody's in the Jesus game; thinking also: Those two birds don't know anything about hats.

But he could not go back to sleep. The brief nap before the doorbell rang had reawakened his mind, the effects of the party were still with him, and even though his body coursed with untraceable pain, he knew his vital capacity was at flood level. What besieged him was the need for forward motion, the need to obliterate the failed past. Where does Bailey go now? he wondered. Should he go back to the library and reconstitute his solitude, or was solitude akin to a death wish? There had to be prophetic wisdom somewhere in his head. The old books, the old newspaper files had activated some things. He had changed some things. But he needed to change more, be done with passivity. Useless to play into a Stanley. No point. No reward beyond the private building of spiritual muscles. Ascetic self-indulgence. Not even any joy in that. Only ecstasy for the narcissistic soul. But joy is Stanley's word. A man could almost buy Stanley's message unless he knew better. Stanley. Always goes back to Stanley. Forget Stanley. Obliterate Stanley. Leap over Stanley. Disintegrate Stanley. Ah, Bailey, you poor simp. If you could only get some advice. But there were no Bailey specialists, and he always knew it. I have a bad case of fallout, Bailey said to his corner druggist. But while he waited for his prescription to be filled the druggist's skin fell off.

He looked at Irma, still sleeping. He stroked her beautiful hair, gently kissed her ears, her neck. She smiled without waking. He thought of making sleepy love to her, then taking a shower with her. They would wash one another, then eat breakfast slowly and carefully. But he could not bring himself to wake her. It was mid-evening, life all turned around. He got up from bed and called Rosenthal.

"I can't sleep," he said.

"Stanley murdered sleep," Rosenthal said.

"You've been home long?"

"Couple of hours. The party went downhill after you left. You're a bag of tricks."

"What did I do?"

"You hurt Stanley's feelings. He thought he was being a good host. He never expected anybody to shoot him."

"I didn't shoot him."

"Intention counts for something, so he feels like you did. He thought everybody was having fun."

"Wouldn't you say that was an unreal thought?"

"When it was all over, some people said it was a gas. Shirley claims she had a good time."

"How is Grace, and the old man?"

"Grace scratched the hell out of herself. Black eye too. The old man? He's a swinger, that fellow."

"And Deek?"

"He made out nicely. At least twice, I'd say."

"I need a drink. Badly. Can I persuade you?"

"What time is it?"

"Some hours after armageddon, is my best guess."

"It's midnight plus. I can't see the minute hand."

"How about Fobie's in half an hour?"

"As you like it," Rosenthal said.

At Fobie's Bailey bought six beers from the fat bartender, a new man with tight curly hair, saucer eyes and mean nostrils. The purchase reduced Bailey's funds to twenty cents. He carried the beers to a booth, quaffed three swiftly and sipped a fourth as he waited. Rosenthal arrived at last, hung up his cape and hat and sat across from Bailey.

"You know," Bailey told him. "I don't remember whether phylogeny recapitulates ontogeny or whether ontogeny recapitulates phylogeny."

"Well, you're slipping," Rosenthal said.

Bailey pushed a beer at him, but Rosenthal shook his head and pushed it back. He signaled the bartender and asked for a glass of Bristol Cream sherry. Bailey looked up at the bartender when he brought the wine.

"It's phylogeny that recapitulates ontogeny, isn't it?" he asked him.

"Paradigmatically speaking," the barkeep said. Then he laughed one nasty burst. "That's a phrase I picked up tending bar in Cambridge. I save it for jerks."

"Even barmen hate us," Bailey said when the man went away.

"Especially barmen," Rosenthal said.

"It wears you down."

At the bar a drunken scab sportswriter raised his voice to the barkeep, "You syphilitic son of a bitch."

The barkeep's evil nostrils flared as he reached under the bar for a miniature baseball bat and stroked the scab alongside the ear, knocking him off the barstool. Two other scabs lifted him into the booth behind Bailey. Fobie left his owner's high chair at the end of the bar and came over to look at the man.

"He went down like a count," Fobie said.

"He's got a bad mouth," the barkeep said.

"He gets it from his mother," said Fobie.

"He's still out," one scab said.

"Call him an ambulance," Fobie said.

Bailey raised his head over the back of the booth and looked into the drunken man's face.

"You're an ambulance," Bailey said. "You're a scabby fucking ambulance."

"You keep out of it, wise ass," the barkeep said.

"How's that again, Mr. Syphilitic?"

"Punk dog. I'll cool you too."

He came around the bar with the small bat in his grip, and Bailey and Rosenthal stood to greet him. As he lurched toward Bailey, who began to bob and weave like a boxer, but with arms at sides, Rosenthal hit him. The punch lacked force but it staggered the barkeep and he stepped on himself and fell. Bailey put a foot on his wrist and took away his bat.

"You win," he said, looking up from the floor.

"Too easy," Bailey said.

"I can't afford to get kicked. I just paid four hundred bucks for teeth."

Bailey opened the bar door and scaled the bat across to the empty parking lot. He started to come back inside, but Rosenthal had grabbed his clothes and pushed him out onto the sidewalk and up the street.

"I didn't finish my beer," Bailey said.

The bar door opened behind them and the barman stuck his head out. "Come back again sometime, punk dogs." He waved a beer bottle like a club.

"You do make it tough to live in the world," Rosenthal said, pulling Bailey away by the muffler.

They walked through the streets with Bailey talking, streaming out the story of Smith, Stanley, drugs, dust and the sweetness of endings with nothing but freedom beyond them, freedom to do everything or nothing or the same again.

"Ballareebennyohdallydooderrydoy," Bailey yelled into the night. Then he admitted the yell meant nothing at all, only a sound on the Bailey tongue. He was liberated from so many things that now even language seemed new.

When they passed Mahar's flower shop he looked up: "Is it M-a-h-a-r, or is it really M-a-h-e-r, I mean truly. Is it C-o-n-n-a-c-h-t, or is it C-o-n-n-a-u-g-h-t? What's the precise truth? Do you think Jack Kennedy was the American Parnell? And how about the Pope? You think he's as dead as God? A gypsy forged the nails that crucified Christ, did you know that? That's why God hates a whistling woman, because the gypsy's wife whistled while he made the nails, five nails, the sharpest to pierce his lung, but they only used three because another gypsy stole two as an act of mercy, at least that's what the gypsies like to believe. That's why his feet are stuck with only one nail. Gypsies did that; twelfth-century gypsy metalsmiths crossed his feet for the first time to fatten their legend. Amazing that we still talk about it. You can't get away from Christ. He keeps coming back like a song, like a weed, like a flower, like the springtime. Sweet as the flowers in springtime. Sweet Jesus. And how is your dear old mother, whom we all love so much?"

"You're rambling quite a bit," Rosenthal said.

"Oyez, oyez, oyez. The court of oyer and terminer hears that you ramble and determines that you rambled. Didn't he ramble? Ramble? Rambled all around. Up and down the town. Oh, didn't he ramble? Ramble? He rambled till the fuckers cut him down."

"Great tune."

"Swings. Rambled till the fuckers cut him. Fuckers cut him. Fuckers. Cut him. Cut. Him. Down."

"Are you all right, Bailey?"

Bailey smiled at Rosenthal, feeling boundless goodwill toward the man. Partners in failure have a bond unknown to winners. Winners tell funny stories. Losers keep the game going.

"Where we walking to?" Rosenthal said. "It's starting to snow."

"I hadn't noticed," Bailey said. "But you're right. Look at all those little fuckers coming down. Sneaking up. Trying to bury us very quietly. Shhhhhhhhh."

"We'll get inside someplace."

"By the time you figure out where, you're on the way under."

"We'll go to my place," Rosenthal said.

"No. Too depressing."

"Your place."

"No. Irma's sleeping."

"How is Irma's condition?"

"Very suitable. In fact, great. Yes, great, goddamn it. And come to think of it, she's had enough sleep. Where is she when I need her? Call Irma. Get Irma to join us. Irma is a constant, joyous temptation. Tempts me unwittingly, titillatingly, cuneiformly, asteroidally, oral pro nobisly and in other extravesicular ways."

"Call her, then."

"We'll all go to the Guild room. Do you have a key to the new lock?"

"No."

"We'll get in," Bailey said.

They stopped at a grill and bought more beer and wine, and Bailey spent his last dime calling Irma. He told her to meet them at the Guild room. Then he went back and drank his beer and wondered: Did he really make it tough for himself to live in the world? He had never looked at the problem that way. He drank his beer and remembered when his own response, not necessarily in a higher cause, had lost him what he wanted most. So many absurd things happened to himself and others because of his response. Things bloomed or died according to how he behaved. It was unfortunate. He felt he should do some serious worrying about such behavior. But when he thought about it, the cause of it all fanned out into every corner of his being. He could not change everything. He had changed some things, but he could not become a different man. So what if he failed? If he hadn't failed, what would he be today? Nothing but a cheap success. So the hell with it. Bolly it. Bollywolly it. He drank his beer. Bolly the whole bleeding mess. Whatever was wrong, it hadn't killed him. He could still pour in the beer and pump out the syrup.

"Let's get on with it," Bailey said.

He and Rosenthal left the bar and walked through the snow, which was falling in large flakes in a quiet and beautiful way.

When Irma arrived, the Guild-room door was open, the snow blowing in. Bailey and Rosenthal were on the floor in their coats, leaning against the wall, where a row of chairs

had been. The room was empty and dark, the walls stripped
of signs, photos, clippings, notices.

"Look at the door," Rosenthal told her.

"I did. The glass is broken."

"Bailey put his fist through that. I mean look at the notice
tacked to it."

By the light of a streetlamp Irma read a note typed on
International Guild stationery:

To Former Guild Members

This is to advise you that this local of the International
Guild has been permanently dissolved by fiat of the international body. All financial and other support of strikes,
demonstrations, negotiations or other forms of contact
with the former employer by Guildsmen is officially and
irrevocably rescinded. In view of recent developments in-
volving violence, death and costly recriminations, this
decision was taken in the best interests of all concerned.
Those seeking further information on this decision may
contact the undersigned. Guild cards of former members
of this local will be honored, should their holders find
employment in other firms where the Guild is the collective bargainer. Anyone having unfinished business
with this local may consummate it through Mr. D. O.
Jarvis, former Guild local chairman, who after the 15th
of the month will be an assistant superintendent of main-
tenance at the Greyhound Bus Terminal.

(signed) ADAM POPKIN
Third Alternate Delegate

Irma went inside and stood in the middle of the empty
room.

"They took everything," Rosenthal said. "Even my coffee
cup."

"I'm thinking of an aphorism," Bailey said. "It's got something to do with fun. Also the clap."

"How did they do it so fast?"

"I think the company and the Guild were in league for months," Rosenthal said. "It came to me in a dream."

"So there's nothing left." Irma paced up and down shaking her head.

"You walk very like a pooka," Bailey said to her.

"How is that pooka of yours, anyway?" Rosenthal asked.

"Unreliable. I'm trading him in for a winged pig."

"It's so rotten," Irma said. "And sad."

"Instead of an aphorism," Bailey said, "I'm beginning to think in terms of a syllogism."

"Your trouble, Bailey," Rosenthal said, "is that you never know when to be solemn."

"So that's what my trouble is."

"When I was a little girl," Irma said, "I remember being in the front yard when a woman in a lacy nightgown came running down the road. She was barefoot, and when she saw me she stopped and asked if she might pick a flower. I said yes because she was so beautiful, and she broke a yellow rose off the trellis. She held its stem in her hand just as if it didn't have any thorns on it. Then she thanked me and ran on down the street. Somebody was chasing her, I found out later."

"Did they catch her?" Bailey asked.

"Down by the garage. I always felt she died after that."

"That's not how you die," Bailey said. "They never really catch you."

"Oh, glop, Bailey," Irma said.

"I can't stand unhappy endings. Why do you suppose I'm thinking about fun? However, I'm no longer thinking of a syllogism, but of a riddle."

Irma walked to the back of the room, looking in all the corners with matches to see if anything had been left.

"Nothing at all," she said.

"No. Nothing," Rosenthal said.

She looked in the closet and found that even the dust was gone.

"The dust is gone," she said. "Why do you suppose they took away the dust?"

"They've got a use for all sorts of things," Rosenthal said.

"My riddle," Bailey said, "should prove to be a challenge to Guild people like yourselves. I know the sound of one hand clapping, but what is the fruit of the fun tree?"

Irma stopped walking and sat down on the floor and stared at Bailey. Bailey was sitting on the spot where the mimeograph machine had been. Irma looked above his head at the wall where the streetlight hit it.

"Say," she said, "they took down the sign."

They all looked up at the spot where the DON'T SIT HERE sign had been. When they each had exhausted the sight of the empty wall, they again looked at each other. After a long silence they got up and left the room.